STABLE HILL

JODI PAYNE

Tygerseye

This is a work of fiction. Names, characters, places, and incidents either are the product of author imagination or are used fictitiously, and any resemblance to actual persons, living or dead, business establishments, events, or locales is entirely coincidental.

Stable Hill

Cover Art 2019 Alexandria Corza

http://www.seeingstatic.com/

Cover content is for illustrative purposes only and any person depicted on the cover is a model.

This is the Second Edition, published September 2019, Tygerseye Publishing, LLC.

First Edition published May 2019, Dreamspinner Press

Print ISBN: 978-1-951011-07-9

CAN THREE MEN FROM VERY DIFFERENT BACKGROUNDS FIND A HOME AND A FUTURE TOGETHER?

After losing his husband to cancer, Oscar Kennedy has his hands full with their four girls, the house, his job, and his mother-in-law. When he loses his father too, keeping Stable Hill, the old horse farm where he grew up, becomes impossible. Oscar hires Jeffrey Stokes, a slick-looking real estate broker with a roll-up-his-sleeves work ethic, to get it on the market.

Russell White manages the day-to-day at Stable Hill. Russ had loved Oscar's dad like a father and took on even more responsibility when the old man fell ill. He is shocked and saddened by Oscar's decision to sell.

All three men have a stake in Stable Hill, and it's not long before they start to invest in one another too. But their complicated relationship doesn't make having to sell Stable Hill any easier. Will the fragile triad they're building last when the farm that brought them together is gone?

To my beautiful wife, who loses time with me to the laptop more often than she should.

CHAPTER ONE

Oscar Kennedy sat at his dining room table and stared at his cell phone, then glanced again at the business card beside it on the table. He'd read the card so many times in the last month, he didn't need it anymore—he had the damn number memorized. There was no reason not to make the call, but he'd procrastinated for weeks anyway. He'd asked himself why a hundred times over and hadn't found an answer. Maybe it was because he'd grown up in that house. Maybe he wasn't ready to close the book on his father's life. Maybe he didn't want to let anything else he cared about go.

But ready or not, without Dad living there, the old farm was costing him money in utilities, wages, taxes, and general upkeep every month it sat empty, and he had mouths in his own house to feed. He'd thought about it long and hard. He'd even thought about moving the family out there, but he just couldn't find a way to make it work.

All right. Enough. He had to make the call. He took a deep breath, picked up his phone, and dialed.

"Jeffrey Stokes Realty. This is Janie. Can I help you?"

Jesus, that was quick. The phone had barely rung on his

end. He fought a strong urge to hang up, and cleared his throat. "Uh, yes. Hello. My name is Oscar Kennedy. Bob Keller gave me one of Mr. Stokes's business cards and suggested I call him about selling my father's farm out in Lancaster County. Is he available?"

"One moment please, Mr. Kennedy."

The Realtor's hold music wasn't bad. It sounded like the actual radio, tuned to an eighties rock station. Oscar tapped his fingers—decorated with pink sparkly nail polish—in time to Duran Duran and smiled as he discovered he remembered all the words.

The receptionist picked up again, and the music ended. "Mr. Kennedy?"

"Yes?"

"May I please get your number? Mr. Stokes is on another call, but he would very much like to speak with you."

"Uh, sure." He gave her his cell number, thanked her, and hung up with a sigh.

Wasn't that just his luck? He'd finally gotten up the nerve to make the damn call and the Realtor wasn't available. Now he'd have to find the courage all over again to actually pick up the phone when the guy—*if* the guy—called him back.

"Dinner will be ready shortly, Oscar."

"Thank you, Rose." Oscar stood and stuffed his phone and the business card into his back pocket.

"So... were you able to reach the Realtor?"

He knew she was going to ask. Hell, that was probably the only reason she'd come into the dining room. He leaned toward her, smiling indulgently. "Yes, Rose. I made the call."

"Honestly, that wasn't what I—"

"That was exactly what you meant," he interrupted, smiling at the woman he'd come to think of as his own mother. "You and I both know it." He bent down and kissed her on the forehead. "Hopefully he'll get back to me. He wasn't able to take my call."

"Oh, I'm sorry, darling. That is frustrating."

Oscar shrugged. "It'll get done. Now if you'll excuse me, I need to visit the nail spa." He waggled his pink fingers at her.

"You're such a good sport."

"The things I do for love." Oscar left the dining room and headed through the living room and upstairs. "Riley, honey? Did you find the polish remover?"

"Yes! You want me to bring it downstairs?"

Oscar stuck his head into the twins' room. "Nope, I'm here."

"Oh! Come sit, Oz," Riley said, smiling and patting the little stool that went with the vanity the girls shared. "Sit, sit. Right here."

"Zoe, go on down and help your grandmother set the table for dinner, please?"

"It's not my turn. It's Sophie's!" Zoe pouted at him.

"Well, all right, then. Please go tell Sophie I asked her to do it?"

"Okay!" Zoe ran out of the room, shouting Sophie's name, and Oscar carefully took a seat on the little stool and let Riley start to remove his nail polish.

"I'm sorry you didn't like the pink."

"Oh, no. I loved the pink. I just have a meeting tomorrow, and I don't want to distract my client with the beautiful sparkles."

Riley nodded seriously. "I understand. Would you like something less sparkly instead?"

"Not tonight, baby, but thank you. Maybe over the weekend?"

Riley beamed at him. "Okay!"

God, he loved that smile. Riley and Zoe both had it, and it was Emmett all over—the wide lips and the dimples. The twins looked just like their dad, whereas Sophie and Emily looked more like Linda, their mother. She was killed in a car accident when they were very young, and he had only ever seen pictures, but their eyes were definitely hers.

It was hard to believe that he—that *they*—had lost Emmett nearly three years ago. The year leading up to Emmett's death had seemed like an eternity, but somehow the three since had practically evaporated. He honestly didn't know what he'd have done if Emmett's mother hadn't insisted he allow her to move in and help with the girls. He and Rose had joked, since the first time Emmett introduced them over dinner, that something had to be wrong that he actually got along with his mother-in-law. Despite her own unimaginable grief, she had been an absolute godsend through those excruciating first days and every single day since. Being together had been good for them both. It had to have been impossibly painful to lose a son, likely even more impossible than losing a husband, and they'd been able to grieve together, but they both knew they had to get up in the morning and soldier on for Emmett's girls.

The girls were growing up now too. They'd seemed so young when Emmett passed away, but now Emily and Sophie were seventeen and fifteen, and the oopsy twins, Riley and Zoe, had just turned ten and were still sweet as anything.

"Oz?"

"Hm?" Oscar blinked. "I'm sorry, baby. Did you say something?"

"I said you're all done."

"Oh! Well, look at that. Thank you so much." He leaned over and kissed Riley on the cheek.

"Maybe purple next time?"

"Perfect."

"Dinner!" Sophie shouted from downstairs.

"Coming!" Riley and Oscar shouted back together. They

laughed their way out of the bedroom and down the hall. Oscar knocked on Emily's door on the way by. "Dinner, Emily."

"I heard."

Oscar just shook his head and headed downstairs.

Rose had made her famous baked ziti, everyone's favorite. There was a huge pan of it sitting in the middle of the table, along with some garlic bread and a big bowl of broccoli.

Sophie was putting out milk for her sisters, and Rose was setting down a glass of iced tea for herself.

"Can I get you a glass of wine, Oscar?" she asked.

"Thank you. You sit down and eat, Rose. I can get it."

"Ziti! Oh, it smells really good, Gram."

Oscar had to look back over his shoulder to be sure, but yes, that was in fact Emily's voice.

"Have a seat, dear. Dig right in."

Oscar poured himself a small glass of wine and joined his family at the table. "Everyone got their homework done?"

The answer was a chorus of yeses.

"Good. So, thorns?" He looked at Riley. "Go."

"Bobby kicked me at recess. Not on purpose but it hurt."

"I'm sorry, baby. Is it better now?"

Riley nodded. "Gram gave me ice."

"Excellent. Zoe?"

"I can't find my favorite hair tie."

"The pink-and-white striped one?" Rose asked.

"Yeah."

"I washed it, sweetheart. It's in the bathroom drying for you."

"Oh! Thank you, Gram!"

Oscar nodded approvingly. "Thorn to a rose. Boom. I like it. Sophie?"

Sophie sighed and answered in her shy voice. "I had a math test today. It was hard."

"I was going to ask about that. Hard like bad?"

"No, just hard. I was the last one to finish."

He smiled at her. Sophie was a good student, but she needed a lot of encouragement. "No worries, Soph. It's good that you didn't rush." He looked over at the last one, knowing already what she'd say. "Aaaand... Emily?"

Emily shrugged. "Same as usual."

"School is boring and you have no life?"

"Pretty much."

"I like the consistency." There wasn't any point in forcing her to play along. It just made everyone aggravated. "Now roses. Riley."

Riley started, "Zoe and I—"

"Got to pet puppies this morning!" Zoe finished for her, bouncing in her seat.

Riley continued, equally enthusiastic, "They were at school today."

"They were so cute!"

"How cool is that?" No, they were not getting a puppy. He moved on quickly before either twin could ask. "Sophie?"

"Um. I bought a new journal on the way home from school."

"You really like the writing, huh?"

Sophie nodded at him. "I got a cool pen too."

"Nice. The right pen can be inspiring. So...." Dare he ask? "Emily?"

"This is my favorite dinner. Thank you, Gram."

Oh. That was so unexpected and sweet it made his heart ache. Every so often Emily showed them a tiny, little bit of the lovely young lady he knew was in there, if a bit repressed by teenage hormones.

"Thank you, lovey." Rose smiled at Emily and patted her hand. Their grandmother made dinner every single night of the week. It was nice that the girls said thank you spontaneously once in a while. Oscar said it all the time, but he knew it wasn't quite the same as when the girls were happy.

"I think I'm headed out to Grampa's farm this weekend if anyone wants to go with me," he said, not really expecting anyone to be interested. The girls didn't have much attachment to the place. "It will be going up on the market soon, so I don't know how many more chances you'll get."

Looking back, he wondered if maybe he should have made more time for the family to spend out at the farm with Dad, with the horses. But back when Emmett asked him to move in, the girls were still young, especially the twins. Emmett had worked very hard to create routine and stability for them after Linda died and adding Oscar to the mix was another big adjustment for them. Emmett wanted them to spend weekends at home together, trying to find the family's new normal.

That was one of many reasons he'd decided not to keep the farm and sell this place. The farm was in the middle of nowhere, and this was a busy neighborhood with lots of kids, biking distance from town. The girls had very few memories out there, especially since Emmett died and Dad got sick. Why would they want to move?

Hopefully he'd be meeting the Realtor there, but either way he had to talk with Russ about getting the farm ready to sell.

He got some version of maybe from all of them, and he thought about trying to persuade them, but his cell phone rang, interrupting him. He didn't answer the phone during dinner as a rule, but tonight he was expecting the Realtor, and he really didn't want to play phone tag.

"It's him," he said to Rose. "I'm sorry."

"Go on, Oscar. It's okay."

He nodded and answered the phone as he headed into the kitchen. "Hello?"

"Mr. Kennedy?"

"This is Oscar, yes." Not that anyone confused him with his father anymore.

"Mr. Kennedy, this is Jeffrey Stokes returning your call."

"Yeah, hey. Thank you for getting back to me so quickly, Mr. Stokes."

"Please call me Jeffrey, and I was very glad to hear from you. Bob Keller mentioned your farm to me a couple of weeks ago, and I took the liberty of looking it up."

"Oh, hey, that's great. So you're a step ahead of me."

"Well, yes and no. Bob says you're looking to sell soon?"

"I am, though I'm sure you're going to tell me the farm needs some work before it'll sell."

"That's usually the case with these older properties, yes. Twenty acres, right?"

"Twenty-five."

"Got it. Main house, guest cottage, three barns?"

"Four paddocks with run-ins, outdoor ring." There was also half an indoor ring that Dad never finished. Before getting sick, his father had intended to hire instructors and offer lessons.

"Horses still on the property?"

"The barn has eighteen stalls, and we have fourteen horses. We can rehome them or sell them with the property." He hadn't ridden them in ages. Years, he thought.

"I'm interested in the details. Do you have some time in your schedule this weekend?"

"I do. Maybe Saturday morning?" He was hoping for Saturday. Sundays he tried to spend with the girls.

"Like, tomorrow Saturday? That would be perfect. How about we meet out there about ten o'clock?"

"Yes, like tomorrow. Sorry. That'll do fine." How did he forget it was Friday? Sometimes the routine just ate his brain.

"Thank you for getting in touch, Mr. Kennedy."

"Oscar."

"Oscar it is. Have a good evening."

"See you tomorrow." Oscar hung up the phone.

Okay. He sighed.

So that was done. He wished he understood how he felt about it. He'd think more on it later. Right now he was hungry and had girls to herd, so he headed back into the dining room. The girls always ate fast if someone didn't keep them talking, and the twins were already heading toward the kitchen with their plates. So much for family dinner. It was his own fault; he shouldn't have answered the phone. He had a rule and he'd broken it, but he really needed to get that call over with.

"Are you sure you've had enough, Emily?"

"Ugh. I am so stuffed, Gram."

"Me, too, Grandma."

"All right, ladies. You may be excused."

Oscar watched them walk right past him. He shook his head. "Well, I'm still hungry," he said, taking his seat.

"I'll sit with you, darling. What did the Realtor say?"

"We're meeting at Dad's tomorrow morning."

"Good. I'll stay with the girls."

"I was hoping maybe they'd want to go with me, but Em and Soph probably won't even be out of bed before ten."

"Maybe the twins will take the ride up there with you."

"Maybe." He wasn't optimistic. If only he'd thought about how much he'd regret not taking them up there. He'd just convinced himself there'd be time later. Like when the girls got to know him better. When the twins were a little older. When work was less crazy. When Emmett got better.

And then Emmett didn't get better.

He dug back into his dinner even though didn't have as much of an appetite now. It had cooled, but he didn't want to be rude and stick it in the microwave, so he ate it like it was.

It still tasted good, like Rose and home, and he felt a little better with each bite he took.

"I'll be taking Sunday, if you don't mind." Rose told him that every Friday night after dinner.

"Of course." She would go to services first thing Sunday morning. There was altar guild and then the service and fellowship; she'd be there until well after lunchtime. After that she usually went to the library and did some shopping or something. Whatever it was she did all afternoon, she usually arrived home just in time to put something simple on for dinner.

He'd tried to explain that she should feel free to come and go as she pleased, that he only needed to know so he could make sure to be home if she couldn't be, but she wouldn't hear of it. "I'm here for those girls," she'd told him time and time again. "Sundays are lovely." It was a load off his mind to be sure. It meant he could focus on providing for them and paying the bills, and it kept his career as a compliance officer on track. He'd managed a promotion since she'd moved in, with a significant financial gain that had gone a long way toward making up for the loss of Emmett's salary.

Emmett had been an accountant, and he'd worked at home. Rose used to help out a lot from January to April but otherwise he'd been a hands-on dad, driving the girls to school, making lunches, helping with homework, coaching soccer. He'd been an equally devoted husband. A love that had caught Oscar completely by surprise. No promotion of any kind would ever make up for that kind of loss.

"I've got the dishes." He stood up, needing to snap out of that train of thought.

"Are you sure?"

"Of course. Maybe you'd like to tuck the twins in tonight? They'd love that."

Rose gave him a smile, the look in her eyes knowing and

compassionate without pity. They'd created a whole silent language of knowing looks between them, every one of them full of things that were hard to say.

"I'd love that as well." She kissed his cheek and gave the other one a pat, then headed for the stairs. Sixty-five wasn't that old, and the girls were pretty well-behaved, but they still took energy, and he knew that by Friday, Rose was tired. Sending her upstairs early meant she could turn in early too.

He washed every single dish by hand, even though he had a perfectly good dishwasher, letting himself reminisce a little in his mind. Not a day went by that he didn't think about Emmett, but the crushing grief that had left him breathless for so long had slowly, subtly subsided. Lately the thoughts had been more in passing, and more often brought a smile.

He was trying to remember the last time he and Emmett were in Dad's house. There was nothing terribly remarkable about it. They'd gone for a trail ride, Dad leading with Emmett in the middle as he brought up the rear. It had been a long one because the day was gorgeous, and then after the ride they'd come home, watched a ball game, and made dinner. He couldn't remember specifically what it was, but it was probably something simple and hearty like spaghetti and Dad's famous homemade meatballs. Emmett had probably made a blueberry pie for dessert, which was always Dad's favorite.

Emmett had been pretty sick even then, but the treatment hadn't totally wasted him yet. It wasn't long after, though, that Emmett really wasn't able to leave the house anymore. Oscar held on to the picture in his mind of Emmett sitting awkwardly on horseback, smiling happily, framed by trees and blue sky.

Good night, Emmett. He shut off the kitchen light and headed for bed.

CHAPTER TWO

OKAY, THEN. Jeffrey leaned back in his office chair. He had a new client. Sweet.

Last month had been a slow one, but this one was picking up. Jeffrey hung up with Mr. Ken—with Oscar, and made sure to put their appointment down on the calendar for Saturday morning. He took a minute to fill in the few details he had in the notes for the appointment and also to make a short list of what he needed to prep and to bring with him.

He was about to take another look at the property when a knock at his door interrupted him. He looked up. "Come on in."

"Hey, Jeff."

"Hey...." *S. An S name*. "Stacie, is it?"

"Stephanie." She smiled at him.

"Stephanie. Right. I'm so sorry." Because that wasn't embarrassing or anything. In his defense, he didn't spend a lot of time actually in the office. This wasn't even his own desk; he shared it with two other Realtors.

"No worries." Stephanie struck a flattering pose in his doorway that showed off her hips and stretched her blouse across her chest. *Pretty.* He wasn't interested tonight, but she was lovely. "How's your month going?"

"Oh. Good. Much better than last month. I just landed a new client."

"Yeah? Nice. What is it?"

"It's a working horse farm."

"Oh, that's a shame. I always hate to see those go."

"Go?"

"Developers, you know? Housing developments, condo complexes, shopping malls? You lucked out. That's good money."

"Oh, I think he wants to sell it as a farm. To farmers." Bob had given him the name after all, and he knew why.

"Huh. Well, that's possible too, I'm sure." She sounded doubtful or incredulous. He wasn't sure which.

"Sure it is." Of course it was possible. He'd sold two other working farms, and Bob Keller's was less than a year ago. He'd found a great buyer for Bob, and he knew that was how he ended up with Kennedy's place. What had Bob called it? Stable Hill Farm. He hoped it lived up to its name.

"Not the same money, though." She grinned at him. He'd been told Stephanie was one of the top earners at the agency, so she knew what she was talking about. He'd already planned to pick her brain at some point. He had a face to go with the name now at least. Assuming he remembered it.

"I'll land something high-dollar soon too, I'm sure. I just want to do right by this client."

"You're a good guy, Jeff. I'd heard that about you." She stepped into his office, brushing her blonde hair to one side. "You have plans tonight? I was thinking of getting some dinner and a glass of wine."

He'd expected that. And, truthfully, if she were his type, he'd have totally taken her up on it. "I do have plans," he lied. "I'm sorry."

His plans were to find a man. Hopefully a hot one. If he had to pick a label, and he really didn't like labels, he'd say he identified as bi. But he only ever went out looking for men. The relationships he'd had with women were far fewer and less casual. He'd even had one serious one as the boyfriend of a married couple. Amy was lovely, and no question he'd been attracted to her. To them both.

"Mm. Shame." Stephanie straightened up, giving up on her seduction.

"I liked the whole doorway pose, though. You looked hot."

"Thanks." She made a face at him. "That's one of my signature moves."

He laughed. "Don't lose it. It works for you."

She headed for the office door. "Whoever you have plans with is very lucky."

He winked at her. "Thank you."

"Good night, Jeff."

"Night, Stephanie."

He watched her leave his office.

Good Lord.

Okay, back to work.

Selling a big farm in the current market wasn't going to be easy. He'd already figured that out. But he'd done his research after his conversation with Bob Keller. It was a nice place, built from the ground up by Oscar's father, who owned it until the day the man died. Only one owner in its history was a big deal, and they still kept horses. Should be a decent price point, but he'd know more after he saw it.

Jeffrey sat down at his computer, googled the farm, and found a workable aerial view of the property. Rough forest, a creek or something along one side of the property line, a bunch of good-size buildings. A couple of fields that looked to be growing hay, though it was hard to tell how old this picture was. Nice. Assuming it was really in decent shape and this Kennedy guy had a little bit of cash to throw at it, they should be golden. And if Kennedy was broke, well, there were ways to get a spit shine for a song.

It sure had taken the guy a long while to call, though. Bob said he'd passed on Jeffrey's info weeks ago. Hopefully that just meant Kennedy was disorganized or busy, and it wasn't a bad sign.

All right, it was time to head out. He needed some dinner, maybe a drink or two. He locked up the little office right on Main Street and got into his car.

Did he want to go out or stay in? Weeknights the bars were easiest because he could get home early enough to be worth something the next day. He enjoyed the clubs, but he usually saved them for weekends so he could dance, people watch, find a hookup a little more organically, or at least in person, and stay out late. Or all night.

Maybe tonight he could stay local. He pulled out his phone and opened Grindr to see who was nearby and looking, and set his display to "Top 31." He scrolled through the grid, flipping right past "SugarDaddy4u," "Bruh," and any numbers under twenty-five, no matter how hot, finally clicking on "Visiting 29." Great body shot, online now, presumably leaving town in the near future. That would do. He tapped the flame and then the chat icon.

Hi. U looking for casual tonite?

Hey Toppy. Yes. Like ur pic. Hot. What are u up for?

Drink at the bar, penetration, no flip. Pretty much the same thing every time.

OK

Limits?

No kink, no power play

No problem. *That works*

Drink sounds great. Play safe?

Oh good. He often ended up asking that question first. *Always. Interested? Got a room?*

Marriott on Dempsey. Meet in the lobby.

He sent his deets so the guy would know how to spot him. *Dark suit, blue tie, clean shave. See u in 20*

Okay, then. A little close-to-home fun. Worked great for him. He turned up the radio and headed for the Marriott. Jeffrey used to have guilt about doing this, meeting random men, enjoying the night together. He really preferred to meet guys in person, but it had been forever since he'd met someone he was into. He was kind of interested in this one guy he'd met at the River, a bar outside town. It wasn't a gay bar, and it was just shy of being a dive, but the drinks were cheap, the music was good, and there was always a game on. One night he'd been in the right place at the right time.

He'd run into the guy there a couple of times since, but Jeffrey wasn't interested in giving out his cell number, so that was hit-or-miss. It was nice when it was a hit, though. They'd park someplace and rut like goats in the back of the guy's pickup. Something about the possibility, however unlikely, of being caught was a huge turn-on, and the guy was lovely, young and wild, and it made him feel that way too.

But hitting the River and waiting the guy out required a patience he didn't have tonight. He had a new client to celebrate, and he wanted some contact. Going home disappointed wasn't going to sit well.

The Marriott was lit up and busy. Clearly a wedding was going on, judging by the women in matching teal dresses and all the men looking hot and handsome in gray suits and matching cravats. The white rose boutonnières were a nice touch too. He waited in his car as they disembarked from the shuttle that had brought them all, and watched them laughing and smiling as they headed inside.

He found a parking spot off in a corner, far away from

other car doors, and pulled his Mercedes across two spaces. It was a dick move, but he was far enough out of the way that hopefully no one got their nose out of joint.

He straightened his tie and pulled his jacket back on, then headed inside. Finding him might prove a challenge in this lobby full of people, so he stayed kind of out in the open and let himself look like he was looking for someone.

"Dark suit, blue tie, clean-cut?"

He smiled at the handsome man in jeans and a designer T-shirt, who approached him. "That's me."

"I'm Nate."

They shook hands. "Hello, Nate. I'm Jeff. Can I buy you a drink?"

"You can. Hotel has a nice bar. Thanks for showing up."

"My pleasure." Sometimes these meetings started out awkward. Nate was obviously not a first-timer, and the easy way they just headed for the bar was refreshing. He smiled, thinking about Stephanie and hoping she was lucking into someone hot tonight too.

CHAPTER THREE

SATURDAY MORNING, Sophie and Emily were both still asleep, as he'd predicted, and the twins got invited for a play-date, so Oscar took the trip out to Stable Hill Farm alone. The drive from Ardmore out to his dad's farm in Lancaster County took about an hour, and he sang along with the radio and played the drums on his steering wheel to keep himself entertained. Once he got close, it was amazing how quickly civilization just fell away and the land turned green. The last bit of road before his father's driveway was lined with some mix of grass and alfalfa that would soon be cut down for hay and sold.

The driveway at Stable Hill had never been paved. It was a stubborn mix of hard-packed dirt, gravel, and metal grating that ran over drainage gullies, and it wound its way from the hayfields up a little hill to the main house in a wide S pattern.

He'd texted Russ before he left home, so he wasn't surprised to see the blond-haired barn manager out on the porch when he pulled up. Russ looked as good as ever—tan and fit from working outdoors.

"Hey, Russ."

"Oscar." They shook hands, Russ's fingers rough in his grip.

Oscar fondly recalled the day he met Russ. It was just over two years ago now, before Dad got sick, when Dad was still full of plans for the new barn and the indoor ring. Lamont, the previous barn manager and a longtime friend of his father's, had decided at the age of nearly seventy to retire to Florida with his wife. Dad hired Russ to replace Lamont, and all Oscar knew before they met was that the new guy was young. He remembered the way Russ rode up on horseback to meet him and slid right down to shake his hand. Russ rode like a cowboy born in the saddle, and Oscar had been struck by the way Russ's smile lit up the overcast day.

He'd been struck by Russ's green eyes too. It was the first time he'd really noticed anyone that way since he'd lost Emmett, barely six months before. He remembered that little spark, like something in him had struggled to come alive but lost the fight to his still-grieving heart.

He looked at Russ but looked away again as soon as he caught those green eyes—as stunning now as they'd always been—and glanced out over the hayfield instead. "So how have things been going here?"

"Fine. Horses are all healthy at the moment. Can't ask for better."

"Good." He nodded and stuffed his hands into his pockets. "Good," he repeated just to fill the dead air. Why did conversations with Russ always feel so awkward?

Dad's fight had been fierce but short. After his father finally moved to rehab, Oscar pretty much stopped coming out here, except to place orders with Russ and pay the bills once a month. He told himself it was because he was plenty busy with monitoring Dad in rehab, working full-time, and parenting the girls, but deep down he knew it was really that he couldn't bring himself to deal with another loss. Russ never complained, never said a word, just kept on very capably taking care of the horses and the rest of the property.

Russ was young, that was true, but also smart and experienced with the animals. Oscar discovered he wasn't as good with managing the farm itself as Lamont and Dad had been. It wasn't that the man couldn't do it—no, Oscar was sure Russ was more than capable. But the money end of things wasn't Russ's interest; he didn't want to sit with books and ledgers. He was more of a hands-on guy.

It hardly mattered now, Oscar supposed, since they were selling anyway.

He felt bad putting Russ out of work, along with the few guys who were still keeping the farm going, but he didn't have a choice. It was too expensive to run the place, keep up his and Emmett's house, and provide for the kids at the same time. Stable Hill was barely breaking even with the hay sales, and Dad had known that; that's what the half-built indoor ring was about. Dad had planned to start boarding, giving lessons, making that a business. But when Dad couldn't manage it, all of that fell away.

Oscar was going to have to help Emily pay for college next year. Sophie was going to need a car and wasn't too far off to plan for collegewise either. The farm couldn't sustain itself, and he just didn't have the money to keep the property up, let alone finish what his father had started. He regretted having to sell, but hard decisions had to be made. None of the options were easy.

Have to be practical. Right? He sighed, resigned. *Right.*

Russ coughed, bringing him back to their conversation. "So... we're meeting a real estate guy?"

"Yeah. His name is Stokes. Jeffrey Stokes. Have you heard of him? Bob Keller, you know him, Dad's tractor guy? Stokes sold Keller's farm about six months ago."

Russ shook his head and squinted down the long driveway.

"Nope, don't know the name. Stokes, I mean. I know Keller, of course."

"Keller is straight up. Should be a good recommendation."

"Yeah."

This time when the silence fell between them, Oscar tried to let it be, but Russ seemed way more comfortable with it than he was. He watched the waves of grass blowing in the hayfield and examined the porch railing, which Russ must have painted recently because it looked great. He did pretty much anything but look at Russ; if he were honest, he was a little intimidated. The guy knew the farm inside and out, as Oscar had once when he'd lived with Dad, but didn't anymore. Russ also knew damn well that he hadn't spent any real time out here in, well, years really, the last year especially. Russ and Dad had become friends, and sometimes he worried that Russ was closer to Dad than he was.

"I tried to get the girls to come out here with me today."

"Yeah? Bet they're getting big. Been a while since I seen 'em."

"I know." The last time they were here, the twins were fascinated by Russ's tour of the barn, and Russ let them ride Lollipop, Dad's ancient pony, walking them each around the ring on a lead. That had been a nice day for them.

They'd buried Dad that morning, so it wasn't his best day, but it was great to see the girls enjoy the property.

"Car."

He looked up. "Sure is." It was a hell of a car too. A sleek black Mercedes coup. He'd never seen anything so shiny in his father's driveway before. Stokes parked it alongside his incredibly not-sexy, seven-year-old minivan, and not far from Russ's old dusty, rusty, red pickup.

Talk about out of place. And as it turned out, the Mercedes was second only to the man who got out of the car.

Jeffrey Stokes was shiny himself—tall, dark-haired, embarrassingly well dressed.

And sexy as hell.

Russ whistled softly. "Oh. Damn."

"Yeah," he agreed quietly, just for Russ's ears, pretending it wasn't weird that they were both ogling the Realtor. He cleared his throat. "Welcome, Mr. Stokes."

"Please call me Jeffrey," Stokes said, climbing the stairs onto the front porch and going right to Russ first with a smile. "Well, hello."

Russ's return handshake was curt, and he pointed to Oscar. "Oscar over there is the owner. I'm Russ. I just manage the place."

"Oh. Of course. I see." Stokes gave Russ a nod. "Hello, Oscar." The Realtor turned a breathtaking smile on him, giving him goose bumps and making him swallow.

Down, boy, he told himself, more amused than anything. That hadn't happened to him in a very long time. Stokes's hand hung between them for a moment and he blinked at it.

"Oh." He shook with Stokes, forcing himself to smile back and think clearly. "Hi. Welcome."

"So, this is a great piece of property you have here. Big, huh?"

Oscar raised an eyebrow. "Thank you." *No, I'm not interested in going commercial.*

"You're looking to sell it as a working farm, right? It's a little off the beaten path, but it's so beautifully situated, I don't think you'll have much trouble."

Okay. He relaxed; this guy got it. *Thank you, Bob.* "It's a working farm now. I'd like to see it go to someone that will keep it that way."

"Great. I'm completely on board. I already have some thoughts, and I'm sure you do as well, but I want to work logically here and do a proper evaluation. If it's all right with you, my preference would be not to discuss anything related to pricing or get too deep into any fix-up costs until I've seen the whole property and have a chance to sit down with the numbers." While he was talking, Stokes took his jacket off, folded it in half and draped it over the back of one of Dad's old porch rockers. Then he added his tie to it and rolled up his sleeves.

Oscar watched Stokes with interest as the man transformed into someone ready to get down to business before his very eyes. He also couldn't help but admire the way Jeffrey's dress shirt stretched across that broad chest. "Oh. Sure, that'd be great. Thanks." He only had a vague idea of the property's value anyway. He was sure it would bring in a good amount, though—hopefully enough to be of real help with college for his girls.

He saw Russ cross his arms over his chest, but the man didn't join the conversation.

"And don't worry, I understand farms need work all the time. It's never ending. Please don't spend time apologizing for something you think needs work. I'll just make a note, and we'll discuss the priorities later. Okay? From where I'm standing the bones look pretty good. That's what matters most."

He took a deep breath and exhaled, giving Stokes a smile. The guy really did get it. "Russ is ready to take us around. Where do you want to start?"

CHAPTER FOUR

Russ sat on the front porch in his favorite old rocker with a cup of coffee, took a deep breath, and let it out slow.

"Damn."

That Realtor? Once he'd let his hair down, he seemed pretty sharp, and he'd had no problem keeping up. He asked a hell of a lot of questions, though. Seemed like every time Russ answered one, he had two more. Was the perimeter fencing no-climb? What was the spring thaw like? How did water flow through the property? Was the horse barn dry? Was the hay barn protected from critters? Were the tractors part of the sale? What about the horse trailer? On and on. He seemed to know farm structures, took notes, used all the right terms and what all. Russ was pretty sure Bob Keller did right by Oscar in suggesting the guy. Oscar was going to owe Keller a debt.

Russ sighed. Sure was awkward, though.

He and Jeff needed no introduction. They'd met a couple of months back at this bar called the River. They'd never exchanged anything but first names. No phone numbers, last names, or really any relevant personal information. But after running into each other a couple of times and having a couple of drinks together, Jeff had become fairly familiar with him physically—and with the back of his truck. He'd wanted to see Jeff again, maybe even wanted more, but that didn't seem like a good idea in light of—it was just sex up until now, just getting off and nothing more. Russ wasn't sure if that made the situation better or worse.

"Damn."

He was going to have to learn how to stay out of the way.

The longer they toured the grounds, the more Russ could see how much Oscar loved Stable Hill. The man had a story for everything. One about the year right after they started building the indoor ring, when all the construction made the hay barn flood during a nor'easter. A story about hacking out in the woods behind the property as a teenager and riding through some kind of wasps' nest that sent him and his horse into a tizzy. The night a skunk got into the barn, and the day the dogs dug up a mess of baby bunnies. Oscar had stories about the house too, about how the sideboard in the dining room was custom-made, with a drawer big enough to hold the huge platter his mother used for Thanksgiving dinner, and about being the first one out of bed on winter mornings and stoking the woodstove wearing nothing but boxers and goose bumps.

Considering Oscar seemed broken up about having to sell the place, and that Russ was happy living and working here himself and would rather not see it change hands either... it was a decent day. At least it seemed like Jeff wanted to do right by the place, and by Oscar.

But man, Oscar and Jeff together were a whole lot of company.

A whole lot of very confusing company.

The two of them had finally left, and Russ sat quiet, drinking his coffee and letting all the whirling energy settle.

He just needed to breathe and soak up the late-afternoon sun while all the noise and mixed emotions floated down and drifted away.

He'd been hoping Oscar would stay a little bit and check in with him, even if it was only to talk farm business—placing orders or writing checks, whatever. He'd thought about asking if Oscar wanted to stay for supper, but of course the guy probably couldn't with all those girls to get home to and all. Oscar was a good dad, from what he knew, and kind. The man was every bit as handsome as the day they'd met too. Right or wrong, he wouldn't kick the man out of bed for eating crackers.

He'd had a thing for Oscar since the first time they shook hands. He remembered that moment so clearly even two-plus years later. Tall, bright blue eyes, thick salt-and-pepper hair reflecting the sunlight. Oscar had given him a friendly smile to welcome him to the family that had made him warm all over. But it wasn't even a full day later that Jonas—Oscar's father had insisted Russ call him by his first name—told him all about how Oscar lost a husband to cancer barely six months earlier. He'd cursed his luck all night long that the man he'd just met, a man with a smile so warm it made his chest ache, was available, but not. Into men but grieving and completely out-of-bounds. Though, truthfully, at that point Russ wouldn't have dared proposition the boss's son, anyway.

But it had been what, nearly three years since Oscar lost Emmett? And they'd lost Jonas months ago, you know? Damn near six months. He was starting to think maybe it might be okay to think about Oscar again, especially since he wasn't gonna have to worry about losing his job if it didn't go over well. If the new owner didn't keep him on, he wasn't gonna have it for long anyhow.

"Damn," he said again and stood up. That was enough daydreaming. He had shit to do. He needed to help get the horses turned out and fed. He had the farrier coming because Manny slipped a shoe. And after the little tour today, Oscar had asked him to personally do an inspection of the fences. All the fences. Every goddamn inch of fence. That was going to be a chore.

He walked through the house, set his empty coffee cup in the sink and filled a water bottle, then headed out the back door toward the stables. He didn't get three steps from the house before his cell rang, though.

Other than farm-related folks, only two people in the whole world had that number—Mama and Oscar—and Mama only called on holidays.

This time it was Oscar.

"Long time no see, stranger."

"Right? Ugh." Oscar sighed into the phone. "I am so sorry to interrupt your day again, Russ. I know you have better things to do than listen to me talk."

"Not really. You're the boss, Boss." Oscar hated when he said that, and he did it now just to needle him.

"Ha-ha."

"So, what can I do you for?"

"Okay. So, I would have stayed and had this conversation in person, but I had to pick up Sophie at—"

"No worries. Really. Family first." *Christ. Please don't fire me over the phone.*

There was a pause, and then Oscar said, "Thanks. So, I'm really hoping that whoever ends up buying Dad's place keeps you on."

Okay... not fired. Yet. "Me too."

"Great. And I want to try to make that happen. So, can you make me a list of the people we still have on staff, including part-time and any regular day hires, and give me an idea of what they each do? I'd like to present you all as a team, you know? Essential staff. Keep everyone working."

"Can do." How fast was this happening? He was under the impression they had some time. For sure there was the fences, there was a buttload of inventory to go through for Jeff, and then there was that half-built barn that was gonna need something. And what about the—

"You there? Did I drop?"

Oops. "Uh. No. I got you." He blinked a couple of times.

"Oh. Good. So, Monday night, then?"

"You need it by Monday?"

"If you can manage it."

"Sure." He needed this job more than he needed sleep. And he needed to make sure he was irreplaceable, right? Nobody better to run this operation than him. "Hey, why don't you bring some beer and I'll make us supper?" *Shit. Christ.* That damn invitation skipped past his brain and came right out his stupid mouth.

"Uh. You think we need that much time?"

Well, fuck. That was about the most straight-up rejection ever, huh? "Oh, well. I suppose not. You probably want to get home to your family."

"No. You know what? We haven't had dinner together since before Dad passed. Let's do it."

"Yeah?" Well, hell. Now what was he going to make for Oscar? "Grill?"

"How about I bring beer and steaks and you do the rest."

He smiled because it all sounded great. The grill, some fresh air, and Oscar was a beer snob and would bring the good stuff. If he couldn't get everything he wanted, he could handle just hanging out and grilling on a decent night. It was still early fall, so it wouldn't be cold yet. "You're on."

"Sounds great. I'll see you Monday, then." Oscar hung up the phone.

It was all good. Oscar was a fair boss, a good guy, and had always put a lot of trust in him—gave him a lot of elbow room, didn't sit over his shoulder on anything. Good thing for Oscar he was worthy of all that trust, or he damn sure tried to be. Probably best not to mess that up with everything else going on.

He didn't need romance right now anyway, right? A steady would just complicate things. He found sex, which he wasn't ashamed to need, pretty much every time he went looking for it. He was good. For now it was him and a stable of horses, and that was enough.

When he was growing up in South Carolina, as a teenager he'd actually fallen in love with a horse. It sounded weird to put it that way, but it was basically the truth. She was a paint, pretty as could be, with a white muzzle and a dark spot over one eye. He called her Matey because she reminded him of a pirate, though she had some longer, fancier name his dad had given her. She was smart and mischievous, had a stubborn streak, was a sucker for a peppermint, and rode like a dream. She was his confidante, and he told her everything. He told her how early one morning he'd caught his uncle in the hay barn making love to another man, and everything he'd been feeling, everything he thought was wrong with him suddenly made sense. He told her about every hurried hand job or blow job behind a dumpster that he gave or got. He told her about the blond-haired boy he kissed all over in the bed of his truck, the one whose daddy beat the devil out of him one night less than a week later, and who he never saw again.

Matey had been his best friend. She listened, she didn't judge, she played with him, took care of him, ran like the wind. He hadn't ever had a friend like that before or since, but he'd survived. And now he had a whole stable full of beasts to talk to. They weren't quite the same as a lover, but they'd do.

He made his way down the aisle, opening stalls, careful to leave Manny in hers. This crew knew the drill. They followed him in a line or in pairs, until he got to the final stall, which belonged to a gigantic mare he called Angel. She'd been a gift from Jonas, and she'd come to him named Angelica, but he felt like that was too stuffy. In his time at Stable Hill, he'd added four horses to the stables and turned two older ones out to pasture. Angel was one of his picks. He'd had a mind to get a mare for Sophie. He'd even seen a slightly smaller roan with a good temperament he thought would suit, if Oscar agreed. The few times they'd been up, Sophie was the only one who had no fear of the animals. He saw something in her, something still and quiet that reminded him a little of the boy he'd once been, something that would serve her well if she ever wanted to ride. But there was no point in asking Oscar now, was there? That was a shame.

Once the lead mare was out of her stall, he got himself out of the way, and they took off in a pack for the turnout pasture, two and three across through the open barn doors.

He followed them up more slowly and far enough back that he didn't have to breathe in the dust they'd kicked up. He could have taken the four-wheeler, but he felt like he needed the walk. Soon it would be time to switch their days and night again. Kids had been back at school for a while, and the days weren't so hot anymore. When he finally got up to the pasture, everyone had made their way through the gate, and all he had to do was close it behind them. Angel came over and knocked his chest with her nose.

"No more peppermints today, pretty girl. You help me get everyone back down to the barn in the morning and we'll talk." He rubbed her nose and scratched behind her ears until she got bored of him and shook him off. "Be good, now."

From out here, if he turned in a circle he could see most of the property. Much of Oscar's farm it was surrounded by undeveloped forest, especially back behind the turnout pastures. There were three big barns—or, two and a half, anyway. The stables and the hay and equipment barn, they used regularly. The third one was only partly finished. Jonas had had plans for an indoor ring, but the old man got sick and the extra cash had to go to his care. The barn had been sitting unfinished ever since.

His cell rang again. It was the farrier. "Hey, Hank."

"Hey, Russ. I'm ahead of schedule. I'm only about fifteen minutes out. That okay?"

"Sure thing. Manny's ready for you."

"See you in a few."

"Sounds good."

He hung up and headed back down to the stables to get Manny on crossties for Hank.

CHAPTER FIVE

"I'm pulling up now."

Jeffrey turned off the access road, eased the nose of his car through the gates of Stable Hill, and headed up the long driveway.

"Are you sure it's okay that I can't be there?" Oscar sounded uncertain on the other end of the phone.

It was fine by him. Russ would be.

"Of course. I'm just getting some sample pictures for the listing. From what I saw last time I was there, it's full of great antique furniture and accents already. If I think it needs some extra staging, I'll let you know, and we'll get some stuff brought in. Okay?" He'd bring in a professional photographer once he saw how these came out. For the price tag he was considering, it was worth doing right.

"Yeah, that sounds good."

He took another turn, this one in a direction that took him away from the main house. Such an odd entrance to the property. "Oscar, why does this driveway meander all over the place on the way up to the house?"

"Dad said if the driveway went straight up from the road, it would be too steep a drive for the horse trailer."

Oh. "Well, that makes sense. Makes me a little dizzy, though."

Oscar's laugh filled his car over the Bluetooth system. "Yeah, I know. So, Russ knows you're coming. He'll give you access to the house and whatever else you need."

Mmm. Yeah, he was looking forward to the "whatever else he needed" part. Hopefully Russ would be game. "Thanks, Oscar. I'll give you a call later and let you know how it went."

"Great. Talk soon, then."

"Later." Jeffrey hung up, taking the last turn back toward the house. He parked in front and got out, grabbing the bag with his camera in it off his front seat. He took the porch steps slowly, checking his email on his phone as he went.

"Mr. Stokes."

Jeffrey looked up from his phone, grinning at the voice that greeted him. Russ wasn't grinning back. "Ah. Is that how it has to be?"

Russ nodded at him soberly, and Jesus, that look was hot. So serious. He wanted to kiss the frown off that stubborn mouth. "That's how it is. Least while we're working together."

"Oh. Well." *Shit.* "All right, then, Mr. White."

"How did you find out my—"

"I asked Oscar."

Russ shook his head and sighed. "Where did you want to start?"

"Well, that would probably be easier to figure out from inside the house." He winked.

"Oh. Right." Russ pushed open the screen door for him. "Sorry."

Wow. Russ seemed anxious. All right. It was disappointing —and frustrating as hell—but he understood. He'd play it cool. He dropped his bag on the couch and pulled out his camera, then handed Russ a notepad and a pen. "I'm going to move some things around and take a bunch of shots. Would you take some notes for me? This will go faster that way."

"Okay." Russ's tone was uncertain, but he took the paper.

The house could use a fresh coat of paint, but it was immaculate. Everything had a place and was in it. Room after room, the house hardly looked like anyone lived there. He moved a few things around, taking personal items and family photos out of the shots, adding throw pillows or blankets from other rooms sometimes, but mostly it looked like he wanted it to. It was a family farmhouse.

"Where do you stay, Russ?" Jesus. He couldn't call the man he'd just been hoping to fuck *Mr. White*. "Do you not live in the house?"

Russ looked at him. "I do. I have a room upstairs."

"Well, you'd never know it, looking at the rooms downstairs."

"It's not my house."

He looked over at Russ. "Seriously?"

"What?"

He shook his head. That was a nice TV in the living room. He'd sure use it if he were living here. He followed Russ up the stairs and into the first bedroom. It was delicate and sweet, with lace curtains and a pretty quilt on the bed. "Wow."

"This was Oscar's mom's room."

"She had her own room?"

"Oscar said she used it like a dressing room, and then she'd nap in here sometimes."

"How sweet." He took a few pictures, but this room wasn't going to sell the house. He knew it wasn't a palace, but he was hoping the master was a little bigger. There were a handful of bedrooms up here, and he shot those too. Oscar must have a big family.

"Over here is the room I use," Russ said finally. "It was Oscar's."

Russ didn't go in. He leaned against the wall in the hallway and waited, letting Jeffrey check it out alone.

He kept his comments to himself, but he couldn't believe how Russ was living. Along one wall, there was a twin bed with a dark comforter and a couple of pillows. A tall dresser with almost nothing on it sat in one corner. A guitar leaned against the wall in one corner next to a black boom box with big speakers and a tall rack full of CDs. The guy lived like a kid who should have left home five years ago. A grown man in a boy's bedroom.

"You play guitar?" he asked, taking pictures.

Russ shrugged. "A little."

The guitar looked like it belonged to someone who played it more than a little, but he didn't push. "That's cool." He finished up in Russ's room and stepped back into the hall. "The master?"

"Yeah, next door." Russ led him into a large, almost entirely empty room. There was a dresser at one end, an old rug, and a pair of nightstands that had been pushed together against one wall.

"There's no bed."

Russ nodded and stuck his hands in his pockets. "Yeah. Toward the end, when Jonas was too weak to get out of bed, Oscar tried to keep him here with a full-time nurse. He rented a hospital bed and had it moved in here, and had me get rid of his parents' double bed."

"Jonas was Oscar's father?"

"Oh. Yeah."

"And staying here didn't work out, huh?"

Russ shook his head no. "Not for long. Oscar got great help and really tried, he did. But eventually Jonas got... hard to handle. Combative and... it just wasn't possible. Oscar had to move him to rehab."

"That's rough."

"We lost him about six months ago."

"I'm sorry."

Russ nodded. "Thanks."

"So, I guess you were close?" The question was out of his mouth before he realized that it was kind of personal and probably none of his business.

"Yeah, actually." Russ squinted out the window. "Seems weird, I guess. I just worked here and all. But he was a friend. He was good to me."

Jeffrey had to wonder if Russ had said any of that out loud before. It didn't seem like it, the way his voice sounded rough and his breathing measured.

To be honest, he was having a hard time recognizing the man he'd hooked up with a handful of times for a blow job or a quick fuck in the back of a pickup truck. That guy in the bar didn't have much to say about anything, and when he did speak, it was either to ask the bartender for another beer or to comment about whatever game was on TV.

But this guy... this guy obviously cared about things—horses, the farm, music, Oscar's father.

He put his camera down on the dresser and moved close to Russ's back, breathing in stable and sunshine. "Hey."

Russ shook that mess of blond hair. "Don't."

He had to. He reached out and rested a hand on Russ's shoulder. "Russ."

"Don't, please." Russ stiffened and turned to look at him. "Do you have all the shots you need?"

He held Russ's eyes for a long moment, hoping to find the right move. Finally, he just nodded. "Yeah." He turned around and picked up his camera. "Yeah, I need to talk with Oscar about some staging. We need to get a bed in here, maybe a new rug."

Russ walked past him, and he followed the man down the stairs.

"Did you need pictures of the barn too?"

"I will, but not today. We'll probably need a couple of your people for that one, so we can move equipment and horses around. I'd like to do that late this week or early next. Maybe you could let me—or uh, let Oscar know what works for you, and we'll set something up?"

"I'll do that." Russ waited without another word while Jeffrey packed up his camera bag, but he had plenty to say after he saw Jeffrey through the front door. "Listen. I didn't tell Oscar we knew each other, and I'd prefer you didn't either. I'd rather not have to explain, you know?"

That he got. "Sure, Russ."

"And I'd like it if you kept what I said about Jonas to yourself too, as I shoulda done."

He sighed. "Okay, Russ. I can do that." Jeffrey hardly ever noticed Russ's Southern accent, it had obviously faded with years of living farther north, but his background sometimes slipped through in his turn of phrase, especially when Russ was drinking. Apparently, it also made an appearance when the man was emotional. "I can't imagine it would be a big deal, Russ. Oscar would probably appreciate—"

"You don't know what he'd appreciate."

Russ shut him down hard, so Jeffrey bit his tongue. There was something more going on, and he had to wonder what he'd stumbled into. "Right. Sorry."

"Thanks. Have a nice afternoon."

"You too, Russ. You too." He got into his car and pressed the button to start it up. He wasn't sure how he felt about any of this. The only thing he knew for sure was that he was going to miss Russ's company at the bar this weekend.

CHAPTER SIX

RUSS MADE sure they got everyone tucked into their stalls and fed and loved on a little early today. He knew it was ridiculous, but he was looking forward to spending some time with Oscar tonight. Yes, it was part business meeting, part hanging out. Yes, he knew Oscar wasn't into him. Didn't matter. He liked what he liked, and hell if he didn't like looking at Oscar.

He'd gotten a head start on the beer while he started up the grill. Just one to make him a little less self-conscious and loosen up his tongue. He wasn't the best with small talk, and he knew silence made Oscar uncomfortable for some reason. He wanted to put his best foot forward.

The rest of the world had switched to gas grills, but he liked good old-fashioned charcoal. Jonas had a big grill, so big he was only cooking in half of it, but it had plenty of room for the coals, and also some mesquite chips he'd put in a foil packet to smoke up some flavor on the steaks.

He was just thinking about another beer when there was a knocking on the kitchen window. He turned, and Oscar gave him a wave, so he headed inside.

"Hey, Boss."

"Don't start that, Russell." Oscar glared at him but grinned at the same time.

"Only my mother ever called me Russell. Does that mean you're schooling me?"

"You bet your ass."

He laughed. "Okay, I hear you. Hello, Oscar."

"Russ." Oscar smiled. "You started without me."

Russ looked at the empty bottle in his hand and set it on the counter. "Oh. Yeah. Long day."

"Not judging. Just means I can have one too. Check out the steaks. They've been marinating for a couple of hours. Rose put them in for me while I was at work."

"No kidding? That was nice of her." Oh, they looked amazing. Thick and lean. He'd have to wait a bit on the fire. These babies needed a good sear and then slow heat. "How do you take your steak?"

"Rare." Oscar popped the tops off of two beers and handed him one. "Like really rare. You?"

"Trot the cow past the coals, I'm good."

"Nice." Oscar held up his bottle. "To... uh. To a beautiful night."

"To a beautiful night," he agreed. They knocked the bottoms of their bottles together before drinking deep. God, he really appreciated a good beer.

"I'm going to start the sides. I've got some sweet potatoes and brussels sprouts to throw in." He set his beer down and picked up the pan of veggies to roast.

"Wow. Sounds great."

He shrugged. "Easy stuff, just took a little prep."

"I'm spoiled. Rose does all the cooking at my house, and Emmett did it before she did. I never learned."

"You don't cook at all?" That seemed absurd.

"I make a mean peanut butter and banana sandwich. And I'm told my toast is perfectly browned."

He laughed. "And here I thought you had it together."

"No. Oh, no. *Together* is not a word that most people use to describe me." Russ watched the way Oscar's Adam's apple bobbed as he swallowed his beer.

Damn.

"Were you going to put that in the oven?"

He looked down at the pan of vegetables in his hands. "Oh. Yeah. Thanks." Jesus. The man had only been here five minutes and he was already getting distracted. What was the matter with him? "You wanna check out my fire?"

"Sounds good."

He set a timer on his phone for the veggies and led Oscar out the back door. He trotted down the back steps, but Oscar froze on the porch.

"Oh, man."

"What's up?"

"That sunset. I'd forgotten how gorgeous it is from here."

It was the perfect spot to watch. He looked up at the deep oranges and pinks in the sky. "Jonas once told me he built the house—"

"So Mom could watch the sunrise from the front porch and the sunset from the back."

He nodded and opened up the grill. Everything was ashy and perfect. He started shifting most of the coals to one side of the grill and popped the foil packet of mesquite bricks in, tucking some of the coals around it to make things smoke up.

"Looking good." Oscar joined him, standing shoulder to shoulder and smelling so good. "Mesquite?"

"Thanks. Yeah. Really wakes things up."

"Cool."

"You know, this is actually ready. You want to grab the steaks?"

"On it." Oscar disappeared back into the house, and he breathed a sigh of relief, reminding himself to cool it.

Twenty minutes later they each had fresh, ice-cold beers, and big plates of steak and veggies. They took their supper out to a picnic table on the side of the house where he'd hung some lights under the umbrella that stuck up through the middle of the table. Oscar pulled out his phone and put on some alternative station on Pandora.

"This looks so good," Oscar said, cutting into his steak. "You know, I can't remember the last time I had dinner out without the kids that wasn't work-related. Like just an adult thing? Honestly, I can't."

"For real? That's too long, man."

"It is. Thanks for suggesting this." Oscar put a bite in his mouth and smiled. "Oh, so good."

"Cool." He cut himself some and took a bite too, and he had to agree it was fantastic. "That marinade is perfect."

"I'll tell Rose you said so. And seriously. Thanks for the invitation."

He looked up at Oscar and smiled. "Sure. It's just... been a while since we hung out."

"Since Dad died." Oscar nodded. "That's way too long, and I'm sorry. I didn't intend to dump this place on you. I—"

"I know." He looked into Oscar's eyes and realized with a strangely calm acceptance that if Oscar wanted it, he'd let those brilliant blues cut right into his soul. "It's all good. No worries, okay?"

Oscar watched him for a long moment. "Yeah. Thanks, Russ. I appreciate that."

"You bet." Oscar's smile made him blush, and he looked back down at his supper, cutting himself another piece of his steak. "So, tell me how the girls are doing."

"Oh, wow." That smile was different now, affectionate. Oscar did have a soft spot for those girls. "The twins are adorable right now. They're not babies anymore, you know? And the older they get, the more different they become. Riley's girly and Zoe is a tomboy. They get along great, but they look at everything differently. It's going to be quite a ride, I think."

Russ laughed. "Kind of the point, right?"

"Oh, absolutely the point. Yes. I'm grateful for every minute of it."

"I believe that." He did. One thing he knew about Oscar, the man didn't take family time for granted. "And Sophie?"

"She's... good, I think. She's a solid student. She seems to have a couple of nice friends, but she's so quiet. I'm honestly hoping I'm not missing something. I don't think I am, but she's a tough one to read."

"Maybe you should get her over here to ride." God, who was he to give parenting advice? But Sophie needed to ride; he just knew it. "She's got a way with the horses."

"She does?"

"Honest. I saw it in her the day we buried Jonas. She was great energy in the barn, so calm. Might be good for her."

"We could try it, I guess. We'll have the farm for a little while yet. Though I'd hate to get her hooked and then —well."

A little while. He still couldn't believe it. He'd better start putting out some feelers for a new job. "And Emily?"

Oscar sighed and took a long pull on his beer before answering. "Emily is good, but she's got this one last year in high school, and then she's going to college. She wants to go Ivy League."

"She's a smart kid, isn't she?"

"She is. Driven."

"I bet she gets in, then. College will be good for her."

"Oh. Yeah. I mean, she's been working her butt off for the

grades. I want her to go. She needs to go. I just... this farm better sell well. I don't know how else I'll pay for it."

"I guess loans and all suck, huh?"

Oscar shrugged. "I don't want to go that route. She's got three sisters, and Sophie is only a couple of years behind her."

"Emily could work to help pay, maybe?" He was on his own and working at sixteen after all.

"She'll probably have to, yeah. But I want to do as much as I can. I'd hate to see her in debt when she graduates."

He smiled at Oscar. "You're a good dad." He wasn't feeling like such a good person right now, himself. He wanted the farm to sell well on the one hand so Oscar and the girls could have what they needed, but on the other hand he didn't want it to sell at all.

Oscar laughed. "I do my best."

"You want another beer?"

Oscar nodded. "Just one, I'm driving."

When he got up, hands full of beer bottles, Oscar got up with him and cleared their plates. In the kitchen, they spent a few minutes cleaning up without really talking much. He kept glancing at Oscar, but the man seemed relaxed, busy hands loading the dishwasher.

"You do that a lot, huh?"

"Dishes? Every night. Rose does all the cooking, I don't make her clean too."

There was nothing not to like about this man. Nothing, dammit. Not a thing he could twist into a good reason to let go of his feelings. He turned and opened the fridge, then pulled out Oscar's beer.

"I've got the—" Oscar was right there when he turned around, church key in one hand. Right there, in Russ's space, not hardly a step away. "Bottle. Opener."

They both froze. He swore it wasn't just him. Oscar was

staring at him, blue eyes shining, and he couldn't breathe. "Oscar."

"I—sorry." Oscar started to step away, but Russ reached for him, caught him by the back of his neck, and pulled their lips together.

Oscar fought him for a few seconds but then relaxed into the kiss like a dream, which was what it was. A dream coming true. He rested a hand on Oscar's hip and leaned, and Oscar answered with a soft sound and tangled their fingers together.

Fuck, Oscar smelled so good. Musky and warm, a little hint of beer. Oscar's kiss was gentle and a little tentative, but he could feel a hunger brewing under it, lighting his skin on fire. He moaned softly, and Oscar cut the kiss short with a gasp, pulling just an inch away. Those beautiful eyes were cast down where Russ couldn't see them, but he could see the knot in Oscar's brow well enough.

He didn't move right away, he didn't dare. But he could only stand like this—this close—for so long. Russ grew impatient and kissed Oscar again, and Oscar leaned in, this time cupping his jaw with warm, trembling fingers.

This was the real deal. This was happening. *That's it, babe,* he thought. *Just relax. Breathe, and let me do this for you.* He covered Oscar's hand with his own, but Oscar whimpered at the touch and froze suddenly, breaking their kiss again.

"It's okay," he whispered.

"No." Oscar dropped his hand and took a step back, and Russ felt the panic rise in his throat.

Don't spook him. Take it easy. "It's hard; it's got to be. But it's been a long time, Oscar. Maybe I—"

"No, Russ. We—I can't." Oscar stepped farther away. He reached out and scooped up the keys to the minivan off the kitchen counter.

"You can. Oscar, please. Wait." Russ didn't understand what was so awful about him. He was a good man. Oscar had felt that pull between them; he knew it. "We can take it slow, you know? I can do that. Really slow."

I want to help. I want to be there for you. I can be that guy.

"I'm sorry, Russ. I shouldn't have done that—let you... I can't. I just can't."

"You gotta start somewhere, Oscar. Why not—"

"No. No, I don't. I don't have to start."

Russ swallowed hard against the cold ache in his chest and jumped as the screen door slammed shut.

CHAPTER SEVEN

OSCAR TORE out of the driveway of Stable Hill like he was being chased, but barely two minutes down the access road, he pulled over, turned on his hazards, and put the minivan in Park. The tears in his eyes blinded him and his hands shook so hard he didn't trust himself with the steering wheel. He wrapped his arms around his ribs and let it out.

He missed Emmett.

It was hard, selling Dad's farm.

He wanted Russ.

He'd be okay; he knew that. He was just overwhelmed. He let his head drop to the steering wheel and tried to breathe.

God, he just *wanted*—

He'd wanted Russ then. Russ was kind and warm. But then again, Jeffrey made him ache the other day with a smile. This obviously wasn't about either of them. It couldn't be. It was about him, about everything he was losing and how much he missed being touched.

It took him a long while with the windows rolled down and the cool night air coming in to begin to breathe again, to pull it together enough that he could drive.

Back on the road, he tried to turn the raw, empty feeling left by all that violent emotion into something that made some kind of rational sense, but it was so... big. So much bigger than he could get a handle on all at once. There was his responsibility to the girls. There was Emmett's memory and the unpredictable grief that still, three years later, would catch him by surprise at a movie, in the hardware store, at the car wash. There was grief over losing Dad and losing the farm.

There was the guilt.

The longing.

His own undeniable need.

And then there was Russ. He felt awful for doing what he'd done. The man's kiss had been real, he knew, genuinely and freely offered. He understood it came from a good place. But it reached right out to him and wrapped itself around a heart he thought had died with Emmett, finding one small, sensitive corner still beating. A fragile little piece that took joy in connecting—real joy in a validating, honest moment with someone else.

It was shocking, and he didn't know what to do with it. All he knew was he couldn't stay in that space for very long. It was too personal. He felt too exposed. And he wondered if he'd ever stop feeling like he was betraying Emmett when he thought about dating again.

Russ wasn't the right guy, anyway. He was an employee and had been a friend to Dad. Oscar was sure it wasn't Russ he wanted, not really; he just... wanted. It had been such a damn long time.

He wasn't any closer to answers when he pulled into his driveway, and he frowned at the beat-up black Honda Civic parked behind Rose's car. He looked at it curiously. Some of Emily's friends were driving now. Maybe it was Jessie or Keisha.

He ducked into the garage so he could go through the kitchen and grab a beer. Rose met him before he got to the fridge. "There's a boy upstairs."

"A what?"

"A boy. With Emily."

"What? You let her take a boy upstairs? To her room?" He tossed his coat over a kitchen chair.

"I didn't let her do anything, Oscar. She just did it."

He looked at Rose. "Sorry. I'll take care of it. Thanks, Rose." They hadn't talked about boys in the house. They hadn't talked about boys much at all. That was his fault. He didn't know what to say or how to say it, and Emily was a good kid, and—

He stopped outside her closed bedroom door. Music was playing inside, and he leaned closer to the door to listen, but all he could hear was low voices. He was thinking about knocking, but then a deep voice let out a low laugh and instead he just barged in.

Emily and the boy she was with looked up sharply from where they were sitting on Emily's bed. The boy was sitting beside her, close, but both of them were fully clothed and the kid was showing her something on an iPad.

It took him less than a second to regret not knocking.

"Oz! What the hell?"

"Emily. I would like to talk with you, please. And your friend needs to go home now."

"Oh my God, Oz. We're watching videos! What's the problem?"

He took a deep breath. If this boy meant anything to her, he didn't want to embarrass her any more than he already had. But the kid needed to go home now. "I'll meet you in the kitchen."

He left the bedroom door wide-open and headed back

downstairs, where Rose was waiting for him. Surprise, surprise. "He's going home."

And sure enough, a breath later, Emily and the boy came downstairs. The boy seemed pretty relaxed, but Emily stormed right by them, pulling the kid out the door.

He sighed. "I know. She's seventeen. Not twelve."

"She is," Rose agreed softly.

"What would Emmett do?"

"Exactly what you're doing, sweetheart."

"Panic?"

"Parent her the best he could." He felt her hand on his back, warm and reassuring as ever, and he nearly burst into tears again. He was sure Emmett would do a better job right now. He went to the door and caught Emily kissing the boy, who was leaning against the Civic. He watched for half a second, feeling horrified, and then took a breath, shook his head, and paced back into the kitchen.

When Emily finally came back in, she was upset. "You couldn't have knocked, maybe?"

He nodded. "I should have knocked. I'm sorry."

She looked at him for a long moment and then sighed and sat on one of the stools at the breakfast bar. Rose had suddenly disappeared.

"We need some rules, Emily."

"I'm seventeen, Oz. Come on. And I really like him."

"What's his name?"

"Brian."

"Does Brian have a last name?"

"Schulman."

"Okay. Good. And you really like him?"

"Yes. We weren't doing anything, Oz. He was showing me iFunny videos. That's it."

"He had his arm around you."

"Really? So what? He still had his stupid sneakers on. Jesus!" She pushed back from the counter.

He rolled his eyes. "Wait, Emily. Hang on. Stay a second."

She did stay. But she was looking at him expectantly, like there was something specific she wanted him to say.

Shit. Think, think, think. "Uh. I would love to meet Brian."

"Yeah?"

"Yes. So how about you see if he can come for dinner this weekend."

"For real?" Emily relaxed. He'd swear he saw it in her shoulders.

Oh, hallelujah. "You like him, right? He likes you too? You want me to trust him?"

"Yeah. I do, Oz."

"Okay, well, then, I need to meet him. Then we'll talk about rules."

"Okay. Yeah, cool. I'll ask."

"Cool." He smiled at her. "Good."

Emily jumped off her stool, slipped around the counter, and threw her arms around his neck. "Thanks, Oz."

He hugged her tight. Emmett's firstborn, his husband's namesake. He loved all of Emmett's girls, but Emily had been his buddy since the first day they'd met. She was the first one of the girls to understand how Oscar felt about her father, and she had simply accepted that Emmett could love a man the same way he'd loved her mom. She was the only one old enough to understand what was really happening the day they stood up together in court and Oscar adopted them all as his own. And she was going to be the first to leave the house, to move on and begin her own life.

"You can let me go now, Oz," she chastised softly. But it was said with love, he knew that. He could hear the affection in her voice.

"Sorry. I think maybe I'm jealous." He grinned at her.

Emily laughed. "Oh, Oz. You're such a derp."

He was. He was a total, uh, *derp*. "Good night, Em."

"Good night!" Emily took off for her bedroom, and his eyes followed until she disappeared up the stairs.

He let out a long breath. *Jesus*. This single parenting gig was not for the fainthearted, but it seemed like maybe he wasn't a total disaster at it.

"Beer," he said out loud. That's where he'd been headed when he walked in the door. He was just reaching for the refrigerator handle when his cell phone rang. He sighed, pulled it out of his pocket, and answered as soon as he figured out who it was. "Hey, Jeffrey."

"Oscar. Sorry to bother you in the evening, but I wanted to let you know that I'm having some of the things we talked about delivered to Stable Hill tomorrow."

"Oh, great. I'll let Russ know. And I'll get over there early next week sometime to look at the paint and the floor in the upstairs hall. I guess I need to deal with Mom's room too." Oscar sighed. He felt like he was being haunted by memories today.

"Not easy stuff, I know. You have a little time, Oscar. I won't show it for a couple of weeks yet. Russ and I need to address a couple of issues with the barns first. You're going to have to put a little money in, but I want to make sure you put it where it'll get you the most return. You're lucky, though. It's really in fine condition and well looked after."

He smiled. Dad had been proud of the place, and Russ didn't like to have time on his hands. It was a good combination. "Thanks, Jeffrey."

"Sure thing. Have a good night."

"You too." He hung up the phone and pulled open the fridge.

"Is Emily okay, Oscar?"

He sighed and started to close the fridge again but

changed his mind. He wanted that goddamn beer. "Yes. I told her I wanted to meet *Brian*, and she should invite him for dinner this weekend. I hope that's all right."

"Oh, that's grand, sweetheart. Just lovely."

"I guess."

"I'll make lasagna. That's what I made the first time Emmett brought you over to my house, do you remember?"

"I do. And garlic bread, and a lovely red wine." He remembered everything about that night. He'd brought her a rose plant in a green-and-white planter. She'd seemed so happy to meet him, and if she'd had any issue with Emmett dating a man, she hadn't let on. He'd felt instantly welcome.

"Well, we won't have the wine for young Brian, hm? But men like hearty comfort food. It'll put him in a mind to talk."

"You're a wise woman, Rose."

"I won you over, didn't I?"

He laughed and opened his beer. She had. He thought it was Emmett's smile, but maybe it had been the lasagna. He toasted the air, hoping to hell her lasagna would be enough for Brian.

CHAPTER EIGHT

RUSS HAD just returned from a ride out to the east pasture when he spotted the truck coming up the driveway. He shook his head. Seriously? How much stuff was Jeff bringing in? He nudged Angel off the grass and walked her down toward the house as the truck pulled up in front. Right behind it was Jeff's damn shiny Mercedes.

"Hey, Russ."

"Mr. Stokes."

"Oh, come on. Really?"

Russ looked at him. "Door is open. I'm going to take Angel up to the barn, and then I'll be down to help, okay?"

"Sure. Sounds good, *Mr. White*." Jeff's tone was annoyed and sarcastic.

That was just fine. Russ nodded and nudged Angel in a circle, and then they made their way back up to the barn. She went without an argument, but she tossed her head and fussed at him all the way up there.

"Okay, what is it?" he asked her, getting her on crossties. "You think I was rude to him, huh?"

Angel stood there, eyeballing him.

"I know, he's a good-looking man. You're right. But he's one of those guys you meet in a bar, you know? A fuck buddy is all. This is business. This is Oscar's deal. I need to respect that." He loosened her girth, opened the buckle, and let the saddle slide off into his arms.

She stomped a foot at him as he hung the saddle pad to air out and set her saddle on a stand.

"I'm telling you, girl. I know what I'm talking about."

He got a snort for his trouble.

"Oh, fine." He groaned. "Do you have to be so right all the damn time? I'm a little wound up, okay? I had a rough night last night. Oscar and I had this great supper and all. We were talking and getting along good. The steaks were amazing." He took out a brush and started working her over with it, smoothing out her coat and combing out the dust. "I wasn't gonna make any moves. I decided that before, I swear. I was just going to let the night be, keep it friendly, have a good time. I already knew he wasn't interested. I don't know what I was thinking. But he was right there all of a sudden, and...."

Right there. Warmth and breath, and those beautiful eyes. "Something told me to go for it." He sighed and started working over her withers with the brush. "I shouldn't have listened."

She flicked him with her tail.

"Very funny. I'm serious. I scared him off. That's done." Oscar had shut it down hard.

He switched to her other side. "I shouldn't take it out on Jeff, though. You're right. That's kind of a dick move even if he is... or was... just a fuck buddy." He took a deep breath and let it out, then tossed the brush back into the tack bucket. "Okay, girl. I'm going to tuck you into your stall, and we'll do turnout together later. Yes?"

As soon as he took her off the crossties, Angel nudged his chest with her nose.

"Angel."

She did it again. He grinned at her.

"Okay, but only one, and only because you're so full of good advice." He pulled a peppermint out of his pocket and pulled off the wrapper, then held it out in the palm of his hand. She lapped it up, and he swore somehow she grinned at him.

By the time he got her put away and made it back down to the house, the truck was gone and Jeffrey was inside unpacking. In the living room there was some artwork stacked against the couch, a whole bunch of fake flowers on the coffee table, and an upright piano stood against the far wall where a long table used to be.

"Piano?"

"People who buy these old farmhouses want a homey feel." Jeff's voice was flat.

"And a piano does that?"

"It does. Among other things."

"Huh." He starting picking through the artwork. "Where'd the table go?"

"Upstairs."

He glanced at Jeffrey, who was pulling a couple of vases out of a cardboard box. "You uh... you need any help?"

"No, Mr. White. I think I can handle it."

He sighed. "Look. I'm sorry, okay? Oscar is my boss, and... I'm in a tough position."

Jeff looked up and gave him a wicked smile and a hot stare. "You look like you're in a pretty good position to me."

Motherfucker. That look went right to his balls. He swallowed hard.

Jeff laughed and started separating the flowers on the

coffee table and filling the vases like he knew what he was doing. "You could make the bed upstairs."

"Bed?"

"Oscar told me to go ahead and pick up a bed for the master bedroom. There are sheets and pillows and stuff in a bag up there."

"Oh. Uh. Yeah, I can do that."

"That's not too weird for you, is it? I mean if it is, you could—"

"No. I got it." And an excuse to leave the room right now wasn't a bad thing either.

"Great, thanks."

He headed upstairs to Jonas's room. It was weird seeing a real bed in here again, but it felt right somehow. He hadn't realized how much worse it felt to have the room just sitting empty until it wasn't. The long table from the living room was in here now too. It fit very comfortably under the window, and Jeff had moved a little silver tray off the dresser to sit on it.

He picked the bag up off the floor and dumped it out on Oscar's mother's Queen Anne chair that sat on one corner of the room, then found the sheets and started making the bed. He was pretty sure it was a king mattress, and although it felt huge, it fit in the room just fine. No wonder Jonas had always seemed so small in that hospital bed; the room dwarfed the bed and the bed dwarfed him.

He got the sheets on, put all four pillows in their pillowcases, and was getting the comforter out of its bag when Jeff appeared in the doorway.

"Hey, looking good in here."

"Thanks."

"I was worried the king might be a little big for the room, but the queen didn't seem to be enough."

"Naw, I think it's perfect. It's the biggest room up here, the only room with its own bathroom. Probably ought to look like a master, right?" He grabbed the corners of the comforter and shook it out across the bed. "Oh, this is nice."

"I confess, I've used the same one before in another house. It's got a classic look and kind of fits in anywhere."

"Sounds like someone I know."

Jeff turned to look at him, and it was his turn to stare. Tailored suit pants, pressed shirt, blue tie loosened at the throat. Jeff always had such a squeaky-clean look. Not everyone needed to put their back into a hard day's work to make a living. Jeff's soft hands and clean shave suited him just fine.

Last night stung bad, but if he couldn't have that, maybe he could let himself have this after all.

"Yeah?"

"You're looking pretty good to me right now too."

"Well, well. If I didn't know better—"

"You don't know shit." He reached for Jeff, his fingers tangling in that fancy tie.

"What happened to your tough position?" Jeff grinned, letting him pull them closer together, those eyes flashing with the heat that had set him on fire earlier.

"Mm. It's still really hard."

"Fuck." Jeff went for him, teeth biting into his lower lip and hands tugging at his waistband and fly. He ached, his balls felt heavy, and his cock shoved against his zipper. He reached down to help, but Jeff shoved his hands away with a grunt.

"Wow." He grinned, throwing them up in the air in a hands-off gesture. "Okay, okay."

Jeff leaned on him until his back hit the closet door.

"Jeff." Russ barely got the name out before Jeff pinned his hands over his head and kissed him again, harder, tangling tongues. He rolled his hips up against Jeff's, the resistance making him gasp.

They rubbed together, grunting and moaning until finally Jeff broke off the kiss and dropped to his knees.

"Fuck, yes."

Jeff tore open Russ's jeans and shoved them down, then smoothly took Russ's aching cock into his mouth.

"Oh fuck, Jeff. Please." He needed. Fuck, he needed this. He dropped his hands to Jeff's head, threading his fingers into dark hair as his cock disappeared into glorious wet heat. "Yes!"

Might have been that look Jeff gave him earlier. Might have been the moment. Might have been the rejection from Oscar the night before or the fact that this was the first time he and Jeff weren't parked behind a building, getting off in his truck. Might have been any combination of those things, and it hardly mattered. Right now he just needed to come. He wanted it like he wanted nothing else in his whole fucking life.

He started to thrust, and Jeff let him, strong fingers digging into his ass, spreading him, fingering his hole. He looked down, watching his dick slide in and out, and in and out of Jeff's mouth, watching that little vein pop out in Jeff's forehead. Jeff swallowed around him, and he squeezed his eyes shut and made a wild keening sound, feeling everything in him drop into his balls.

"Fuck. Fuck yes," he whispered. *Come on, man. You need this bad.*

His hips started to jerk, and he pulled back a little. Jeff replaced that amazing mouth with a tight fist and pumped him hard and fast, two fingers still putting pressure on his ass. He couldn't breathe, he gasped and panted and kept his eyes closed against the dizzy feeling, and a second later he shot so hard he had to lean on the wall and flatten out his hands to keep his knees under him.

"I want to fuck you." Jeff stood and took a deep kiss. "I want to fuck you, Russ. Please."

"My room. Bedside table."

Jeff couldn't have been gone half a minute. Russ was still leaning against the wall, still trying to convince himself to open his eyes, when he heard the tearing of a foil wrapper. Jeff turned him, and he braced his hands on the wall, letting Jeff coax his legs wider and spread him with lubed fingers. He moaned as Jeff slipped one inside him.

"Jesus, you're tight, Russ."

"It's been a long time, man. Gonna have to start slow, okay?"

"I won't hurt you." A second finger joined the first, making him moan. "See? Feels good, right? Just relax, Russ. I'll make it so good."

He nodded, not able to speak. Between the head rush, Jeff's voice, and the incredible sensation of Jeff's fingers, he was long gone, floating on hormones, his senses overwhelmed and raw. He felt Jeff's cock nudge him a couple of times, heavy pressure, and then he groaned as Jeff entered him.

"Jesus, Russ." Jeff panted behind him. Strong arms snaked around his chest, and Jeff started to move, rocking him gently, slow and deep. "That's it. So good, babe."

It was good, the thick cock filling him up, making him burn. It was better than he remembered—better than he'd ever had. He was a total slut for Jeff, moaning and arching, rolling his ass to meet Jeff's thrusts. He knew it, and he didn't care. He couldn't help it. He begged with his body, letting Jeff take him.

Jeff took enough time that Russ's cock came back for more, and he jerked off just because Jeff wanted him to, fisting his own prick in all the right ways until he came again.

Jeff grunted and built up after that, rutting fast and hard behind Russ until he came in shuddering waves. The two of them hung there in silence, arms braced and hips rocking together slowly as they found their breath again.

"Jesus Christ, Russ."

That about said it all. "It had been a while."

"That was incredible. You are incredible. My God."

He laughed softly. "I was desperate and horny. And it wasn't the back of my fucking truck."

"So if I make you wait a few weeks, you'll do that again?"

"Shut up, asshole."

Jeff laughed and moved away, leaving cool air at his back. The man disappeared into the master bathroom, and he headed for his room, feeling a little like he'd been scrubbed with sandpaper, inside and out. But man, he liked that feeling. He collapsed on his twin bed and looked at the ceiling, trying to get his brain to fire up again.

Jeff joined him a couple of minutes later, sliding into the little bed with him, and kissed him slow, a hot, curious tongue sliding over his.

"I don't think I've been in a twin bed since I was in college."

"Cute. Don't make fun of me." He hadn't really intended that remark to have a bite.

"I'm not making fun of... what? Russ. Come on."

"Sorry. I'm sorry. I guess I'm tired. That was mind-blowing, Jeff, no lie. You were amazing. I just... wow. Took off. Me and the clouds."

"You're hotter than a four-alarm fire, Carolina."

"Hey, that was pretty good for a Yankee."

Jeff chuckled. "Now who's making fun of whom?"

He just grinned and nipped at Jeff's chin. Jeff settled back, and he curled in, resting his head on Jeff's shoulder. "I'm gonna fall 'sleep."

"Good, me too. I've got time."

"Gotta bring the horses in 'fore it gets dark, but Miles can manage without me if I'm late." He yawned.

"Close your eyes. I've got you."

That was the last thing he heard before he passed out.

CHAPTER NINE

HOLY SHIT, he got his hottie.

Jeffrey had been awake for a few minutes, but he hadn't dared to open his eyes yet. He was a little afraid to find out it was all a dream or a hallucination or something. He had a few rules for guys he picked up. Things like not using last names and not sticking around after they both got what they needed. He was very used to safe and sane one-nighters, and perfectly happy to keep those men out of his daily life.

But his little Southern hottie from the River had just become more than a hit-or-miss exchange of incredibly satisfying blow jobs in the back of a pickup truck.

Finally.

Jeffrey wasn't going anywhere. Russ not only had a last name and a job, but the farm manager had relevance to his life now. He ran his fingers down one muscled arm and breathed in deep. Russ smelled like horses and sex, and probably needed a shower, but he wasn't complaining. He liked it. Loved it even.

He wondered what Russ would say when those green eyes

opened up again. Would Russ toss him out? Would they have some nice pillow talk and dinner together? Would he be all business and get back to work?

To be fair, he did have to make a couple of phone calls—it was the middle of the workday after all. And Russ had said something about the horses too. What a strange choice in lovers he'd made. Assuming that was what they were now—lovers. He wouldn't argue with being a recurring booty call, as long as they got to hook up in a real bed once in a while. His back wasn't going to miss that truck. Or his knees either.

He finally let himself open his eyes and discovered that the light had gotten low. He looked around Russ's bare room, astonished at how simply the man lived. No pictures, no posters. Just a guitar in one corner and a stereo, a chair and a small empty-looking desk, and a beat-up cowboy hat and a couple of baseball caps hanging on the wall by the closet door. And this damn twin bed that was threatening to do his back in.

He needed to get up. He slipped out of the little bed and stood stiffly, trying not to wake Russ. He found his shirt and pulled it on, then ran his fingers through his hair to straighten it. He watched his little hottie sleep for another minute, then shook his head at himself and headed downstairs to snoop through Russ's kitchen.

He put on a pot of coffee and made himself a peanut butter and banana sandwich, then took a cup and his plate over to the vintage farmhouse dining room table, where he sat on one of the benches and pulled out his phone to check his email. The appraisal on the Van Dyke property came through with a good number. The Dorfman house failed the mold test, and the chimney had some issue... maybe they could deal with that in escrow. He was about to forward that email on to Jessica in the office, but then his phone rang.

Oh, look. Oscar. Life was so interesting.

"Hello, Oscar."

"Hey, Jeffrey, I was just checking in to see how things are going at the house."

"Things are good." *Fucking amazing. Your manager is a firecracker in the sack.* "I brought a truck in this morning with the piano and the king bed, some other details. I think it looks pretty good."

"Awesome. Thanks for taking care of that. Russ let you in okay?"

Boy, did he ever. "Oh, yeah. Got in fine. Hey. How does Thursday work for you? I'll need about an hour. Can you meet me here after work? I'm going to come out early in the day and should have a good idea about what else needs work before we can list."

"Yeah, I want it on the market ASAP. Thursday is good. I won't get there until at least 5:30 or quarter of six. Is that okay?"

"Do I smell coffee?" Russ appeared at the bottom of the stairs, hair slightly mussed and looking adorable in jeans, a T-shirt, and bare feet.

Jeffrey held up a hand in a *stop* gesture. "Sure. That should work fine, Oscar."

Russ froze on the bottom step, eyes wide, and he covered his mouth with his fingers.

"Okay, I've got you on the calendar. I'll see you then. Thanks, Jeffrey."

"My pleasure. Take care."

"You too. Night."

Oscar hung up, and Jeffrey double-checked that the call had disconnected before saying another word. Then he grinned at Russ. "I assume you don't want him to know."

"Well, seems like a bad idea. Yeah." Russ strode over and offered a kiss. Their lips met almost curiously, gently, exploring like they were new to this. Like they were learning each other, and really, he supposed they were; everything was different now, wasn't it?

Russ pulled away with a smile and headed for the coffeepot, leaving him blinking and bemused.

Okay, then.

They'd gone from first-name privileges-only to domestic bliss in an afternoon. It was enough to make his head spin.

"I wouldn't mind, you know. If Oscar knew."

"No?" Russ sounded less sure.

Interesting. "Well, it's not a conflict of interest or anything. I'm selling his house, not writing your employment contract."

"I guess, but it feels—"

"Because you didn't tell him right away?"

"Well, yeah. Partly." Russ sat down at the table opposite him with a cup of black coffee.

"Let me ask you something, *Mr. White*."

Russ sighed at him.

"Sorry. I'm serious here, though. What's next, in your mind? Was this a one-off? Are we still just fucking around? You think I can have your cell number, now?"

"You can have my cell number. I don't know about the rest yet, you know?"

That was fair. Jeffrey wasn't entirely clear on what he wanted yet either. "Okay. Then there's no need to risk pissing Oscar off yet."

"I'm not an asshole, Jeff. I'm just not sure how these things work."

"And I'm not pushing you. I can give you an honest answer, though. I loved that. I like you. If you give me your cell number, I'm going to use it."

Russ smiled at him. "Okay. Unlock your phone and give it to me."

He handed it over, and Russ dialed in his number and

created a contact. Russ White. And for "Company," Russ typed in *The River* and handed the phone back with a grin. "So you don't confuse me with your Grindr buddies."

"Oh, there's no forgetting you. Not after that encounter. That was transcendent."

Russ blushed hard. "Jesus, Jeff. You're making me all self-conscious."

"I'm telling you, Russ. I want more. I want more of you."

He saw Russ swallow before getting up from the table. "I gotta deal with those horses. I gotta move some hay. And I'm not done checking all that fence."

All right, that was fine. Russ had to sit with this for a bit and so did he. In the meantime, he had Russ's number and he'd check in on the man in a day or so. "I'm going to be back on Thursday to look over the barns with a contractor. Oscar's meeting me here after work. 5:30 or so."

"Sure thing."

He stood up from the table and watched Russ, who was filling up a travel mug with coffee.

"I've got a couple things to wrap up...."

Russ looked at him sidelong, then made his way back over. "Really. I'm not an asshole. I just need to—"

"Stop." He pulled Russ into a hard kiss, deliberately cutting off the guy's words. Russ relaxed against him and accepted his lips, his tongue, and gave him a long moan. Jeffrey smiled as he pulled away. "Everything good takes time."

"Okay. Thanks, Jeff." Russ smiled at him.

"You want me to lock the door when I go?"

"God, I haven't locked a door since the day I started here. I've got a key on my ring, but I never use it."

"I love that."

Russ stomped into his boots, pulled on a cap, and screwed the top on his travel mug. "See you Thursday, man."

"See you Thursday." Jeff watched Russ head out the back door and then looked at the new contact in his phone. *But I'll talk to you sooner*.

CHAPTER TEN

OSCAR GREEDILY guarded his Friday-night custom of binge-watching shows on Netflix. It was like a reward after a long week. It wasn't so much about whatever show he picked, but the chance to sit on his ass and drink a beer, and know he was going to basically be left alone for most of the evening.

Tonight, though, wasn't a Netflix night. It was meet-Brian night.

Brian. The boyfriend.

The boyfriend with the black Civic. With tinted rear windows. Who kissed his daughter right out there in his driveway last weekend.

Jesus Christ, Emmett. Emily's almost done with high school. She's almost a freshman in college. She's almost a woman.

And he was pretty sure Emily was in love right now too. Sweetly in love, kind of how he thought Emmett would have wanted. He didn't pretend that there wasn't some pressure on Brian, being the first serious boyfriend of his late husband's eldest daughter. Pressure the poor kid probably had no clue was coming. But Oscar understood it well. He was under the same pressure to raise every one of their girls well, to keep them safe, to deliver them to adulthood without their biological father.

Leaving aside the pressure of paying for four girls to go to college, it was already a stressful responsibility sometimes. Add that detail back in and the stress often felt crushing. But somehow it was going to happen.

The doorbell rang and he looked at his watch. The kid was almost fifteen minutes early. That seemed like bad form, didn't it? Emily appeared at the top of the stairs as if she'd planned to open the front door herself, but no, he was going to take that on, thank you very much.

"Oz."

"I've got it." He smiled at her. "You look pretty." She was in jeans and a sweater, nothing fancy, but her eyes were bright, and her cheeks were pink. Despite her figure and her height, she looked ten years old to him still. He wondered if she always would.

Oscar stepped to the front door and opened it, but the man standing there wasn't Brian. This guy was in a suit and tie and had a smile that made his throat so dry he had to swallow. Again.

"Hey, Jeffrey...?" *What are you doing here?*

"Hey, Oscar. Sorry to drop in but I... are you okay?"

"Oh. Oh yeah. Fine. I was just... I was expecting someone else. A date."

"Oh, I... sorry." Jeffrey looked decidedly uncomfortable all of a sudden.

Oscar shook his head. "Emily's date. Boyfriend." *Jesus H. Christ.* "He's coming for dinner."

"Oh." Jeffrey smiled at him. "Gotcha. That sounds a little stressful."

He huffed. "A little."

"I texted you about that paperwork we talked about when

I saw you yesterday, but when I didn't get an answer, I thought I would leave it with you."

"Oh, sure. No problem. Come on in."

"Is that Brian, sweetheart?" Rose called from the kitchen.

"No, Rose. It's Jeffrey Stokes, the Realtor." He led Jeffrey into the kitchen. "Jeffrey, this is my mother-in-law, Rose Fisher."

"Oh. Well, hello, Mr. Stokes. It's a pleasure to meet you."

"And you, Mrs. Fisher." Jeffrey set the paperwork down on the kitchen counter. "I… didn't realize you were married."

"I'm not. I mean, I was. My husband, Emmett, died three years ago." *Awkward. God.* He'd never figured out a simple way to deal with all of that.

"Oh, I'm so sorry. I had no idea." Jeffrey's eyes lingered on him a second longer than was just polite, and he held the gaze.

"No, it's okay. Really."

Jeffrey gave him a nod and then smiled at Rose, turning on the charm. "Are you making lasagna? It smells divine."

"I am."

The doorbell rang again.

"I better get that. Excuse me a minute, Jeffrey."

He hurried for the front door, but this time he arrived seconds behind Emily, just in time to see the way she glowed when Brian smiled at her.

"Hi, Em."

"Hi. You look amazing."

Oscar wasn't sure what the criteria was for "amazing." Brian was in jeans and a button-down shirt, and he had an odd little fuzzy patch stuck to his chin. He couldn't remember if the kid had that a few days ago.

"Hello, Brian."

"Hi, Mr. Kennedy." Brian held out his hand to shake, and

he shook it, getting a nice firm, confident grip. "Thanks for the dinner invitation. It smells amazing in here."

"Emily's grandmother is making lasagna."

Sophie was setting the table in the dining room and smiled as Brian came in. "Oh, you're right, Emily! He *is* cute!"

"Oh my God, Soph." Emily turned bright red.

Brian laughed. "What? I am, actually. I am totally adorable. My mother says so all the time." Brian winked at Emily, and she smiled back and relaxed.

Hey, he might like this kid. *Well played, would-be boyfriend.*

"Sophie, why don't you call your sisters down and have a seat. I'll be right back." He headed back into the kitchen and walked in on Rose and Jeffrey laughing and singing the U of M fight song. He listened to them as they finished their choruses of "Hails," loving the pure joy on Rose's face.

"Wolverines!" he called out when they were done, laughing.

Jeffrey had one of Rose's hands in both of his. "This lovely woman and I have found something in common. Her husband went to my alma mater."

"Small world." He grinned at Jeffrey, noticing the way the man's brown eyes absorbed the light in the kitchen. He had to tear his gaze away to speak to Rose. "Brian's here."

"Oh, goodness. Yes, everything is done. Jeffrey, why don't you stay for dinner? There's plenty, and Oscar never has adult guests."

Wait, what? Wait. Did she just— "Rose."

"I'd love to, Rose. Thank you for the kind invitation."

He blinked. Wow, so smooth. Jeffrey was good at that. The two of them must have really hit it off, because not only were they on a first-name basis already, but Rose wasn't given to spur-of-the-moment invitations like that.

Jeffrey moved around behind Oscar to hang his suit jacket on the back of one of the kitchen chairs and pulled off his tie, rolled it neatly, and put it in his jacket pocket. With the top couple of buttons of his shirt open and his sleeves rolled up, he looked very ready to assist in Rose's kitchen. "What can I do to help?"

He looked so handsome, Oscar couldn't help but admire. The crossover of dressy and casual really worked on him. If Jeffrey had any idea Oscar was looking, he didn't let on.

"Goodness, aren't you sweet. Could you pull the lasagna out of the oven for me? You can put it right on that rack there. Thank you, Jeffrey."

Jeffrey got right to work, and the kitchen wasn't really big enough for the three of them to be working at once, so he excused himself to make sure things were ready in the dining room.

The twins seemed equally infatuated with Emily's boyfriend. Zoe was looking out the window. "Is it a fast car?"

"It's... uh." Brian glanced at Oscar as he came in. "I always drive the speed limit."

Oscar grinned and herded the twins into their seats. Jeffrey brought the lasagna out, hands gloved in Rose's floral oven mitts. "Oh, put that here." He cleared the way and tapped a trivet with his fingers. "Sophie, can you pull over another chair from the living room, please?"

"Who are you?" Riley and Zoe asked at the same time, staring at Jeffrey.

Oscar laughed. "Shall I do introductions? This is Mr. Stokes. He is the Realtor who is helping me sell Grandpa's farm. Mr. Strokes—"

"Jeffrey, please. Mr. Stokes is so—"

"Stuffy. Like a teacher," Zoe interrupted.

He gave Zoe *The Look*. "Zo-zo."

"Totally stuffy. Please call me Jeffrey."

Zoe smiled at Jeffrey, and the little meter next to Jeffrey's name in Oscar's mind jumped from "handsome" to "hot."

"Okay." He cleared his throat. "So. Jeffrey, this is my family. The twins are Zoe on the left and Riley on the right, that's Sophie, and this is Emily and her... friend who happens to be a boy, Brian."

"Oz!" Emily protested, but Brian laughed.

"Wow. You set the bar high, Mr. Kennedy."

Oscar gave Brian a pat on the shoulder. "You're doing fine, Brian. Jeffrey, have a seat."

Rose brought out a salad, and Oscar took the bowl from her.

"Oh, thank you, darling. I'll just get the bread."

"You sit, Rose. I can get the bread. Jeffrey, would you like a glass of wine?"

"If you're having some, I'd love a glass. Thanks."

Oh, he was definitely having wine. How many men was he going to have to work to get off his mind this week? It was like he'd been asleep for three years and suddenly something in him just randomly started working again, like Mother waking the crew aboard the *Nostromo*.

He got the bread on the table and poured wine for Rose, Jeffrey, and then himself.

"So, Mr. Kennedy, what do you do?"

Oscar raised an eyebrow. "I'm a compliance officer for American Express."

"A what?"

"He makes sure the bank is following all the government's rules," Sophie clarified for Brian.

"That's basically it, yes." The food went around the table, everyone helping themselves.

"That sounds complicated."

"It can be. It's brain work for sure." And most people found it boring as hell to talk about. "What are you into, Brian?"

"Me? Uh... I don't know. Right now, I'm finishing my college apps."

"He plays the violin. He wants to go to music school," Emily said proudly. "He's so good. You can tell him, Brian."

"Music school? Sounds great." Maybe the kid really had talent. Of course, he would give his own kids the practicality lecture first, but if one of his girls had talent and drive, he'd be supportive.

Brian looked up from his lasagna. "Yeah?"

"Sure. Do you love it?"

"I do."

"I played the violin." Everyone at the table turned and stared at Jeffrey, and Jeffrey casually sipped his wine.

"What? Did you really?" He probably could have phrased that better.

Jeffrey glared at him. "Yes, Oscar. I really did. I still pick it up sometimes." The words were stern, but the smile and the way Jeffrey's eyes twinkled betrayed the sarcasm.

"Sorry."

Brian was interested. "Did you go to music school?"

"I didn't. Sometimes I wish I had. I hope you find the right conservatory."

"I hope I can get in."

Jeffrey shrugged. "Takes drive and a little luck."

So, wait. First Jeffrey won Rose over, and now Emily's boyfriend too. The man didn't have to try, didn't have to make small talk. Jeffrey just fit right in.

And the guy was hot.

The rest of dinner was really nice. There was lots of conversation from everywhere. Jeffrey and Rose traded stories about their alma mater, Emily and Brian talked about college worries and a round of midterms that was coming up soon. The twins sang everyone a song they'd learned at school. Rose's lasagna disappeared from the pan like vultures had been at it. There was nothing left of the bread either, and the adults polished off a bottle of wine.

Brian, the whole reason for this get-together, was pretty relaxed and seemed like a nice kid. So when Emily wanted to know if they could go hang out in her room, he agreed.

"Just leave the door open."

"Oz!" She rolled her eyes at him. "Fine. Let's go sit in your car, Bri."

Rose looked at him and laughed.

"Thanks for dinner, Mr. Kennedy. Grandma Rose." Brian gave Jeffrey a wave, took Emily by the hand, and out the door they went.

"His back windows are tinted," Jeffrey offered, helpfully.

He snorted. "Yeah, yeah."

"Come on, girls. Reading and bed." Rose herded them toward the stairs. "It was lovely to meet you, Jeffrey. Do come around again."

"I will. A pleasure meeting you too, Rose. Dinner was out of this world. Good night."

Rose smiled, looking pleased and charmed, and disappeared up the stairs after the girls.

He started gathering dishes off the table. "You are one smooth operator, Mr. Stokes."

"She is darling."

"She is, and a lifesaver too. I couldn't do this single-dad gig without her." Okay, that was maybe too much information to share with his Realtor. Damn the wine.

"She told me some more about Emmett. Such an awful loss. I'm so sorry. She thinks you're a wonderful father."

He knew that. He was fairly confident that the fierceness with which he loved those girls made up for most of his shortcomings. They were his sun and moon, even more so after losing Emmett. "She doesn't give herself enough credit.

She moved in here a few weeks before we lost Emmett, and she never left."

"Lucky. She's a damn good cook."

He laughed. "That she is. I had to learn to eat carefully to keep the waistline in check."

Jeffrey brought dirty dishes in from the dining room, and Oscar washed. He started to suggest that Jeffrey didn't need to help, but decided to let himself be selfish. He was enjoying the man's company. It was nice to have another man in his kitchen again.

Jesus, hadn't he just blown off Russ? That had been a hell of a kiss too. What was he doing?

They finished the dishes together and cleaned up the dining room. Jeffrey even helped him put the extra chairs away. All this domestic stuff was easy and wonderful, but it was starting to break his heart.

Jeffrey seemed to know when it was time to go.

"The paperwork I brought is on your desk in the kitchen. Why don't you just bring it with you on Tuesday?"

"Sounds good."

"Thank you again for a nice evening. Your girls are lovely. And I think you could do worse than that boyfriend."

"Oh, I definitely could. Tinted windows notwithstanding." He grinned, but it faded a little and an awkward silence fell between them as he saw Jeffrey out the door.

"Well... good night?" Jeffrey looked at him, brown eyes searching his, and reached for him.

God, he could, he really could. He wanted to, but—

He took a step back. "Yeah. Good night. Thanks for indulging Rose."

Jeffrey's face fell. Oscar knew he was blowing it, first Russ and now Jeffrey. "Yeah. Rose. She's something else. Night."

Shit.

Jeffrey tossed his jacket on the front seat and climbed into his car.

Oscar stood in the doorway and watched as the fancy Mercedes taillights disappeared.

Dammit.

Emmett, I wish you could tell me what I should do, baby. What you'd want me to do. I don't know what's right anymore.

He had feelings for Russ and a hard-on for Jeffrey and didn't know how to handle either one.

CHAPTER ELEVEN

ALL OSCAR had been able to think about all morning was how much money today was going to cost him. He turned up the radio to distract himself, got on the road straight from work, and headed out to the farm.

Jeffrey was at the house with a contractor, a carpenter, and whoever else, poking through the barns, evaluating the indoor ring Dad never finished, and checking out the foundation on the little cottage on the property that hadn't been used since his grandparents lived in it years and years ago.

It seemed so ironic that he was going to have to put money into a farm he needed to unload as soon as possible. Jeffrey had reminded him that the return would be much greater, and while he knew that was probably true, it didn't stop him from wincing at the idea of out-of-pocket costs when things were already fairly tight.

He sighed, put on some Springsteen, and drove, trying not to obsess about it. His mind wandered instead to Emily and the colleges she was looking at, two of which were Ivy League. That brought him back to the money issues, so he moved on to her boyfriend. Brian seemed like a genuinely nice kid, but Oscar had been seventeen once. Nice or not, he knew what was on that boy's mind. He'd tried to have the safe-sex talk with Emily, but that went over like a lead balloon. She insisted she knew it all, and at this point he wasn't sure he had much choice but to hope to hell that was true.

Still, Brian had been a gentleman, and he'd treated Rose with respect, so there had to be someone decent in there.

Right?

That train of thought got Oscar thinking about Jeffrey again, only this time about how he'd said he played the violin. That was wonderful to know about him but seemed to be so incongruous with the rest of the guy's life.

Bet he looks good with a violin in his hands, though.

Oscar could picture it, sleeves rolled up, shirt unbuttoned, eyes closed and brow furrowed, moving with the notes he was playing. Shirt unbuttoned a little more....

He snorted as he pulled off the highway and headed up the access road to Stable Hill. Good grief. Wasn't he trying not to obsess?

Oscar had been so stressed about what was going on without him at the farm that he'd left work a couple of hours early to head out here, hoping to catch the guys Jeffrey had brought in and hear what they had to say firsthand, instead of filtered through a Realtor. He trusted Jeffrey; it wasn't about that. There was just something about looking a contractor in the eye and understanding what they were thinking that he felt would be reassuring, especially if the estimates came in high.

He pulled into the driveway and parked next to Jeffrey's Mercedes but didn't see a contractor or anyone else's truck. He must have missed them.

Dammit.

He climbed out of the minivan but stopped in the

driveway and looked around. Dad had been inspired when he decided to build the main house right here. It was a beautiful spot. The sun was low and setting on the back side of the house, he knew, but the view from here was all long shadows and bright colors on the fields and the treetops. Beautiful.

He smiled and let himself in. The front door was unlocked, as it had been his entire life. But the scene inside wasn't anything he'd seen in the living room before. The sounds were all new too.

"Fuck, yeah."

His Realtor was standing, shirtless and pants open, back against the living room wall. Jeffrey hissed and looked down at another man.

Russ?

Russ was licking and biting at one of Jeffrey's nipples with a hand down Jeffrey's pants, the other holding on to Jeffrey's hip.

Oh. God.

He stood in the doorway, staring. He couldn't help himself, though he knew it wasn't right. He should leave now. He should tell them he was standing there. He should break them up—this was his father's living room, right? He should... he should do something... he....

Oh, Jesus.

They were beautiful together.

"Mmm." Jeffrey hummed, and then his eyes flicked up. Deep, deep, brown eyes locked with Oscar's. A hot, knowing grin tugged at the corner of Jeffrey's lips, and he licked them as that smile grew wider.

Oscar was frozen in place. His feet felt heavy, cemented in the spot he was standing. Jeffrey held their stare, tangled long fingers in Russ's hair and pushed down.

"Yeah." Russ moaned and knelt, then licked the bulge in Jeffrey's open jeans through bright white cotton briefs.

"Come on," Jeffrey mouthed soundlessly across the room to him.

Oscar's skin broke out in goose bumps, nipples growing stiff and hard. He licked his lips and swallowed back a moan.

"Come. Here," Jeffrey whispered again, extending a hand out, beckoning, palm up, toward him. The other hand was still combing through Russ's tousle of blond hair.

He wasn't sure what he was feeling. His dick was liking this, though—his balls had begun to ache, and he was half-hard, his cock filling enough to make his pants uncomfortable.

He knew he had a real connection—a pull, a longing, a need for each of these men, though he didn't quite understand how that was possible. Emotion was coiling tight in his chest and making it hard to breathe, and there was an all too familiar stinging at the corner of his eyes. What did it mean? What was it telling him? He didn't know what to do with any of it.

But some part of him must have known, because his feet were moving slowly toward them.

Later. He needed this contact so desperately. He could sort it out later.

He put a shaking hand in Jeffrey's, and that dark gaze held him, smiling at him again, but something softer was in Jeffrey's eyes now. Jeffrey pulled him a step closer, and then closer still, until Russ was trapped between them, and their lips met in a light, sensual kiss.

"Oscar." That was Russ's voice. "Oh my God. Oscar."

Russ stood up slowly between them and stole his kiss away from Jeffrey. Oscar made a sound that was more of a whimper than a moan and looped an arm around Russ, pulling the man in close. He was aware of Jeffrey moving around to his back, starting to undress him, damp lips running over his bared shoulders and warm hands settling against his abs.

The kiss left Oscar reeling, and he gasped as Russ released him to pull off a worn T-shirt.

"I... I—"

"Shh," Jeffrey hushed him in a soothing tone and placed a kiss between his shoulder blades. "We've got you, Oscar."

Oh God. Oh dear God.

He swayed a little, and they caught him—Jeffrey a strong, steady presence at his back and Russ cupping his jaw with one hand and looking into his eyes.

Every nerve was suddenly alight, buzzing, and every touch of Jeffrey's lips and Russ's fingers set another little bit of him on fire. He had no desire, let alone the will, to resist them. His fear was countered by their reassurance and his reservations replaced with guileless need. It was foreign and forbidden, but it felt so right. Their single-minded seduction was absolute. Inescapable. He surrendered willingly and completely.

He tried to touch and kiss them, to return some of the sweet sensation they were giving him, but they kept him off-balance. He was distracted and confused by whose hands were where, whose mouth was on his, and he was consumed by the constant heightening of his own arousal.

"Upstairs," one of them whispered. As if they shared a mind, they moved together, bound by tangled fingers, bumping hips and elbows, trading kisses, and leaving behind a chaotic mess of clothing on the living room floor.

At the top of the steps, he lingered for a moment by the door to his old bedroom, the room his father had given to Russ, but Russ herded him forward. Jeffrey went ahead of them and yanked the covers off a big bed in his parents' old room. A bed he'd never seen before.

"Whoa."

He didn't get to say much more than that. Russ leaned in again, openmouthed, offering. He took Russ by the back of the neck and kissed him deeply, sweeping tongue over tongue. Russ's return kiss was laced with an affection Oscar recognized from their kiss that night in the kitchen. He didn't understand it, really, but his heart wanted it, needed it as much as his body did.

"Mmm. You two kiss like tomorrow isn't going to happen." Jeffrey ran his hands over Oscar's chest, rolling and lightly pinching one nipple and then the other. Russ reached down and cupped his balls in one hand, and Oscar groaned.

God, it felt so good.

It had been so long.

Jeffrey nudged Russ and cut in, kissing Russ quickly, then took Oscar's mouth himself. Jeffrey's kiss was hot and hungry, not in a hurry but not holding back the level of his own need either. Jeffrey put a hand on Russ's shoulder and leaned on it, a gentle directive that sent Russ down to kneeling again.

Just that move, the anticipation, made Oscar moan again and his cock stretch. "Yes," he said, his voice breathy and garbled by Jeffrey's mouth. He felt Russ's tongue run up and over the skin on either side of his balls, and then Russ drew them in, one at a time, massaging them with a talented tongue.

He and Jeffrey kissed forever. Minutes, hours—he had no way of knowing. They tasted and tested each other, took control and gave it up, asking and telling. Oscar had never learned so much from a kiss before. But when Russ finally took his full length into a hot mouth, Oscar tossed his head back with a gasp, the wet heat something he'd missed more than he'd understood.

"Russ. Fuck." He mumbled words of praise and scratched his fingers through Russ's hair.

Russ moaned around him, held his balls in one hand, licked and kissed and swallowed him deep, making him pant and his thighs tremble. Jeffrey was all hands and teeth, biting his earlobe, his neck, his nipple.

"Oh. God."

Russ stood, and Jeffrey herded Oscar to the bed and onto his back, where Russ picked up where they'd left off. Oscar stayed lost in it, his cock stiff and his need rising steadily until the attention became erratic. He looked up to find Jeffrey standing behind Russ, fingering Russ's ass.

"Oh. Mmm." Russ's eyes rolled back. Such a goner.

Jeffrey's grin was filthy and betrayed everything the man was thinking. Oscar licked his lips as their eyes met again, only this time he wasn't nervous or hesitant. He just grinned right back.

Jeffrey slapped Russ's ass and headed around to the nightstand. Oscar pushed Russ onto his back, staying to one side to be out of Jeffrey's way, and licked up the length of Russ's cock.

"Fuck. Oscar!"

Oscar went after him, sucking hard, stroking the line behind the man's balls with two fingers. Russ arched and moaned.

"Oh, look at you, Russ." Jeffrey stood at the end of the bed, rolled on a rubber, and fingered Russ, making Russ howl and groan. "You like that?"

"Fuck. Fuck!"

Oscar pulled off Russ and kissed him instead as Jeffrey slowly eased that hefty cock inside. Russ clung to Oscar, panting and moaning, and Oscar watched as the two of them put on a very impressive show. Jeffrey had a lovely strong rhythm, and Russ was no complacent bottom.

Oscar found himself watching them, listening, as he alternated between touching them and pumping his own erection.

"Ah. Fuck." Jeffrey's eyes slammed shut, and he started to piston hard. Russ was gone, moaning almost constantly. Oscar looked at them both, as close to orgasms as they obviously were, and bent back over Russ's straining cock and took it right down his throat.

That set them off like fireworks. Russ cried out and bucked, coming hard, cock punching Oscar's soft palate. Jeffrey made a strangled sound, thrusts becoming insanely erratic, and let out a shout, and that lean sculpted body was rocked by tremors.

Oscar's balls drew up hard and he gave them a tug.

Russ laughed softly. "I saw that."

"God, the two of you."

"Us?" Jeffrey asked, snorting. "Us? You set us off, Oscar." Oh, Jeffrey's voice had dropped to this sexy purr. "Lie back."

When he hesitated, Russ gave him a light shove, and he fell back in the pillows. Oscar started to protest, but Jeffrey and Russ shared a kiss, and he lost his train of thought. The two men exchanged a look, Russ settled by his hips, and Jeffrey kissed Oscar so hard, he thought he might bruise. Russ teased him with a hot tongue and nimble fingers for a moment before taking Oscar's needy cock into his mouth to suck him off. He groaned, the heavy sound muted and muffled by Jeffrey's kiss.

The pair of them didn't let up until he was sweating and shaking, on the verge of his first orgasm in years that didn't involve his own hand.

"I... oh God gonna...." He felt like he was spinning. Flying. Blood roared in his ears and his pulse pounded in his skull. He gripped the back of Jeffrey's neck with one hand and tugged on Russ's hair with the other, his hips jerking hard as he shot. "Oh fuck!"

Everything went into slow motion and he shattered into bits.

Little pieces of his mind and heart exploded outward just beyond his reach and then slammed back into place, leaving him aching and breathless. His chest felt heavy, his eyes burned, and every breath was a struggle. He felt disoriented and lost but not afraid. He was aware of the arms holding him and the soothing voices, even if he couldn't understand the words yet.

The room came back slowly, and he nodded to let Jeffrey and Russ know he was okay. At least he thought he was okay. "Okay?" he managed to say, bewildered that it came out a question.

"You're okay, Oscar. We're right here."

"It's all good. We've got you."

The weight in his chest, the ragged breathing—to his horror, he realized he was sobbing.

"I don't... I can't. S... sorry." God, what was the matter with him? He was ruining such an incredible experience for all of them.

"Shh. No, Oscar. There's nothing to be sorry for."

"Sorry. I'm sorry. I'm—"

"Stop it." Jeffrey's voice was stern, and Oscar looked up but didn't see anything but warmth in those brown eyes. He let them ground him, bring him back to the moment. Finally he nodded.

"It... so good, it... it hurts."

Jeffrey smiled at him. "Impossibly good."

"So good, it was unreal." Russ kissed him gently.

A little sound escaped Oscar, just a small release, but enough that he was suddenly back with them, his breathing deeper and his vision clear.

"There you are." Russ smiled.

He tried a smile and thought he even managed something close to it. "Hi."

Coming back to the room whole was just as wonderful as all of that shattering had been awful. The bed was luxurious and comfortable, and he had Jeffrey close on one side and Russ warm on the other, each with arms over him.

"So... you showed up early." Jeffrey laughed.

"I... did. I thought I'd try to talk to the contractors myself if I could, but they... they'd left." Jesus, his voice sounded like he'd swallowed glass.

"I thought for a second when you walked in the door that we were about to be in some very big trouble. Like, really big."

"I suppose if my brain hadn't shorted out when I saw you leaning on that wall, you might have been." Oscar laughed then too, happy to join in the fun.

The three of them lay tangled together, kissing and touching and being lazy. Oscar still felt overwhelmed but also safe lying between them. He decided not to overthink it all right now. He was a grown man, and he was entitled to intimacy. He could enjoy this for a couple of hours.

He hadn't felt this good in so, so long.

CHAPTER TWELVE

"Yes, I'll need to talk to my client, but I think that's exactly what he'll want to do." *Score*. Jeffrey pumped a fist in the air. "You can start right away?" He'd finally found Oscar a contractor.

"Yeah, I can slot you in Monday, if you like. Have the job done in a couple of days."

"Perfect. I'll text you in a bit with the go-ahead."

"Thanks for the rec, Jeff."

"Always a pleasure working with you, Mark." Jeffrey hung up the phone with a grin. *Always a pleasure.*

Speaking of pleasures, now he needed to give that client a call. His client, turned one-night stand, turned someone he couldn't get his mind off of. He'd had dozens upon dozens of one-nighters over the years, and he rarely gave men a second thought, let alone a second date. Russ was one rare exception, and now Oscar had left quite an impression too.

Start with looks, right? Oscar was a tall silver fox. The man was business casual, not outdoorsy like Russ, and not a suit-and-tie guy like himself either. Jeffrey thought Oscar was probably in the mid- to late-thirties range. The man's bright blue eyes had a depth that called to him in a way he hadn't felt before. Of course he'd had infatuations. In fact he'd have put Russ in that category until very recently. But this was something else. Something more.

He wanted to get to know Oscar better, and that feeling hadn't just started up when Oscar walked in on him and Russ. It had started several nights ago at dinner with Oscar and his family. That had been an experience he'd never had before, all of that domestic stuff. He'd stayed for Rose's lasagna because he liked Rose and because Oscar had the potential to become an important client. But that's not what made him hang around to help with the table and the dishes.

That had been Oscar himself.

Because that was personal and this was business, this was one of those phone calls that had the potential to go sideways. But he refused to overthink it. He made the call, waiting to see what kind of reception he got.

"Hello, Jeffrey." Oscar's voice was smooth and deep and gave him absolutely nothing to go on.

"Hey, Oscar. Got a minute?"

"I do. Hang on, let me go somewhere I can talk."

Ah. He smiled because that told him what he needed to know. He waited patiently for Oscar to get back to him.

"Back, sorry. I needed to get to my office. What's up?"

"Well, I have business and pleasure. What are you up for first?"

"Business."

Oh. Damn.

"Okay. I just got off the phone with the contractor. It's pretty good news. The only thing that he really thinks you need to address before listing is the roof in the functioning horse barn. The southern end looks like it took some damage from something—tree branch, bad weather, hard to say. It needs repair. There is water leaking in, and that's what's causing exposure of the foundation in that corner. He says repairing the roof and then shoring up that corner should do it."

"And that's in the budget I gave you?"

"Yes, well within. I still think you should paint the house inside and out."

"Yeah, I know. It's overdue on the outside and not exactly neutral inside. I was thinking about taking some time off and doing it with Russ."

He laughed. He could think of much better ways to spend his vacation time. "Better you than me."

"Asshole. Is that it? Just the roof?"

"And paint."

"Great. Done. Can we move on to the personal part of the conversation? I think I'll like it better."

Oh, he did like the sarcastic side of Oscar. "Hell yes. I want to see you."

"Yeah. I... I want to see you too."

He smiled. "And by see you, I mean—"

"I know what you mean."

"When?"

"Tonight. Can I come to your place? It might be late. After dinner."

Should he bring up Russ? Oscar hadn't. "Of course. Too many girls in your house, huh?"

"Many too many. Text me your address."

"Text me when you're on your way."

"Deal. See you later."

"Right, I—"

Oscar had hung up. He looked at his phone. "I'm looking forward to it." Wow. Someone was hot to trot. Suited him just fine.

He opened up the MLS and started working on the listing

for the farm. With the roof repairs on the schedule and painting planned, he could go ahead and start showing.

RUSS TILTED his head back and let the hot spray rain down over his face and shoulders. God, that felt good. He'd spent a very long day checking the fences, and he was tired. He didn't mind the work so much, except that it was slow going. He liked being out there with Angel in the sunshine and the chilly weather.

He actually liked work. No lie. He was at his best with a lot to do and busy hands. Without them, he spent too much time in his own head. Of course, busy didn't stop him from thinking too hard. He was in a fantastic mood, but he'd been preoccupied with thoughts about Oscar and Jeffrey all day. Especially Oscar, who'd been such a surprise.

He was still working out it all out in his head, but it sure was a fun time. Oscar's heated kisses had been everything he'd hoped they would be, just exactly what he needed. He could still feel Oscar's mouth on his dick too, sure and hot and not taking no for an answer. Fuck.

But sharpest in Russ's mind was the look on Oscar's face when he came. Oscar had disappeared at first, kind of blank and faraway, but then he got this look like his whole world had turned upside down, then suddenly righted itself again. And when Oscar opened his eyes, he'd looked right at Russ.

Right into his soul. He felt it; he was sure of it. Or pretty sure. Fuck, he really wanted it to be true. He'd had a little thing for Oscar before, but he had it bad now. There was no denying it.

He got out of the shower and toweled off, then headed back to his room. He'd been using the shower in the master bedroom since Jonas passed, because it was so much bigger and more comfortable than the one that in the hall with the little tub, which was technically his. He walked through the room and past the big bed, smiling at it. He'd stripped it and washed the sheets, and now it was clean and calling him.

Did he have to sleep in that single bed when this one was right here? Oscar didn't seem to have any problem with the three of them using the room. Maybe... maybe he could move into this one. Then if Oscar wanted to come over, it wouldn't be weird; it would just be his room. And Jeff, of course. Jeff was so hot it made him stupid. He literally had a hard time keeping his hands off Jeff.

He was making supper when his phone rang, and he smiled at it, a warm anticipation making him tingle.

"Hi, Oscar."

"Hey, you."

He blushed, his smile even wider. "I'm glad you called."

"I wanted to check in, you know? Last night was... pretty mind-blowing for me."

"You were amazing. Beautiful, Oscar."

"Listen, I'm sorry I took off on you the other night after dinner. I didn't know what I was feeling, what I should do. I'm still trying to sort it out."

"Because of Emmett?"

There was a long pause, and he was starting to think he'd said the wrong thing, but then Oscar sighed in his ear. "Yeah. Emmett. And whether that was.... I wasn't sure why I...." Oscar sighed again. "Sorry. This is hard. I guess I didn't know whether it was you I wanted in that moment or if I just wanted. I didn't know if I was ready, and that scared me."

"I understand—"

"And now... I wasn't sure whether I could handle one lover, you know? And now you *and* Jeffrey.... It's a lot. I need to figure it out."

"I don't think we need to make decisions, Oscar." He hadn't asked Jeff's permission, but now that they were.... It was definitely time to come clean. "Jeff and I... well, you should know that's not new."

"What? It's not?"

"We didn't have a thing, like anything real. I met him in a bar a couple of months ago, and we've hooked up a few times."

"A couple of months ago? Why didn't you—oh. Never mind. It wasn't any of my business I guess, was it?"

"That's kind of how we saw it." That was a relief. Seemed like Oscar got it.

"No, you're right. So... wait. Are you two—"

"A couple? Not before, but I guess I don't know now. I think it's okay not to know. I mean, I'm open. I think we should stay open."

"Yeah, that's pretty much what I'm thinking."

"I just want to see you again."

"I do too, Russ. That's really why I was calling. I don't know what the right way to handle this is, but I feel like I should be honest. If we all stay honest, then at least we... well. I wanted you to know that I'm going over to Jeffrey's later."

Going to Jeff's. And it didn't sound like he was invited. Oscar's words felt like a punch to the gut. "Oh."

"I want to spend some time with him and also some time with you, you know? I want to understand what I'm feeling. I think we all should."

Wow. How did Oscar make something that hurt so much sound so reasonable? "You could both come here." That would make sense too, right?

"Yes, we could. But I need a little.... I want to figure out where I stand with each of you. Can I come over tomorrow night?"

"Yes." Jesus. He jumped on that like he was drowning and those words were a life raft. "Please come over."

"Russ. It's okay. But I don't know Jeffrey at all, and the two of you apparently have an advantage on me."

He sighed. Of course that made sense. It felt like crap, but he needed to get over himself. "Sorry, but I feel like we have something."

"We have something." Oscar's tone was frank and reassuring. "Russ, we have something, I feel it. I think it's important we explore it, because I think it could be really good. I hope you can understand that I need to figure out where I stand with Jeffrey."

God, why was he being such a baby about this? It was obvious enough to him that the three of them were something together too. "Yeah. Of course that's fine. I have to tell you, though, Jeff's hot as hell, but I don't know him all that well either. Maybe after this, we could figure him out together?"

Oscar laughed. "Sounds like fun."

He liked the laugh; it made him feel warmer. "Okay. Okay, good. So I'll see you tomorrow night?"

"Late. After dinner. The girls...."

"It's all good. See you then."

"Thanks, Russ. Good night."

"Night."

After supper, he did it; he moved his few things into the master bedroom. It took him all of fifteen minutes because he really didn't have much to move—his guitar and his music, a stack of jeans and T-shirts, boots and coats, his very few pictures and possessions. When he was done, he looked around. You'd hardly even know he was there. His few things were practically lost in the big room.

CHAPTER THIRTEEN

OSCAR TAPPED on Rose's bedroom door, even though the door was open. She was sitting at her little desk, writing something in a note card. "Rose?"

She looked up from her card. "Hello, sweetheart."

"The girls are all in bed. I wanted to let you know I'm going out."

Rose arched one eyebrow at him, but her tone wasn't at all judgmental. "Are you?"

"I'm meeting Jeffrey." That was scandalous enough and offered her plenty to chew on, being that this was the first time he'd done anything like this since Emmett passed away. She didn't need all the details around the event yet.

She smiled, the look both sweet and sentimental. "You deserve to have some fun. Just don't stay out too late."

He ducked into her room long enough to kiss her on the cheek and give her hand a squeeze. "It will be late, but I'll be home long before the girls are up. Call me if you need me."

"You won't hear from me, dear."

"Thanks, Rose. I love you."

"I love you too. Go on now. Enjoy your date."

He nodded and texted Jeffrey on the way out to his car. Rose was a wise woman. She knew damn well this was a booty call and not a date. She might even remember how he and Emmett first started seeing each other in a similar fashion— stolen evenings after the girls were in bed. The big difference was the girls were younger then and had much earlier bedtimes. Leaving the house at nine o'clock was tough on a weeknight.

Hauling his ass back home before sunrise wasn't going to be a picnic either. But he needed to see Jeffrey. He needed what he sensed Jeffrey was capable of, what he'd learned from their long, intimate kiss. They both had a little push and pull in them, but tonight he wanted to be wanted. All of the care and touching the other day had been wonderful—the mouths, the hands. It had been the perfect new first experience for him. But it had opened up something in him, and he felt unable to deny himself now. He wanted to fuck. Hard.

He shifted in the front seat of the minivan as he drove, giving his thickening cock more room, glad that the drive wasn't a long one. He turned onto Jeffrey's road and started looking for the complex. Jeffrey said he had a town house on a cul-de-sac, and even in the dark, Oscar found it easily. He pulled into one of the guest parking spaces across from Jeffrey's front door.

It was a nice brick-front town house, with white trim and black shutters, and when the door opened, he was going to say so, but Jeffrey hauled him inside and kissed him without letting him speak.

The greeting was absolutely everything he wanted.

He pushed Jeffrey against a wall and shoved his hands up under the man's shirt. Jeffrey groaned and tugged on his waistband, pulling their hips together.

"Yeah." He leaned into Jeffrey and rubbed against a muscled thigh with a groan as he pinched one of Jeffrey's nipples. Jeffrey hissed and thrust against his hip. It was beautiful.

"Want you."

"Yes."

Jeffrey placed hands on Oscar's chest and leveraged him backward a couple of steps, pushing fingers up under his shirt to pinch one of his nipples. "Take your shirt off."

Oscar lifted it off over his head, then took another kiss as his fingers found Jeffrey's oxford, opening one button after another. Jeffrey tore Oscar's jeans open and pulled his cock and balls out with both hands, making him ache as Jeffrey stroked him with hot fingers.

"Fuck."

"Hot." Jeffrey let him go and slid a hand from Oscar's belly down into his curls, fingers combing through his sensitive expanse of fur.

Oscar smiled against Jeffrey's lips. He'd always loved it when men appreciated his body hair, and it was even more satisfying now, knowing it had gone somewhat salt-and-pepper of late and Jeffrey seemed into it anyway. He was still coming to terms with looking older but still not really feeling it.

Jeffrey grunted and shoved Oscar's hand against his crotch, moaning softly.

"Mmm. Yeah. I got you." Oscar took it slow with Jeffrey's fly, forcing patience that Jeffrey didn't seem to actually have. Jeffrey arched and rolled those narrow hips until that cock was finally free, and he gave his lover what the man was after. The groan was delicious, and he stroked Jeffrey through it, slipping a thumb over the tip.

Jeffrey pressed his face into Oscar's neck and thrust slowly into Oscar's hand. "Fuck."

He took Jeffrey by the jaw, and they kissed again, deep and hard and long. They touched and stroked each other until they were desperate, both of them panting and wanting. When Jeffrey pulled back and looked at him with those deep dark eyes, Oscar's patience dissolved.

"Please, Jeffrey. I need you."

Jeffrey groaned and started moving them toward the stairs. "Oscar."

Oscar nodded and went up, holding his jeans up with one hand, then slipped them off along with his shoes at the top of the stairs. Their eyes locked, Jeffrey stalking him, backing him into the bedroom. Jesus. Russ was right; Jeffrey was hotter than hell.

Jeffrey undressed as Oscar climbed up on the bed.

"Uh-uh." Jeffrey put a hand on Oscar's hip and pushed him over, off his hands and knees. "On your back. Want to see you."

He didn't argue and kept his eyes on Jeffrey, who was rolling on a rubber as Oscar got comfortable on his back. Jeffrey pushed one of his knees up and pressed slippery fingers against his hole. "How long...?"

"Over three years."

"Sorry to.... I just want—"

"I know. Thank you for asking." He hadn't been fucked since the last time his husband had been able to do that, maybe a year before Emmett died. Maybe longer. It had been forever.

He wasn't embarrassed; he appreciated the question. He wanted it now, though. Like he'd wanted nothing else for ages. "Please."

Jeffrey slipped a finger into him slowly. Oscar reached down and tugged on his cock, remembering, relaxing, and moments later Jeffrey added a second finger. He moaned.

"You like that. Your body remembers, right? Feels good?"

"So good."

Jeffrey took his time, stretching and lubing him up,

teasing and making him want even more. "I'll make sure it's good for you."

"Want you, Jeffrey."

"You're ready? You're sure?"

"I'm sure."

Please. Fuck. Don't make me wait any longer.

Jeffrey slipped his fingers away, and Oscar arched, begging for a moment because he felt so empty.

"Right here." The hot tip of Jeffrey's cock nudged at him, the pressure so sweet.

"Yeah. Fuck, yeah."

"Mm. Tight, Oscar. Jesus." Jeffrey sank slowly into him. Beautifully, achingly slow.

Oscar sighed and moaned, his legs falling open and his eyes squeezing closed as he centered all his attention on the stretch and burn where they were joined.

"Breathe," Jeffrey reminded him.

He took a breath, then let it out in a long hiss. "Oh God."

"Okay?"

"Yes. Fuck, Jeffrey. Just right."

"That's it."

He felt Jeffrey's balls slap against him and the heat of their skin so close together made him sigh.

"Oh, that's pretty, Oscar. I'm going to take such good care of you."

Jeffrey was getting off on this "first time in a long time" thing, and Oscar loved it. Nothing wrong with that; he was too. Eventually, though, he needed more. He moaned and rocked, and Jeffrey smiled at him.

They moved together, humping at first, and then Jeffrey hooked strong arms around both of his thighs, lifting them slightly, starting to thrust. He threw his arms out, gripping the sheets as Jeffrey forced grunts and groans from him, and he let himself go. He let go of all conscious decisions and went with what his body wanted. It was so right. It was exactly what he—

"Oh fuck!" He shouted, shocked, as Jeffrey gripped him, milking his erection and he started to rise fast, his cock hard and heavy and his balls beginning to ache.

"Yeah," Jeffrey panted, flushed now, a light sweat on his forehead. So hot.

"More."

"Oscar—"

"More!" he demanded.

Jeffrey growled like an animal and gritted his teeth, his thrusts going deep and hard as they lost their rhythm.

The next few minutes were full of sound—filthy words, grunts and moans, cursing and begging. By the time he felt the urgent need spiraling in him, he was damp and trembling, panting hard, and Jeffrey seemed somewhere well beyond the moon. Oscar was rocked by the sudden force of his orgasm, and he bucked, his hips lifting higher off the bed. Jeffrey howled and took him by the hips, fingers bruising his skin, and slammed into his ass with a loose, wild motion. Oscar watched as Jeffrey gave it up with a cry that sounded like gratitude, and a beautiful grimace on his face.

"Fuck, Jeffrey."

Jeffrey shuddered again and gulped air, dropping down to rest that damp forehead in the center of his chest. "Yeah."

He slid his hands gently over Jeffrey's back and shoulders, still catching his breath as well.

"Jesus Christ, Oscar."

Oh. Jeffrey sounded pretty shattered. "You were amazing. You're gorgeous."

"I fucking lost it. I don't.... I mean... are you okay?"

"Perfect." It was everything Oscar needed—wild and wonderful, so fucking good. "Are you?"

"No. I'm a disaster, and it's fucking great. I think I forgot my name there for a while. Good thing you kept moaning it." Laughing softly, Jeffrey disposed of the condom and climbed into bed beside him.

"Ha. I would have liked to hear mine, but I think you lost the power of speech." He hooked an arm around Jeffrey and pulled him in.

They lay there for a bit, breathing, recovering, relaxing in each other's arms. Jeffrey combed curious fingers through the hair on his chest. "You're going a little white, stud."

"You'll get there. I bet I have at least ten years on you."

"No way." Jeffrey laughed at him. "Come on, five at most."

"What are we betting?"

"What? Wait, you actually want to wager?"

"Yes. Because I'm going to win." He was incredibly flattered that Jeffrey thought he was under forty, though. "I bet that I'm more than ten years older than you are. How about...."

"Wine?"

"Dinner. With Russ."

"Dinner and wine with Russ," Jeffrey said, and they shook on it. "So how ancient are you?"

"Shut up!" He reached over and pinched one of Jeffrey's nipples, making the man recoil, wincing.

"Ow! Jesus."

"How old do you think I am?"

"Hmmm." Jeffrey tilted his head one way and then the other. "Well? Thirty-five maybe. Maybe thirty-seven, but that's it."

Nice. "I am forty-five." He grinned like a cat in cream, he felt so smug.

Jeffrey truly looked stunned. "No, you're not."

"I am! And I'm getting free dinner, aren't I?"

Jeffrey sighed. "Yes. I'm thirty-one."

"Oh, wow. I'm robbing the cradle." He snorted.

"No, that would be Russ."

He knew that. He wasn't sure he wanted to know by how much. Russ looked like a baby. He was pretty sure Russ wasn't one, but the guy really looked it. "So, he's...?"

"Twenty-eight."

He laughed. "Oh God. I'm horrible. I'm going to hell." Seventeen years. He was seventeen years older than Russ. What was he thinking?

"What? Shit, if that raunchy last half hour doesn't send you to hell, Russ isn't going to be a problem."

He sighed. "I hope not."

"Hey." Jeffrey sat up on one elbow and leaned over him. "Age means nothing, except when you have sexy silver hair. What happened the other day was fantastic."

"It was incredible. But to be honest, it was also confusing." He wanted to just accept that it was what it was, like Russ had. Be open. Have it all figured out. He didn't want it to be complicated. And this time with Jeffrey was both helping and making it harder for him to think clearly.

"I've been with multiples before, but not in this kind of context. I've never thought about having a relationship like this before. You're something, Oscar. I... I'm really drawn to you. I don't know what that means yet, but it's not common for me."

"I'm...." He shrugged. "Not sure what I am."

"Still figuring it out?"

"Still figuring it out, yes. Trying to understand what I'm feeling, what I want. Whether I'm really ready for any of it."

"Well, did this feel good?"

"This felt amazing." Oscar kissed Jeffrey lightly, enjoying their connection. "Amazing."

"So don't overthink it for now."

That was too simple. "I'm trying to be fair, is all."

"Which would be overthinking." Jeffrey patted his cheek playfully.

"Except that I'm here with you right now, and Russ—"

"Russ is in love with you, I think."

He swallowed and shook his head. Part of him knew that, but he wasn't ready to think too hard about it. "Shit. You see what I mean?"

"No, Oscar. You're still overthinking. None of us signed a contract the other day. No one made any promises to anyone else. We had sex together, all of us. It was just sex, you know? Could it turn into something else? Who knows? But you're here in my bed even though you know Russ has a thing for you. I assume that's because you wanted something specific from me that you didn't think you could get from him."

"You're right. And I got it." He smiled, following the line of Jeffrey's jaw with one finger.

Jeffrey laughed. "Glad I could help. Now stop thinking so hard about us. Russ and I both know you have a lot to work through emotionally. You would, even if there was only one of us."

"How do you—you talked about me?"

"Sure. Yes. After you left, we did talk about you. And we talked about each other a little and what we wanted. We were as surprised as you were by what went down."

"But you two already have a history."

Jeffrey nodded. "Russ told you. I'm glad. It's totally physical, though. Or... well, it was until.... Things feel different with you in the mix."

"Oh ho! Now who is overthinking things?"

Jeffrey laughed. "I never claimed not to be a hypocrite."

"Russ knows I'm here, by the way. I called him."

The look on Jeffrey's face was hard to read, but Oscar thought he seemed pleased. "Yeah?"

"Yes. I didn't think it was right to... to do this behind his back. So I called him and told him I was coming over here. He was okay about it. I don't think he was thrilled. He and I made plans for tomorrow night."

"Oh, perfect. Good." Jeffrey didn't seem to have any issues with that at all. It was amazing how different they all were. "So, then, why don't we all plan something together for the weekend?"

"Plan something?" *Plan something like what? A three-way booty call?*

"Dinner."

"Like a date?" *A group date. Huh.*

"Sure. You won the wager, remember?"

"Dinner and wine with Russ. Right." This was all so totally new to him. Of course they should have a date. It still felt so strange, though.

"So, Saturday? I'll tell Russ."

"I'll have to check with Rose." He thought about it. Emily would be out with Brian—or inside with Brian—*God, please, Emmett, watch over her*—and Sophie could spend the night with her friend Leslie, so if Rose could stay with the twins, then it could work. Or... wait. He needed to check the calendar, because Saturday might be Sophie's choir concert and he couldn't miss—

"Oscar."

"Huh?"

"Over here."

He blinked at Jeffrey. "Sorry."

"There you are. Where did you go?"

He snorted. "Uh, Rose, babysitters, the house calendar, um... Brian. Going out for an evening is complicated."

Jeffrey shook his head. "Which is why you had to come over here so late."

"I wanted them to be in bed. I didn't think I should be

explaining anything to them yet. And I will have to leave pretty soon too."

"Sure, so you're there when they get up. I get it. You're a good dad. I don't know how I'd handle all those kids, especially on your own."

"I have Rose. I couldn't do it without her." Well, he probably could; people did. But he'd have lost his mind figuring out how. It took both of them just to handle all the girls' tears. Grateful didn't begin to cover it.

"Come on. Let's have a drink before you go." Jeffrey climbed out of bed, his naked body looking lovely in the pillar of light streaming in from the hallway.

"That sounds perfect." They cleaned up, and he got dressed—searching for and picking up clothing here and there on the way down the stairs—while Jeffrey put on sweatpants.

"What's your preference? Whiskey? Brandy?"

"Oh, have you got a brandy?"

"I have. A nice one." Jeffrey dug out a couple of snifters, and he picked one up and warmed it in his hands. He hadn't had a nice brandy in a while. How adult and... normal.

"So, I've been getting ready to show the farm." Jeffrey took the top off the half-full bottle and poured them each a generous splash.

"Yeah? Already?"

"Well, as long as I can say work is being done, there's no reason not to. Sometimes you can find a buyer who will accept money in escrow for the work, and then you don't even have to deal with it."

"Oh, that's an interesting idea." Would that get it sold faster? The whole sale process was already frustrating, and they'd barely even begun.

"I'm going to activate the listing Monday. Russ and I are going to clean up the inside of the house on Sunday."

He really didn't want to talk about the farm right now. Or business at all. He swirled his brandy and hugged the bowl of the glass between his palms, finally deeming it warm enough to sip. "Oh, this is smooth."

"If I'm going to drink, it's going to be good." Jeffrey smiled. Oscar believed it. Jeffrey was even shiny in sweatpants. He stepped forward, slipped an arm behind Jeffrey, and kissed him. Gently, just for the sake of a kiss.

"Mm. What was that for?"

"To see how the brandy tastes on you." He pulled Jeffrey tighter and danced slowly around the living room, his brandy still in one hand.

"Are we dancing? There's no music, Oscar." Jeffrey didn't seem to be complaining, though. His lover seemed more intrigued and amused than anything.

"It's in my head." He slowed to a stop so they could sip their brandy. He was already pretty relaxed, and the brandy warmed him inside too. After a few sips, he put the glass down. "I'm not going to be able to drive home if I finish that."

Jeffrey grinned at him. "You've seen through my nefarious plan."

He chuckled, found his shoes and socks, and sat on the couch to pull them on.

"For what it's worth, Oscar, I think we should keep ourselves open to this."

That was his plan. "I'm... open. Well, I'm not closing any doors yet anyway. I'm still getting my feet under me."

"Hey, that's fine. No one is in a rush here. We're all taking it a day at a time." Jeffrey kissed him. "Have a good evening with Russ tomorrow."

He found himself searching Jeffrey's eyes, wondering how that was offered so freely. How Jeffrey had enough confidence to hand him off to another man. It was wonderful, and baffling. Mostly wonderful.

"Thanks for... well. It was exactly what the doctor ordered. And the brandy." He pulled his coat on and got out his keys.

"I am really glad you called. Is it cool if I call you or text— I mean, not about business?"

"Oh. Yes. Yeah, that's totally fine. I'd like that." He wanted those calls. He gave Jeffrey a smile that felt as dorky as what he'd just said.

"Cool. Good." Jeffrey saw him to the door and held it open for him. "Good night."

Oscar leaned in and took a light kiss. "I'll talk to Rose and get back to you about plans for the three of us, okay?"

"Call me."

"Night." He didn't linger. It was the middle of the night, and Jeffrey understood why he was leaving. He headed for his van, hopped in, and headed home. He was going to be tired tomorrow, but it would be so worth it. Jesus. Jeffrey was right —he didn't think he could get that from Russ. He really didn't even want that from Russ. Russ was... sweet. Gentle. A different vibe.

When he got home, the house was dark, except for the light in the upstairs hall, which Rose had left on for him. He climbed the stairs, wickedly sore and totally wiped out, and he smiled because it felt great. He was lucky as hell.

CHAPTER FOURTEEN

Russ needed a shower. He'd just help get the horses in, and then he could go get cleaned up and have something to eat before Oscar arrived. He needed a shave, and he should probably deal with his fingernails....

Shit, listen to him. Taking time to be all pretty for his date. Lord.

He'd left Miles and the other guys down at the barn to supervise and he trudged on up to the pasture to open the gate. These beasts were such creatures of habit, they were already heading over when he arrived. Angel must have seen him coming. She tossed her head and greeted him, and he stroked her nose and unlocked the gate.

"Take 'em on down, girl. I'll come say good night." He pulled the gate open, and she strutted through it, then took off at a trot for the barn, everyone following her down obediently. He did the mental count as they trotted by, but really, he could tell by looking these days, and he knew as soon as the last one came through the gate that Mila was missing.

"Shit, Mila. You lazy ass." He pulled out his cell and called Miles.

"Yo, boss."

"Hey. Mila's still dickin' around in the pasture. I need to go pull her in. We'll be down in a bit."

"Sure, man. We got this."

"Thanks." He hung up, looking at Mila out in the paddock. "Mila! Come on, girl!" When Mila didn't budge, he sighed and headed out in that direction. He was annoyed at first, thinking the mare was just being stubborn, but the closer he got, the more he was convinced something was wrong. The mare wasn't standing right.

When he got close enough to see, he realized Mila wasn't putting weight on her front foot. "Oh. What did you do, lady?" He jogged the rest of the way over. "Aw shit. Where did you get that?" Her foot was attached to a three-foot board. "Got a nail in there, girl? Hang on."

Russ kept one hand on Mila's neck and ran the other from her shoulder slowly down her leg. She twitched a little but was pretty trusting, and he was able to eventually get both hands as far as her knee.

Okay. A sixteen-hundred-pound animal with a nail in her hoof. What could possibly go wrong here?

He sighed. "Don't you put my lights out, Mila, you hear me?" He took a deep breath and in as quick a motion as he could manage, he got his hands between the board and her hoof and shoved downward.

She danced sideways, pulling her foot from his hands. He went right for her mane and grabbed it, tugging on it to keep her from going too far. "Hey. That's it, girl. It's gone. Shh. It's gone now."

A couple of minutes later, they were making their way back to the barn, Mila only limping slightly. He brought the board along too, trying to figure out where she'd picked it up. It had to be from the fencing, but he was baffled where. He'd been checking the fences all over the property; tomorrow he'd make that paddock his priority.

"Hey, man. She's got a foot."

He held up the board for Miles. "Kicked a fence, maybe? I'll go see tomorrow." He put Mila on crossties and pulled out his phone. "I need to call Hank. Can you put a soak together for me?"

"You got it."

"Thanks, man." He got on the phone and left a message with the vet's answering service, set his phone down, and then bent to have a look at Mila's foot. He ran his hands over her knee and down to the shoe, pleased that it didn't feel warm. It was sore, though, and she fussed at him, tugging her foot out of his fingers. "Yeah, I know, girl. We'll get a soak on that, huh?"

"Right behind you." Miles came up next to him and sat the bucket down.

"Thanks."

"I'm going to go finish up with the guys, and then I'll come back and check on you."

"All good. I got this."

Miles jogged off, and he picked up the bucket, then it down near Mila's foot. The trick here was to make sure she didn't kick it over. He kept one hand on the bucket's handle and coaxed her foot up and then down into the bucket with the other.

"Yep. That's it." She didn't spook. She hesitated for a second, but he leaned on her knee and she put her foot down into the warm water. "Good girl. There you go." He petted and soothed her, keeping an eye on that leg, making sure she kept her hoof in the bucket. Once she settled, he got out a grooming kit to keep her relaxed, keep some routine, and give himself something to do. She was going to have to soak for a while so the antiseptic could do its work. He wanted it good and clean.

He combed through her mane until it shined, then started in on her shoulders and over her back. She needed to soak for a good twenty minutes, so he took his time and got every nook and cranny, combed out her tail. The vet called and asked a slew of questions, confirmed the record of her tetanus shot booster, and gave Russ some instructions.

"Keep an eye on her, and I'll be by in the morning." Hank didn't sound too worried.

He and Miles pulled her shoe, put some antibacterial glop on the hoof, and packed it with gauze, then wrapped it up in vet wrap and duct tape so she could step on it and not rip open the bandage.

"Looks pretty good, huh?" Russ said, packing everything away in the horse-sized first aid kit.

"That's some good work, for sure."

Russ snorted. "Thanks for sticking around. I'm going to hang out here with her for a while."

"You sure?"

"Yeah, thanks. I won't sleep anyway."

Miles shook a head full of dark curls and laughed. "You treat them well, boss."

"Thanks. That's my job." He said good night and then made his way over to the little corner set up with a heater, a coffee machine, and a stack of books and magazines.

What seemed like barely a minute later, his phone rang, and he sat up, blinking. He must have dozed off. He patted his coat pockets and his jeans pockets, and he looked around, but he couldn't find his phone.

Oh! Right. He'd left it at the crossties. He jogged over, but it stopped ringing before he got there. "Damn." He picked it up to see who'd called.

Oscar.

"Oh shit!" He'd totally forgotten with all the worry over Mila.... "Fuck." He dialed Oscar back and looked at his watch.

"Russ?"

"Hey, Oscar, I'm—"

"I'm in the house. Where are you?"

He sighed. "I'm out in the barn. Mila got a nail in her hoof, and Miles and I were working on it.... I got completely distracted." That sounded great, didn't it? I got involved with a horse and didn't even remember to call you.

"Is she okay?"

"I think so. She'll be on rest for a few days for sure, but it didn't feel infected when I wrapped it up. We'll see what tomorrow brings. I'm really sorry, Oscar. I need to stay out here with her."

"Sure. I get it. I'll be right out."

"Oh, you don't have to—"

"Stop. What can I bring you? Are you hungry?"

He totally was. "Peanut butter and jelly?"

Oscar laughed. "You're serious?"

"Well, yeah." What was wrong with peanut butter and jelly? It was his supper half the week anyway. The other half was canned soup or spaghetti and meatballs. And pizza on Saturdays.

"Okay, peanut butter and jelly it is. Be out in a bit."

He couldn't believe he'd forgotten to call. Mila had him worried. But how sweet was it of Oscar to bring him supper? He was doing his job after all. The boss couldn't get that mad, right?

Oh, man. He was sleeping with the boss. Well? It was way too damn late now, huh? He was pretty sure the boss wanted him right back.

He cleared some tack he'd put off working on from the only other chair in the barn and brought it over to where it was warmer. Then he checked on Mila to kill some time because he realized he was impatient to see Oscar.

It took a while for Oscar to appear, but when he finally did, it was with a picnic basket.

"Special delivery." Oscar smiled at him and set the basket down on one of the chairs. His lover had on a dark green barn coat and a black scarf, a Phillies cap covering silver hair. It all looked familiar.

"Jonas's hat." Russ stepped close. Their eyes met, and Oscar pulled him right in, bringing their lips together in a gentle kiss. He leaned into Oscar, soaking in everything he'd wanted from the brief kiss they'd shared in the kitchen the other night. Oscar offered it so freely this time, affection, desire—his lover was so open to him, it made him feel a little guilty that he'd worried about Oscar spending time with Jeffrey for even a moment.

"Mhm. Dad's coat too. I didn't want to wear my leather one out here, just in case."

"In case what? You gonna get your hands dirty?"

Oscar pretended to be offended. "I beg your pardon? I was raised on this farm."

He laughed. "So defensive. It's adorable."

Oscar snorted and let him go. "It's good to see you."

It was good to be seen. He still couldn't quite believe this was happening. "Oscar, I am so sorry about this. I should have—"

Oscar put a hand up, cutting him short. "You're doing your job. So where did Mila pick up the nail?"

"Looks like that paddock fence needs some work. I hadn't gotten to it yet. I just finished the perimeter this morning."

"Is it bad?"

"No. But we took the shoe off, and she's indoors for a few days, I think. Hank will be by in the morning, and we'll see."

"Okay, good."

"Is this supper?" He already knew he didn't need to explain why he was in the barn still to Oscar, but he felt so bad about ruining their night together.

"Oh, yes. This is dinner. Sit."

He looked at Oscar.

"Sit."

"Okay." He sat, smiling and wondering what Oscar was up to. He found out soon enough, as Oscar pulled all kinds of crazy things out of that basket, starting with a red dishtowel that was spread out on top of the little crate to serve as a tablecloth. "What's this?"

"Well, since our evening got rescripted, I figured I'd bring you a little atmosphere with dinner."

"You're one of those romantic types, huh?"

Oscar smiled at him, not the least bit embarrassed. "Yeah. I am, as a matter of fact. You ready to be disgusted?"

"Oh, I didn't mean…. Romance is great. I like romance." Truthfully, he didn't know the first thing about it, really, but he liked the idea anyway.

Oscar leaned over and took another kiss, the quick sweep of Oscar's tongue across his lips leaving him blinking and grinning like a fool.

"Good." Oscar grinned and pulled a covered plate out of the basket, pulled the foil off, and set the plate down. He laughed, feeling himself smile from ear to ear at the two heart-shaped peanut-butter-and-jelly sandwiches.

"Oh my God."

Oscar looked pleased and sat in the other chair. "Mom's cookie cutters."

He knew his smile was goofy, taking over his whole face. But how sweet was this? "You actually dug out cookie cutters."

"I did," Oscar replied smugly. "I have four daughters,

remember. You have to get creative sometimes. Or, well. Rose is creative, and I learn things."

He laughed and picked up one of the heart-shaped sandwiches, studying it from the side. "Nice thick layer of peanut butter. I approve."

"Is there any other way?"

"Strawberry jelly. The only kind there is."

"I guess. That's all that was in your fridge."

"Damn right." He grinned and made a show of taking a bite. "Mm. Delicious. Thank you."

Oscar pulled out two stemless wineglasses and a root beer and split it between the glasses before lifting one. "To our first real date."

"In a barn." He picked up his glass, still all smiles. "Cheers. I've never had root beer in a wineglass."

"I figured wine was a bad idea with the horse and everything." Oscar clinked glasses with him. "You had these in the fridge."

"So thoughtful."

"Russ, your kitchen looks like a teenager lives there. Milk, cereal, soup, pasta, bread, peanut butter and jelly."

"Doritos. Don't forget the Doritos. And the apples."

"Right. Apples. Yeah, I was impressed you had something good for you."

"Shut up." He laughed, though, because it was pretty simple stuff. He only really cooked on Sundays, and he'd shop fresh in the morning after he turned the horses out. He ate his other sandwich and sipped his root beer, letting Oscar watch him. "Okay, what?"

Oscar smiled. "If things had gone as planned, what would we be doing right now?"

"Making out. And talking. But mostly making out."

"Yeah, that sounds about right."

"How was your evening with Jeff?"

When the question first came out of his mouth, he didn't catch the way it sounded. It wasn't until Oscar sat forward and put his drink down that he realized what he'd asked.

"Oh. I didn't mean.... I really just meant, was it...." God. He was such an idiot. "I'm not trying to be nosy, I swear. I—"

"It was exactly what I wanted it to be," Oscar interrupted smoothly, that deep voice cutting right through all of his stuttering.

"I'm sorry. I didn't mean anything by that."

"Russ. You don't have to apologize. I called you so you'd know I was going there. I told Jeffrey I was coming here tonight. I don't have any idea how this will all work out, if it works out, but I intend to be honest about everything."

He felt chastised on one hand but encouraged on the other. "Yeah. Honest is best."

"So, honestly, Jeffrey and I had a great evening. He's...."

"Aggressive."

Oscar nodded and grinned at him. "Hot. Toppy."

"Confident."

"All of those things. We had a good conversation too."

He laughed. "He talks about something other than football?"

"Remarkably, yes." Oscar chuckled. "He's something. So different than you are."

Was that a good thing? He hoped it was a good thing. "Yeah. I don't have—I'm more—"

"That's not what I need from you."

He blinked at Oscar. "Oh." *Oh, wow. It was a good thing. Cool.*

"And you have different expectations of me too, I think."

Russ's skin started to tingle, and he swallowed. "How do you do that?"

"Do what?" Oscar wasn't really asking, was he? His lover

knew exactly what Russ was talking about; it was in those blue eyes.

"That seduction thing with just your voice." It was hot as anything.

"I don't know. I don't really know what you mean, but Emmett used to say things like that. He liked it too."

"Were you like this with him?"

"You want to know about Emmett?"

"Yes. If you want to tell me."

Oscar leaned back in his chair. "I don't mind. I've never really had anyone ask, you know? Nearly everyone I know knew him."

"Jonas told me some. He said Emmett was a good man, that he loved you, that he was a good dad."

"He said all that?" Oscar looked a little faraway for a second. "Huh."

"Sure. He liked Emmett."

"Well, I knew that. I just didn't know how much."

He smiled. "Parents are funny that way."

"Emmett was all of those things. He was...." Oscar got quiet and thoughtful, like he was remembering, choosing the right words maybe. "He came from nothing. He put himself through college and started a geeky accounting career. He got married, had four beautiful girls, lost his wife in an accident, found me, and fought like hell to keep it all. And then he graciously trusted me with his family when he... when it was time to go. He traveled a short but eventful, vibrant, busy road and spent the last few years trying to outrun a coming storm."

He just stared at Oscar. "Wow."

Oscar sighed. "I loved him. We were good together." Oscar look at his hands as he spoke, his voice deep and steady. "I was unhappy when we met and he was... persistent. Kind. Occasionally a real pain in the ass." Oscar laughed.

"The best thing I'd ever had. He loved hard, and he was a fierce champion for his family. He was stubborn as hell, passionate about everything, so we argued a lot. I mean, *everything* mattered to him. Dinner mattered. Emily's grades mattered. Mowing the lawn mattered. I mattered."

"You matter, Oscar." He wasn't sure where that came from, even though he knew it was true. "You matter to those girls."

Oscar nodded. "I do, I know."

"You matter to me."

"I know that too." But Oscar didn't look up. "I saw it the other night in your eyes. I don't understand it, but I believe you."

He reached over the little table and covered Oscar's fingers with his own. "Thanks for sharing him with me."

"It's nice to talk about him with someone I'm not related to." Oscar looked up and gave him a soft smile. He'd expected to see tears in Oscar's eyes, but he didn't. "It feels good to tell someone about him."

"Anytime."

"It's not weird for you?"

"No. Why? Should I be jealous?" He gave Oscar a goofy grin. Oscar laughed. "Right. So anytime."

"Thanks."

Oscar pulled his phone out of his pocket and put on some music, which blared a little heavy on the treble from the tiny speakers, and stood up. "Come here."

Russ grinned and looked around. "Me? Whoa!" Oscar hauled him right off his chair and he fell into his lover's arms easily.

"Come here often?" Oscar had a strong lead, and Russ wasn't used to dancing backward.

"Uh, yeah. All the time."

"Right, I thought I'd seen you before. You're the guy who has the thousand-pound girlfriend with the black mane."

He laughed. "Yes, sir. That's me."

"I can do better by you than she can."

"Well, she's faster, but you make a better sandwich for sure."

Oscar laughed, holding him close, leading him slow and steady around the barn. "This is fun."

"I've never done this." It was strange and wonderful.

"Danced?"

"Not like this."

"Really? I love to dance. Love it." Oscar spun him suddenly, laughing as he grabbed on with both hands.

"Whoa!"

Time disappeared for a bit while they danced, Oscar's strong lead making it easy for him to follow and just enjoy himself. Oscar was a total surprise. He knew the man as stoic, responsible, quiet—all those things that Oscar had been while Jonas was alive. Then the thing with Jeff.... That had been eye-opening too. Oscar obviously made time for the gym and wasn't shy. But more than any of that, he loved this. Fun, romantic, and Russ felt... taken care of. That was a first. An honest-to-God first. He'd had a couple of lovers, but he'd never had this before.

Oscar hooked a finger under his chin, and he lifted it, accepting the kiss that was waiting for him. It was gentle and warm and without the hesitation. Oscar was confident and strong, the shaking fingers and the pained expression from that night in the kitchen long gone.

"Oscar," he whispered against his lover's lips.

"Tell me, Russ. Tell me that you can—"

"I can. I can make this feel right again. You've lost a lot, Oscar."

"I'm not feeling sorry for myself."

"No, of course you're not. You have those beautiful girls. You have Rose. They are your family. You're lucky to have so many people that love you. I want to show you this can be good too. I want to be here when you need me. Let me do that for you?"

Oscar nodded slowly. "This is what I meant, Russ. This is something I can't get from Jeffrey. Not like this. He's got something I need, and so do you. I don't want to have to decide between you, but I can't live with myself if I don't know that it's okay with you."

"It's okay with me." He went up on his toes and kissed Oscar. "It's okay. I have a little thing for Jeff too."

"Yeah? A little thing?"

"Pretty sure it's mutual. The way he looks at me, it's... he *wants* me. I love that."

Oscar nodded. "So we're going to try this?"

"Yeah. He wants to. I want to."

"Russ." Oscar pulled him close again. "I've been so.... I'm not alone, but I'm lonely. My heart needs this."

"Your heart is safe with me, Oscar."

The barn, the horses, the music on the radio, the chilly night air—everything disappeared as Oscar kissed him again.

CHAPTER FIFTEEN

"THEY LIKED the property, Jeff, but they're concerned about the location."

Jeff shook his head. "It's a very quiet, private road—"

Amy interrupted him. "It's a little out of the way for them. And honestly, the house isn't modern enough."

"It's classic. It was built for a farming family. It's only had one owner."

"Look, I'll ask my clients again in a few days, but I don't think they're interested. The property is beautiful, though, for the right buyer."

"Yeah, okay."

"Maybe see if the seller would be interested in renovating the house?"

"I'll talk to him. Thanks, Amy."

"Good luck."

Jeffrey hung up the phone and leaned back in his chair with a sigh. That was the fourth family to tour the property and turn it down because the house either wasn't modern enough or big enough. He got it, and he didn't get it. It was a classic farmhouse, the kind you see on Christmas cards and in the movies, painted white with black shutters and surrounded by a wide porch, sitting up on a snowy hill, with red barns in the background. It was lovely.

Granted, inside it had some older-home issues. The floors could use refinishing, the kitchen was on the small side, some of the bedrooms had tiny closets, and there were only two full bathrooms upstairs for five bedrooms. The house was what the real estate industry called "charming" or "quaint." It fit in beautifully on the property. He so appreciated all the insight that Oscar had had about it—the stories about how it was built, the east-west facing porches, the odd, snaking driveway. Those were the kinds of details that sold houses like this.

But he was learning that these days horse farms weren't all what they once were. Not in this market anyway. In some circles in the horse world, farms were status symbols like McMansions were in suburbia. Newer owners wanted the fancy white fencing, the big modern home, lots of meticulously groomed green fields. Stable Hill wasn't that kind of farm. It was a working family property, where the small staff was kept very busy and where the animals were always the top priority.

That meant sometimes a coat of paint waited a season, and the fencing was much more functional than fashionable. It meant the condition of the turnout paddocks was more important than killing every weed in the front lawn. It meant the stalls were maintained meticulously but the driveway had potholes.

Apparently when you were a buyer with money and could afford to hire all kinds of people to run the place for you, you weren't satisfied with just how healthy and happy the animals were. You wanted pretty. And you wanted a bigger, more modern luxury home.

He and Oscar had talked budget. Remodeling the house wasn't remotely possible, and even if it were, he didn't think

Oscar would go for it. Jonas had built that house fifty years ago for Oscar's mother, Sarah. There was no scenario he could imagine in which Oscar would say, sure, tear it apart.

The knock at his door startled him.

"Hey."

"Hey, Steph. Come on in."

"I have someone who wants to see your farm."

Oh, thank God. "Yeah?"

"You're not going to like it."

Or... "Why not?" He felt an eyebrow climb toward his hairline. He had the worst poker face.

Stephanie laughed and sat in one of the guest chairs in front of his desk. She reached over and put a folder down on the blotter. "FHI."

"FHI?" *FHI...? Wait, that sounds familiar.*

"First Home Incorporated?"

Right. Yes. "The real estate company. They um... they build developments, right?"

"Fifty-five-plus active adult residential communities."

"Retirement homes. Of course."

"Well, they're my clients, and they're interested. They contacted me today, looking to make an appointment."

"They want to buy a horse farm, huh?"

"Jeffrey." Stephanie's tone was scolding, and she rolled her eyes at him.

"I already told you my client wants to find a farming buyer."

"Oh, that's right. We had this conversation, didn't we? Silly me. And how is that going for you?"

He looked at her. "It's only been a couple of weeks."

"Four."

"Okay, a few."

"A few is three. It's been several. Enough to judge interest."

He sighed. "I suppose you think you're helping by sitting here arguing semantics with me?"

"I am being helpful. It's more than semantics. These guys want to see it. They like the location, and I'm positive they'll make an offer."

He eyed Stephanie and reached for the folder, then read over the email she'd printed for him. FHI's proposal, of course, was to purchase the property with the intention of building one of their residential communities. They had no need for the horses or the equipment, which would mean that Oscar could sell those off separately on his own and bring in an extra profit. And if they did make an offer, it would likely be more than Oscar could get from a private buyer. He closed the file.

"My client wants to sell it to someone who wants an operational horse farm," he said steadily.

"Mhm. You said. My client wants to see the property. I'll just leave that email with you. Does next week work? Tuesday?" Stephanie stood up.

"There's more in it for him than the bottom line, Steph."

"For him, maybe. For you? No. Tell him about it and see what he says. Dollar signs are persuasive. Text me a good time for Tuesday." And with that, she left the room.

She was right; he needed to pay his rent. But his client was also his lover now, and he knew this would not go over well.

He wasn't going to give up. There were places he'd managed to sell that had a lot less to offer than Stable Hill. But this could wait until tomorrow because right now it was time to get home and shower for a hot date with his men.

CHAPTER SIXTEEN

RUSS WONDERED at first how long Oscar was going to let him hang out in the doorway before acknowledging him. After a minute or two, he realized Oscar genuinely didn't know he was there. He broke the silence. "Taking a break?"

Oscar looked up at Russ from the edge of the bed and smiled. "Something like that."

"This is hard for you, huh?" Oscar's mom passed away years before Jonas did. Her name was Sarah, and several items in this room were inscribed with her name or her initials, SRK, Sarah Reardon Kennedy. Jonas told him once that he'd given a lot of them to Sarah because she loved personalized things—stationery, jewelry, pens, a tissue holder, several picture frames.

Oscar held one of those frames with gentle hands right now. "I don't know. It's not as hard so much as it is a 'walk down memory lane' thing, you know? All this stuff that was Mom's. Everything has a story."

He pushed off the doorframe and stepped into the room, then went to Oscar and rested a hand on his shoulder. "You want to tell me one?"

Oscar shrugged. It was hard to tell if he felt like talking or not, so Russ didn't push.

"You haven't hung the new curtains yet. How about I do that while you pack that box?"

"Yeah? That would be great, thanks. I could use the company."

He smiled and gave Oscar a kiss on the cheek. "All you had to do was ask."

"I'm not very good at that."

He knew how that felt. "I get it. Neither am I." He took one of the curtain rods down and slid the delicate lace valence off the rod and onto the bed. "Jeffrey asked me about the separate rooms. Your mom used this as a dressing room, right?"

"Yes. They built the house with all these bedrooms because they wanted more kids. They wanted a huge family. When that didn't work out for them, Mom took this room as a dressing room. She did come in here sometimes if Dad was snoring or if she was angry with him. He didn't like that at all."

He chuckled. "So it was effective?"

"Very." Oscar laughed. "There was this one time I remember, when Mom was upset with Dad about something and she didn't speak to him for days. Literally days. I have no idea what it was originally about, but he was desperate to fix it. He did dishes and laundry, the lawn was mowed, he fixed little things round the house. Finally after he spent like four days not being spoken to, he stood in the kitchen and shouted at her, 'All right, I'm sorry!'"

"Uh-oh. Did she accept?"

"Yep. She said, 'Thank you, dear. Was that so difficult?' and asked him what he wanted for dinner. You had to see his face."

"All of that just for an apology." He snorted.

"Yep. Please, thank you, I'm sorry... Mom was a stickler for saying the right thing."

"I love you?" He was teasing, mostly.

Oscar grinned at him. "You know, it's funny. Neither of them said it much that I heard. It was understood, though. It was obvious to look at them."

"My folks were like that."

"Yeah? Tell me about them."

"Not much to tell. They're farmers. Mother raised a handful of us, and my dad was a cowboy. That's about all there is to it." He didn't have much else to say. There were some good years when he was younger, lots of siblings to chase after him, horses to ride, friends. But he figured out early who he was. Not long after that, he figured out he wouldn't be wanted if anyone found out. He couldn't do it, hiding felt like torture most of the time, and very soon after that someone outed him.

Oscar nodded. "Yeah. My parents were great, but it still took them a little time to warm up to me."

"My dad never did. Mom is... better about it. I left home at sixteen." He threaded the new, boring, solid-color valance onto the curtain rod and set it down while Oscar wrapped the picture frame in newspaper and put it in the box.

"Well, I'm glad you made it up this way."

He grinned. "Seems like a good call so far."

"Thanks for the help up here."

Oscar stepped up behind him and kissed his neck, giving him shivers. This casual touching was strange and new but definitely something he could get used to. He sighed and leaned into Oscar.

"Small wonder no work is getting done in here."

Russ looked over at Jeff, turning in Oscar's arms. "Oscar was thinking too hard."

"I needed some direction." Oscar shrugged against him.

Jeff sauntered over and put an arm around each of them. "Looks to me like you found it." Jeff kissed him a sweet hello first and then Oscar, who gave Jeff the most amazing smile. "Might be the wrong direction, though. This needs to get done today."

Oscar groaned and pulled away, heading back to the dresser. "Taskmaster."

"I beg your pardon. I believe I have been more than patient."

"You have. I'm sorry I haven't done this sooner. It's just—"

"It's difficult." Russ looked between them. "Don't be an ass, Jeff. Leave him alone."

"Whoa. Yes, sir."

He rolled his eyes. "I'm hanging curtains. You want to take all the frilly stuff off the bed?"

Jeff nodded. "You got it."

He grabbed the lace valence and folded it, then added it to Oscar's box. The three of them worked quietly for a few minutes, many hands making the task go by quickly.

"I'll have to ask Rose to wash all that stuff for me. I'll ruin it. Especially those lace curtains."

Jeffrey pulled a valance back out of the box to look at it. "You might even want to do these by hand. They're really fragile."

"Yeah, you're probably right." Oscar went quiet again for a second and then added, "Russ, you should find something of Dad's to take with you."

Russ froze, looking over his shoulder at Oscar. To take with him? Was there something he didn't know? "I couldn't do that. Your girls—"

"I want you to. I wouldn't have said it otherwise. My girls might want a few things from Mom, but Dad's stuff? I doubt there will be much."

He knew exactly what he wanted, but.... "Well, I... I don't know."

Oscar moved closer, smiling. "No?"

He laughed, shaking his head. Of course Oscar would know. "I can't ask."

"Fine. Russ, would you like to have Dad's porch rocker? You're in it all the time. He'd want you to have it."

He leaned in and kissed Oscar. "Yes, please."

"Would you like a couple of his pipes too?"

Oh. Wouldn't that be something? "Are you serious?"

"Sure. Just pick out a couple that you like. None of them are valuable except to us."

He smiled wide. Being included felt good. It warmed him up inside. "I really appreciate it."

"I know." Oscar bent to kiss him but didn't quite get there.

"Isn't this where I came in?" Jeffrey laughed, interrupting them. "I can go have a beer and come back later...?"

"Hey, it's not every day you inherit the world's most comfortable porch rocker."

"If I give you something, will you kiss me too?"

He slid over to Jeff. "I'll kiss you for free." He did, and tangled tongues with Jeff, letting Jeff turn it naughty, as usual.

Oscar snorted and went back to packing. "I'll start taking odds on whether we make it to dinner tonight, shall I?"

Oscar had a point; their track record hadn't been that good.

"They're just kisses, Oscar the Grouch." Jeff pulled Russ a little closer, looking over his head at Oscar. "We can wait."

"Curtains," Russ reminded Jeff, and he was set free.

"I'm taller. You want me to do that?"

He looked at Jeff. "You know how to hang curtains?"

"I'm a Realtor. I can hang curtains, make beds, fold napkins, do the little toilet paper fold-over thing...."

Oscar whistled. "You're hired."

He laughed and switched places with Jeff.

"So we've established that my parents were adorable, and Russ's parents were... conservative. What about yours, Jeffrey?"

"My parents?"

"Yeah."

"They're old snowbirds. They live in Boca."

"Whoa. Nice."

Jeff nodded. "Yeah. I found them the place a few years ago. They love it."

"Wow. Shipped them off to Florida, huh?" Oscar laughed.

"Pretty much." Jeff winked. "My lifestyle is a little too... busy for them to really understand."

He looked at Jeffrey curiously. "By busy, you mean work?"

"You know that's not what I meant."

Oscar snorted. "Busy being a bad boy."

"Well, it's slightly less busy these days."

"Only slightly?" Russ shook his head.

"The two of you are keeping me plenty occupied. And trying to sell this farm, of course."

"Anything new to report?" Oscar asked, and Russ held his breath on the answer.

"No, unfortunately. But I'm not desperate yet. I would like more of a pipeline of people to come see it, but... it'll happen."

Russ wasn't in a rush. He didn't stand to gain anything, and he was very worried he was going to lose his job.

"What's the feedback?"

He watched Jeff's shoulders droop a little, and he looked over at Oscar, but Oscar was putting something in the box and his back was turned.

Uh-oh.

He gave Jeff a look, and Jeff straightened up quickly.

"People love the property, the acreage. They're are happy with the stables, and most see the potential in that unfinished indoor. Someone today told me they thought it was really well-maintained."

Oscar folded one arm over the other across that broad chest and looked at Jeff. "But they're not interested."

"Not enough."

"Why not? Didn't you say most people——"

"It's the house, Oscar." Jeff shrugged.

Russ knew how poorly Oscar was going to take that. Jeff sounded like he knew it too.

"What's the matter with the house?"

Jeff sighed. "You know, we can have this conversation another time, Oscar. Maybe at my office?"

"My father built this house. It's in great shape. What's the matter with it?"

Russ finished folding the bedding and then moved over to hang the curtains that Jeff had stalled on. Nobody needed his input here. Seemed safer to stay out of it.

"Some people... *most* people are looking for something more modern."

"This is a classic farmhouse." Oscar sounded pretty huffy.

"Yes, it is, Oscar. But that's not what everyone wants. People are looking for a bigger kitchen, more bathrooms, open floor plans, bigger bedrooms——"

"Well, why did you take it on if you didn't think that you could sell it?"

Jeff blinked. "I didn't say I couldn't sell it."

"Then what are you complaining about?"

"I'm not complain...." Jeff took a step toward Oscar but stopped abruptly, took a deep breath, and sighed. Russ could see his lover was trying hard. "Look, Oscar, I know all of this ——the boxes and everything——is stressful for you."

"I'm fine." But Oscar's tone was pretty short.

Okay, Russ decided that was his cue. "Hey."

Oscar sighed. "I'm fine, Russ." But when he forced his arms around Oscar's waist, Oscar pulled him close. They stayed there for a minute, quietly holding each other, and then Jeff joined them, reaching out to run fingers through Oscar's hair.

"I will find a buyer for the farm, Oscar. Give me some more time."

Oscar took Jeff's hand and kissed the palm. "I know, I'm sorry. I guess you're right. This is maybe harder than I expected it to be."

"It's not just a house to you."

"It's not," Oscar agreed. "I'm actually pretty grateful to have you both here right now."

Russ smiled. Oscar had had a lot of loss around him, and then to be losing the house too.... It was probably a relief to have something gained instead. "You ready to get this room done? Then we can all start dinner."

"I have one more curtain. Russ, the new comforter is in the hall."

"On it." He leaned up and kissed Oscar quickly. "You don't have to pretend this is easy, okay? We're here."

Oscar nodded and let him go. "Yeah, okay. I'll try to remember that. And I'm sorry, Jeff."

"You weren't really upset with me."

"No. No, I wasn't. I'm not."

"I know." Jeff gave Oscar a bro-hug and went after the last set of lace curtains.

When the room was finished, it looked nothing like it had. The comforter had flowers all over it, the curtains a solid, dark red—Jeff called it cranberry, of course—the dresser and nightstand were bare, and the tiny closet was empty. Russ waited while Oscar took one last look around the room and turned the light out, and then they followed Jeff down the stairs, each of them with a box in their arms.

"Just leave them by the door. I'll put them in my car later."

Jeff put his box down. "Dinner?"

"Woo! I'll start the grill." He set his box with Jeff's, grinning, and headed for the back porch. Somebody swatted him on the ass as he went by.

Jeff followed him. "I'll make the burgers."

"I'll, uh... get the beer?" Oscar offered.

"Man, don't work too hard, Oscar!"

"Aw, leave him alone, Russ. He has to take care of that pretty pink manicure."

Oscar snorted. "It's sexy and you know it."

They were all laughing as Russ headed through the kitchen and out the back door. No one laughed harder than Oscar.

CHAPTER SEVENTEEN

"WHAT IS this?"

"Minions!"

Sophie rolled her eyes. "It's not called Minions, Zoe. It's called *Despicable Me*."

"Who's the minion? That guy?" Jeffrey looked totally confused. Oscar couldn't tell if it was an act or not.

"No, Mr. Stokes! Minions are the yellow guys."

"Oh." Jeff still looked confused. "Can they please call me Jeffrey?"

"Oh, fine. Whatever you prefer."

"Oz! Sit still!" Riley tapped his hand, and he turned back toward her.

"Sorry, baby. Better?"

"Yes. Can I do black?"

He blinked. "Black?"

"Oh, sweetheart. Black like Brian's nails, of course." Rose gave him a knowing wink.

"Brian has... oh. Brian has black nail polish, of course." When did that happen? How did he not notice at dinner?

"Brian says boys wear black."

"Well, then I guess I better have black."

"Mm. Black sounds ho—hard. *Hard* to do." Jeffrey looked at him wide-eyed, and Oscar chuckled.

Riley disagreed. "Black isn't any harder than pink, you know."

"Well, you are certainly the expert. I liked the pink your dad's been wearing."

"That's one of Oz's favorites."

Sophie snickered, knees curled under her in the over-stuffed chair and eyes in her book.

"Soph," he admonished.

She glanced up at him and grinned. "I didn't say anything."

"What are you reading, Sophie?"

She showed Jeffrey the dog-eared cover of her beloved *The Black Stallion*.

"She's read it a million times." Zoe snorted.

"Not a million. Seventeen."

He blinked. "You've read that book seventeen times?"

Sophie gave him a look. "Yeah? So what?"

"Oh. No. No, I'm glad you like it." He hadn't meant his tone to be so... shocked. *Get her over here to ride*, he remembered Russ telling him. *She's got a way with the horses.*

He should have been paying closer attention. All this time she could have—well. It was getting late now. But maybe she could ride somewhere else. Russ was definitely on to something.

Hm. Russ.

"Jeffrey, you seem like you do well for yourself in that real estate business."

"Oh, uh." Jeffrey glanced at him, but he shook his head and grinned. Nothing good came of suggesting that Rose change the subject. "I do all right, I guess."

"That's a nice suit." She tilted her head.

"Okay, a little better than all right."

Rose nodded. "That's what I thought."

"Rose, you're a piece of work."

"Just trying to get to know your Jeffrey, Oscar."

"My...." He looked at Rose sharply, but she smiled at him.

Jeffrey laughed. "Oh, Oscar. I think maybe—" Jeffrey's phone rang, interrupting, and he pulled it out of his pocket. "Oh, hey. It's Russ."

Oscar raised an eyebrow at him meaningfully. "Probably about the paint, right?"

Jeffrey looked at him oddly but seemed to get it. "Oh, yeah. That or the contractors. Excuse me."

Oscar watched Jeffrey head for the kitchen. He had no idea how to explain his relationship status to Rose when he wasn't sure he entirely understood it himself. That's the reason Russ wasn't here tonight. Right or wrong—and, if he were honest with himself, it was starting to feel wrong—Rose already knew Jeffrey was at least a love interest.

He looked back at Riley, who was finishing up with his black nails. "Girls, I think it's bedtime."

Rose nodded, setting her knitting aside. "Riley, Zoe. Come on up and I'll tuck you in. Sophie, love. You too."

"What about Emily?"

He looked around. "Where is Emily?"

"She and Brian went out after dinner." Rose looked completely passive, and he had no idea how to read that expression.

"Oh. Well, it's not curfew yet."

"Come on, girls, up you go. Kiss your father good night."

He was mobbed by girls and hugged and kissed, and he gave it all right back, careful not to smudge his new manicure. "Love you, Zoe, Riley, Soph. Good night, sleep tight. Good night, Rose."

"Is your friend staying the night?"

"No. No, definitely not. The girls...."

"They'll be happy if you're happy."

"I love you, Rose. Good night." He gave her a kiss on the cheek and sent her on her way too.

Okay. Emily was still out, so he wasn't going upstairs yet. He headed for the kitchen to check on Jeffrey.

"Did you get hungry?"

"Yeah. Tomorrow is good." Jeffrey turned dark eyes on him, brow furrowed. Something was wrong, but he couldn't quite read the look. "Yes. I'll talk to Oscar. Saturday sounds great. Good night, Russ. Sleep well."

Jeffrey didn't take his eyes off Oscar as he hung up the phone.

"What did—"

"Why didn't you warn me that Russ didn't know I was here?"

"Oh." He sighed. "I thought we could talk about that. I didn't know he was going to call."

"He's our boyfriend, Oscar. He can call anytime he wants."

"God, that sounds weird. 'Our boyfriend.'"

"It's not weird. It's reality. You better get your head around this, Oscar."

"I'm sorry. I know." *Jesus. Talk about making bad even worse.* "I know. I didn't mean anything by that."

"So now we've both lied to him."

"You didn't tell him?"

"I told him I stopped by to drop off some paperwork."

"Shit. I'm sorry, Jeffrey. I didn't mean to put you in that position or... or to make a thing out of this. I wasn't.... I don't know how to handle things with Rose. She does so much for me, and when she asked to see you, it didn't occur to me to say no, and then after I invited you...." He closed his mouth to stop the awful flow of words. He was digging a deeper hole now.

Jeffrey shook his head. "Well."

"What was I going to say to him? 'Sorry, Jeffrey is okay to visit but you're not'?"

Jeffrey... stared, gaping at him.

Damn. Oscar returned the look. "What?"

"You're serious?"

"Jeff—"

"You could have invited him."

"But... Rose."

"You can't be in a relationship with both of us if it's all good except when it's embarrassing or inconvenient."

"What? I'm not embarrassed by either of you!"

"No? Oscar, you should have invited him or not invited me."

Oscar crossed his arms. He and Jeffrey were destined to work everything out by arguing, weren't they? It was the same with Emmett. Everything had to be fair. Balanced. So fucking left-brained and anal-retentive, and God, he loved Emmett, but it made him crazy.

Jeffrey isn't Emmett.

Jeffrey was not Emmett.

Fuck.

"I've got the kids too, and this is still so new. I've got more than myself to worry about. It's very complicated. I didn't think about it as slighting Russ, but you're right, I did."

He felt terrible. He hadn't intended to do this to Russ. His lover deserved better; he knew that. He sighed, trying to breathe through whatever was happening, and looked down at his feet. "This is... *hard*. You, Russ, the farm, Emily looking at colleges, and this boyfriend thing. I feel like I have so many balls in the air all the time, and it's... emotional and...."

He glanced up at Jeffrey sharply. "Maybe I shouldn't do this. I can't seem to do it right."

Jeffrey was suddenly at his side, one arm going around his shoulders. "Hey. Okay, I hear you."

"I feel like I'm going to keep getting this wrong. I don't want to get it wrong. I'm trying, but...." But he didn't have a blueprint for this one.

"Maybe there isn't a wrong, yet. We haven't laid down any rules. Maybe we can get by on good intentions for tonight."

"The road to hell."

"Oh, come on. I know you weren't trying to hurt Russ, but he's probably going to be hurt anyway. If it were me, I'd be annoyed but I'd understand. Russ is more...."

"I know."

"We'll talk to him. He'll get it once we talk."

"But he'll be upset first." And what was he going to say? Sorry I purposefully didn't invite you? Jesus, he was an asshole.

"Well, you... *we*... might have to pay the piper."

Oscar nodded, and a silence fell on the kitchen for a bit while he tried to decide what he should say. What he should do. He understood his feelings for both of these men. It was the same strong emotion but felt so different, each of them something he needed, something he wanted. He'd changed, grown since he lost Emmett, both in his desires and his needs. Enough that this new relationship made him realize they wouldn't be easily met by Emmett anymore, not this completely. Was that okay? Was it really possibly to be in love with more than one man? Right at this moment, he didn't know for sure, but he was genuinely open to the idea.

He just didn't know if he had what it took to do right by each of them. He didn't know if he had the energy, or the time. And he didn't like feeling as if he was failing them.

"Oscar."

He looked up at Jeffrey, startled out of his own head, and Jeffrey kissed him.

"Relax."

"I don't do relaxed all that well."

"Let me help." They kissed again, deep and long, Jeffrey running strong, warm fingers over his arms and the back of his neck, soothing away the worry. Distracting him. Jeffrey's kiss was so different from Russ's. Russ's was full of emotion at the forefront and the heat at a constant simmer, ready to be fanned into flames. Jeffrey's was always roiling, the desire aggressive, but the need was more than physical.

But he needed to think.

He put a hand on Jeffrey's chest and levered him away, gently but firmly. "Jeffrey."

"What?" Jeffrey went in for another kiss, but he pulled away. "Oscar?"

"I think it's time to say good night."

"Why? Because Granny is upstairs?"

Wow. Jeffrey had gotten a little ramped up. "*Rose* is not the reason."

"Come on, Oscar. Let's work off some of your steam."

"You're the one who's steamed, babe." He gave Jeffrey a smile and put a little more distance between them. "I've really got to get my head around this."

Jeffrey bristled. "You're not sure?"

"I know how I feel, babe. I need to figure out how this relationship fits into everything else. My family. I have to think about the girls and... and their future. There are a lot of pieces to this puzzle."

Jeffrey shouldered past him to the living room to get his jacket.

He followed. "Please, I need you to understand."

"It's your family, Oz. I'm... I'm a little thrown. And a little revved up."

He grinned at Jeffrey. "You called me 'Oz.'"

Jeffrey froze. "I did. Is that okay? I guess... I mean, I've been hanging out with your girls and it just slipped out."

"It's fine. I grew up being called Oz. Emmett called me Oz too."

"Rose doesn't."

"Rose doesn't care to use nicknames. But she likes 'sweetheart' and 'dear.'"

"I did notice that." Jeffrey smiled and gave him a man-hug. "It's all good. Call me."

"I will." He took Jeffrey's arm. "I'm not running you off, I promise. But I need a clear head."

Jeffrey nodded at him. "Okay."

"I promise." Their eyes met and they held the gaze for a long moment.

"I believe you. Call me."

He let his lover go. He hated to do it, but he needed to make a decision, and he couldn't do that with Jeffrey in his house. "Good night, Jeffrey. Thanks for coming."

"Yeah." Jeffrey hurried to his Mercedes, got in, and took off at a speed Oscar was pretty sure wasn't allowed on a residential road.

CHAPTER EIGHTEEN

OSCAR NEEDED to think. That was completely fair. Totally understandable. This was the man's first experience since he'd lost his husband, and that had to be as stressful as it was a relief, right? He had those girls to worry about, after all.

This wasn't Jeffrey's first rodeo. He'd been down the poly road before, and it had ended for him as naturally as it had begun. He had all kinds of advantages over Oscar right now, and he understood that.

But fuck if he didn't have a nearly crippling case of blue balls.

He'd wanted Oscar, really wanted him, and he thought... he'd assumed that Oscar was there with him.

Oscar had been on a different train entirely.

Still half-hard, he shifted in his seat, his prick rubbing against his fly. The clock in his dashboard said it was 9:35 p.m. Not horrible, even if it was a Sunday night.

He was also nearly out of gas.

"Oh. Damn." He turned around and headed back to the gas station he'd just passed and pulled in. While the tank was filling, he looked at his phone, reflexively flipping Grindr open to check out the grid. Very quickly someone with the handle "BTM4U" caught his eye. The guy had a great body, everything from thighs to a slightly stubbled chin was in the shot, shorts riding low on narrow hips. Assuming it was a real pic, it totally looked worth his time.

His thumb hovered over the picture. Oscar had left him wanting for sure. This early in a relationship wouldn't necessarily put them in exclusive territory, would it? He hadn't expressly had that discussion with either of his current lovers.

But....

In this case, he couldn't have Oscar, but he didn't need to find a one-night stand either.

Russ.

He shut Grindr down, flipped to Russ's number, and dialed it as he pulled out of the gas station. It rang three times, but a quiet voice finally answered. "Hello?"

Russ's raspy, sleepy voice finished what Oscar had started, Jeffrey's cock swelling to fill his jeans.

"Russ, I'm coming over."

"Jeff?"

"I'm on my way."

"Are you okay? Did something happen with Oscar?"

"I want.... Christ, Russ, I *need* you."

"Oh. Fuck." His lover moaned in his ear.

"Yeah? You're in?"

"I'm in, Jeff. Jesus. How far away are you?"

"I'll be there as soon as I can." It wasn't a short drive. It would be all he could do to keep his mind on the road.

"Hurry."

He hung up the phone, let his foot drop heavily on the gas pedal, and drove on.

Jeffrey didn't remember much of the ride, but he got there in one piece. He slid out of his car, slammed the door, and took the steps two at a time, arm reaching for the doorknob as soon as he hit the porch. He crashed right through the front door, making the hinges creak and the door bang against the entryway wall.

Russ was waiting for him on the couch and stood up as he appeared in the doorway.

"Look at you, all wound up and wild-eyed. Is that for me?"

He nodded and stalked toward Russ, who grinned at him and bolted up the stairs.

"Little shit!" He took off at a run, taking the steps two at a time and caught sight of Russ disappearing through the bedroom door.

They were both breathing hard by the time he caught his lover in the bedroom. He got hold of one wrist and pulled Russ to him, and they stared at each other for a long moment, panting in each other's faces.

Finally, Russ grinned, breaking the spell. "Come on."

He grinned back and shoved Russ onto the bed, and they both stripped off, clothing flying, filthy words and grunts filling the air.

Jeffrey pulled a drawer open and covered up, slicked his fingers, and dove after Russ's erection with his mouth.

"Oh fuck!" Russ shouted, surprised. That was followed by a lovely arch and groan as Jeffrey pressed two fingers inside his lover, also without warning. "Fuck. Fuck, Jeff!"

"Mm." That was the plan. Russ smelled so good and looked like pure sex to him. He was ready. Now. He hoped Russ was close enough. "Want you. Now."

"Please. Please!" Russ pulled his knees up, offering that beautiful ass to him, giving him a hell of a view.

He dove in, making Russ gasp and pant as his cock sank deep. Fuck, Russ felt so good. Just right.

"Want you. Fuck, Jeff. Come on."

He grunted, Russ's words going right to his balls. The last

rational thing he remembered was that he didn't think either of them was going to last very long.

HOLY MOTHER of God, he'd seen bright green and yellow stars, no lie.

He lay there after with Russ in his arms, sliding fingers over his lover. It was fascinating how rough with outdoor work his lover's hands were, young face a little weathered, skin with a permanent farmer's tan, but how pristine and smooth the rest of Russ's skin was.

Russ shifted and sighed sleepily. Jeffrey let him, enjoying this strange new habit he had of staying in his lovers' beds until morning and waking up beside them with morning breath and bedhead and the whole nine yards. Commitment. He was still a little baffled by it, but it was working for him. Jeff wanted Russ and Oscar and enjoyed their attention, their care. It was amazing to him that he returned it so effortlessly, like it was something he was used to when he definitely was not. They just made it easy.

He must have fallen asleep shortly after that because he woke up to kisses and the smell of coffee. Smiling against Russ's lips, he reluctantly opened his eyes. "Morning."

"Good morning." Russ was dressed and already smelled like horses.

"What time is it?"

"Eight. Brought you coffee."

He sat up slowly, took the coffee, and sipped it. "Mmm. Good. You been working already?"

"Out at the barn at six for turnout, stalls to clean up. It's what I do."

He nodded. "I hope I didn't keep you up too late."

Russ laughed. "Well, last night's going to own me for a few

more hours I think, but I'm recovering. I just need more coffee."

"I better get up." But he pulled Russ in for another quick kiss first. His phone chirped and he reached for it, glancing at the screen. "Oscar."

"Yeah? House stuff?" Russ peered at his phone.

I'm really sorry about last night.

"What happened?"

"Huh?" Shit. He put his phone facedown on the table again.

"What is he sorry for?"

"Oh, well...."

Dammit. Come on, coffee, kick in.

His phone chirped again, and he reached for it, but Russ snagged it first.

"You know it's not that I didn't want you?" Russ said, reading the text. "What? I thought you said you were just dropping off papers?"

"I... uh. Well—"

"You made a move, but he turned you down, so you came for me?"

He blinked. "What? No. It wasn't like that." Or was it? Maybe not... entirely?

Russ pinned him with a look. "You wanted Oscar, but he sent you home. Right?"

"Well, I guess. Yeah. I kissed him, and I kind of... I wanted—"

Russ stood up, tossing his phone on the bed. "Right. I get it. So all that 'Russ I need you' shit was more like 'Oscar gave me a boner and you're the next best thing,' huh?"

"Russ. No. No, I didn't mean it that way.... I didn't intend it to be like that."

"I need to get back to the barn."

"Russ, come on. Give me a chance to explain." Although what was he going to say?

"Go to work, Jeff," Russ said with a sigh and left the room.

"Fuck."

His phone chimed again and he looked at it with a sigh.

You there?

I'll call you later, he texted back and got up out of bed to get dressed.

CHAPTER NINETEEN

GODDAMMIT.

Russ spent the rest of morning in a foul mood. Why did he do this to himself? He knew better.

Fuckbuddies? No problem. Lovers? Dangerous territory. But this? Actually falling for someone? For *two* someones?

Bad idea.

Bad, bad idea. Stupid. He couldn't decide who he was more angry with, himself or... them. His... well, his boyfriends. Did he still want to use that word?

Everything he was feeling right now was his own goddamn fault.

Why? Because people sucked. People disappointed him all the damn time. He'd learned that lesson young, really young, and he couldn't believe he was dealing with this again. The first person he ever met in his adult life who didn't disappoint him was Jonas. He should never have let himself fall for Oscar, let alone open himself up to Jeff, who... who had snuck into his heart at some point and he hadn't realized it until this morning, when he figured out the two of them were fucking with him.

Jesus Christ, something about all of this hurt. It hurt real bad.

"There's a reason that I work with horses and not people." He was cleaning tack like a fiend, scrubbing and polishing so hard his fingers hurt. He normally would be munching on his PB&J at this hour, but he didn't have an appetite, so instead he was sitting with Angel, who had primly refused turnout in the rain, chatting her ear off about Jeff and Oscar.

"You wouldn't lie to me, right? Horses are simple. If you're hungry, I know it. If you're hurting, I know it. If you don't feel like dealing with me, I know that too. You don't want to do something, like today with the rain, you say, 'Nope, sorry, Russ. I'm not going out today,' and I get it. Easy. If I tell you shit, you won't tell nobody, right? Simple, trustworthy, straight-up."

Angel bumped his ear with her nose and nibbled on the shoulder of his coat. He stroked his hand down along her jaw, glad for the quiet company, and laid the bridle he'd finished cleaning down. "See? You love me." He picked up some long reins next. "People are confusing. I don't like confusing."

His feelings were kind of confusing too, but what he wanted wasn't. He wanted them both; it was plain as that. But then again, he wanted a lot of things he couldn't necessarily have. And the thing was, he didn't want either of them if it meant being left out all the time. But what was he supposed to do now? Jeff knew well he was pissed, and so Oscar knew by now for sure. Were they going to gang up on him? Write him off?

Was there any chance they'd apologize? Would he accept it if they did? Would they really understand why he was upset?

Did they love him the way he loved them?

"Mother. Fucker." He tossed the reins down and leaned back against the wall of the barn. "Is it cheating on someone if you're also in a relationship with the other guy? Maybe not, right? So not cheating, but can you still be used? Or... taken for granted? Is it wrong that I feel second-best? Am I just being a brat?"

His phone buzzed in his pocket, but he ignored it because he knew it was one of them. He was too busy to pick up the phone, right? He sat up again and reached for the reins, and his phone went quiet. He tried to put it from his mind, going over the chores he needed to get done before the construction guys came back tomorrow. He needed to think about something else.

But his phone started ringing a few minutes later. *Fuck you, go away, I'm mad.*

Then it was ringing and buzzing at the same time. "What the fuck?" He pulled it out of his pocket and looked at it.

Jeff was calling him, and Oscar was texting that he wanted to talk. Then it switched all of a sudden, and Oscar called him as Jeff started shooting him texts asking him to pick up the phone.

Jesus, he was being double-teamed.

Maybe that meant they both felt like assholes. Good.

Russ. Talk to me. That was Oscar. They'd both given up calling.

No

Russ, we should talk.

No I'm pissed off

I know. It's my fault.

He stared at his phone. Huh. Okay, that was upright of Oscar, but what was he supposed to do with it?

Okay, if you don't want to talk to me right now, that's fine. Will you please call me later?

He thought about that. Thought about what he wanted.

No

...?

He started a group text, looping in both Oscar and Jeff.

Both of you come here Saturday. Can you make that work with the girls, Oscar? I don't want to talk to one of you I want to talk to you both at the same time. We need to all to talk together. We need to have an understanding.

He wanted to make sure they both really wanted him. And if it worked out, he didn't want anyone to have to go home after.

Yeah. I can do that. Rose will be here.

Okay, Russ. I think that makes sense, Jeff answered finally.

And until then we text here, all three of us. Where we can all see what's being said.

Oscar jumped right on that train. *Sure. Good idea.*

Can do.

Good. Done.

There was a short pause, and then Jeff followed up with *Want a dick pic?*

Jesus Christ. But he laughed. All right, then.

Jeff! He could practically hear Oscar's gasp.

Don't be such a prude, Oz, Jeff fired back.

Oz? Really?

That's what his kids call him. Also, faster to type.

Oz. That was cute. He liked it.

Russ, I'm sorry. Last night was my fault. I'll explain it on Saturday, but I didn't want the apology to wait until then. Oscar's text seemed sincere, and it really was cool that he was trying.

Russ, I'll explain too. OK? Honest to God, I had a great night, and I was totally with you. I promise. Every second.

He swallowed hard as emotion pushed up from his gut into his throat and stung in his eyes.

OK. I gotta go guys. He had work to do and he needed to think.

Oscar texted back quickly. *OK. Love you, Russ.*

Jeff sent a picture of his dick.

CHAPTER TWENTY

It was possible his relationship with Emmett had been diffi-cult sometimes, but if so, Oscar couldn't remember much of that at all. Some bickering, sure, but that was who they were. Still, it seemed like everyone believed that relationships required work, so he supposed it was natural that a relation-ship with two men at once would require even more.

He'd had a few days to think about how Russ and Jeffrey were going to fit into his family, but he was no closer to answers than he had been the other night. The only thing he knew for sure was that he'd been well-intentioned and wrong at the same.

He felt completely unprepared for this conversation, armed only with what he knew he wanted and genuine feel-ings for Russ and Jeffrey that seemed to grow deeper every time he saw them. As he pulled into the driveway at Stable Hill, he resolved to stay honest with them and to try to be open to whatever they had to say. They couldn't ask for more than that, could they?

He was running a few minutes late because Zoe needed an extra hug before he left. Jeffrey was already there, that schmancy car parked out front. He parked right next to it and got out, trying to balance how glad he was to be seeing them with the anxiety riding along in the pit of his stomach.

It would be okay. It was just a talk, and one they needed. The whole point was that they wanted things to work out, right?

God, he hoped he was right about that.

He took a deep breath and knocked on the door. He heard voices and Russ answered, the look on his lover's face hard to read.

"Are you seriously knocking on the door to your own house?"

He blinked. "Oh."

"Come in." Russ stepped aside and let him in.

"I know I'm late, I'm sorry. Zoe—"

Jeffrey put a hand on his arm and kissed him, the connection just exactly what he needed. "It's okay, Oscar. Relax."

He nodded. "Trying."

"Breathe. No one's dropping a guillotine, Oz. I'll get you some wine."

"Hey." Russ stepped in front of him. "I want one of those too."

"You do?"

"I do."

He kissed Russ, his lover's acceptance making the knot in his stomach come loose all at once, emotion threatening to spill out of him in tears. He forced them back. He didn't need to embarrass himself further by losing it over something as simple as a kiss. But he knew it meant Russ forgave him, and he was surprised to discover he needed that much more than he'd known.

"You okay?"

"Better now." But he'd had to swallow hard before he could speak.

Russ smiled at him. "Me too."

"Jesus, Oz. Do you need a shot of whiskey before I give you this wine?"

"It's been a long week." He tried out a soft laugh and took the glass from Jeffrey's fingers, stepping farther into the room. There was a pad of paper and a handful of pens in the center of Dad's farmhouse table, and Mom's sideboard was covered in food.

"Eat something. I brought a bunch of munchies, figuring we shouldn't talk on an empty stomach. I've only been here fifteen minutes, and Russ has already eaten half of the pigs in a blanket."

Russ nodded. "It's true. I love those things."

He laughed again. Maybe this was going to be okay. "Smells good." He looked over the food, picked up one of the little hotdogs, and then cut himself a hunk of cheddar cheese.

"Someone's taking notes?"

"I don't know. I thought it might be good to write things down. I just... I want to be sure we understand each other."

"Whatever you need, Russ."

Russ looked at him. "You might want to hear what I need before you say that."

Maybe. But he already knew that as long as the girls would be okay, he'd give them the moon if they asked for it. It only took two kisses to remind him.

Jeffrey pulled one of the benches back from the table and sat down with a glass of wine, and Russ set a beer next to a chair at the head of the table. Okay, then. He pulled out the other bench.

Jeffrey sipped his wine.

Russ played with the label on the beer bottle.

Finally, they both looked at him.

"Me?" They wanted him to start this? He looked at Jeffrey, who shrugged at him.

Okay.

He sat down and took another sip of his wine. "Russ... well. Hang on." He took a deep breath and then looked at them both. "Before I start, is this like a come-to-Jesus thing, or is this really a conversation? Because I mean, I already said I was sorry."

"I hope we're all going to listen to each other. Right, Russ?"

"I'm listening."

None of that made him feel any better, but what was he going to do? He had to man up and see how things played out. He sighed, finally deciding to start at the beginning. "A while back, when Jeffrey was still only my Realtor, he brought some papers by the house one night. There was all this chaos going on with the girls and Emily's new boyfriend was coming over, and while I was dealing with that, he and Rose started talking. Next thing I know, she's invited him to dinner."

"We have the same alma mater. She likes me."

Russ leaned back in his chair and crossed his arms. "Oh, yeah?"

"Jeffrey, maybe let me talk?"

"Sorry."

"So, okay. Rose liked the idea that I might be thinking about dating someone, you know? And I think she liked having Jeffrey over. So the other night she asked me to invite him to dinner again, and... she does so much for the girls and for me, and she knows Jeffrey and I are seeing each other now, so I couldn't really say no anyway, and—"

"She knows about you and *Jeff*." Russ looked at him hard.

He sighed, nodding. He expected that reaction. "Yeah."

"But she doesn't know about me."

"No."

Russ looked at Jeffrey. "And you didn't go by just to drop off paperwork."

Jeffrey shook his head, looking contrite. "No. And I absolutely got caught with my pants down there. I didn't know Oscar hadn't told you I was there, and then I panicked and didn't know what to say because I didn't want to get him in trouble or hurt your feelings. I felt stuck, and I totally lied to you. I'm sorry."

Russ leaned forward and picked up his beer. "Why didn't you tell me what was going on?"

"And say what?" Oscar shrugged. "'Hey, Russ. Sorry, man, only Jeff can come to dinner'? I knew it would hurt your feelings that he was coming, that I hadn't told Rose about you... all of it."

"Russ, if I can speak for Oscar here a second—"

Russ cut Jeffrey off right there. "You can't." Jeffrey blinked, and Russ looked back at him. "When are you going to tell her?"

"Soon."

"When?"

"Soon, Russ. I don't know. You deserve better, I know, but it's not that simple."

"He's got kids, Russ. And Rose is—"

"Don't tell me who Rose is, Jeff. I've known her longer than you have. And I sure don't need you to parse this out for me. You've already got your recognition."

"Russ." Oscar scooted over on the bench so he was closer to Russ's chair. "Listen. I'm going to tell her. I promise you that. It's not a measure of how important you are to me. It's got nothing to do with you at all. It's about my girls. It's about Rose having lost a son, you know? It's about handling this right."

Russ watched him, nodding finally. "Okay. I hear what you're saying. I—"

"It feels crappy, I know. And I'll fix it, I promise I will. The next time Jeffrey comes to dinner, you'll be invited too." That was his intention, anyway. He just had to figure it out.

"Okay." Russ still looked a little wary but seemed to accept his promise. "Thanks, Oscar."

He took a deep breath and reached for his wine, glancing at Jeffrey, who shrugged at him.

"So." Jeffrey leaned on the table. "Can I talk now?"

"Yes. Go ahead." It was kind of hot the way Russ was taking control of this conversation. He was glad, actually. Of all of them, Oscar felt like Russ needed this the most.

Jeff played with the pencil on the table. "So, was coming here after that really the wrong thing to do?"

Wait. What? "You came here?"

Jeffrey gave him a haughty look. "Are you judging?"

Whoa.

"Well, I... uh. No."

Jeffrey looked at Russ. "Are you still upset about that?"

"Only because I didn't know the rest of the story."

"You weren't a consolation prize, you know. I wanted you. *You*, Russ."

Russ nodded. "Thank you, I understand it better now. But that's another thing we need to talk about."

"Okay. Can I start?" Jeffrey looked at Oscar and then at Russ. "This isn't my first time."

"It's not?" He supposed he shouldn't be surprised. Jeffrey had been pretty confident from the beginning. "You've had two boyfriends before?"

"No, a boyfriend and a girlfriend."

"No." Russ stared at Jeffrey. "You're into women? You?"

"What? I prefer men, but yeah. Women, men, it's all good. Women love me."

He just bet they did. "And this makes you an authority?" he teased.

"Ha-ha. No. But I wanted to.... Look. In my experience,

there's really only one way to handle this, you know? We can't expect it to be all three of us together all the time, in bed or out. We don't live together, for one thing, but also our schedules are different, and honestly? Our needs are different. I get different things from each of you. Don't you feel that way?"

He did. Exactly that way. But he craved time with the three of them together too.

"Yeah," Russ said quickly. "Absolutely."

He agreed readily too. "I'm glad you said that. I do feel that way."

"So, being together in pairs has to be allowed, yes?"

Both he and Russ answered at once. "Yes."

Jeffrey laughed first, and he and Russ chuckled too. "Okay. So. We just have to decide how we want to handle that—when it's okay and when it's not."

"It's not okay for family things." Russ jumped right in with both feet.

Oscar sighed.

Again.

Damn.

"No, it's not, Russ. If we're serious, then we do have to consider things like family. That's really only an issue for Oz, though, and I think we need to be respectful of that process, right?"

"We? That's easy for you today, huh? You're already in, Jeff."

"Russ—"

"Russ, please." He leaned closer again, willing Russ to hear him out. "In every way that matters, Rose is my mother. And with the girls in the mix too, I just have to approach things carefully. I apologize that Jeffrey got there ahead of you; that wasn't planned. But I'm going to tell everyone. I will. I'm every bit as proud of you, I promise."

"Oh." Russ smiled at him. "Thank you. Yes, okay. I'll try to be patient a little longer."

"Thanks, Russ." He'd deal with his family. He would. He knew he had to. "So, hey... I like the group text thing. Can we keep making our plans there, and then everyone knows who is doing what when?"

Jeffrey sat forward. "Oh. Yeah, that was a really good idea, Russ."

"It's been good, right? So how does that work? Should everyone always consider themselves invited? Like if I want to make plans with Oscar—"

"Should I assume I can join in? No." Jeffrey shook his head but looked to Oscar for confirmation. "No, right? That defeats the whole idea of—"

"Is that fair?" Russ interrupted.

Jeffrey looked back at Russ. "Are you worried you'll be jealous?"

Oscar held his breath a second. That *was* Russ's issue at heart, wasn't it?

"No."

"No?" Jeffrey sounded doubtful.

Oscar jumped in. "I am."

Russ looked at him. "*You* are?"

"Well, yeah. Is it seriously realistic not to feel a little jealous? If you two are out one night, and I'm home alone, regardless of the reasons why, then sure, I might feel a little jealous. Even if I'm fine with the idea of you two enjoying each other's company. Even if I'm happy you're having a good time. Even though I know you care about me. I mean... I'm only human."

Russ watched him and then gave him a smile so sweet it made his heart ache and his cock take notice. "Yeah. We're all only human, huh?"

"Sure. It would be natural to feel left out, especially if you wish you could join in."

Russ looked thoughtful. "Yeah, okay. But...."

"But?"

"Well, I'm also sort of worried. I'm concerned that... I don't know how to say this right. What if two of us end up, I mean, I don't want to be mean or borrow trouble, but it could happen that—"

"Russ." Jeffrey slid close to Russ this time and he watched how they were together, easy and familiar. Always so physical. "This isn't a marriage contract, babe. This could shake out any number of ways, like any other relationship. We're not writing the Ten Commandments here. We're trying to make sure everyone is on the same page and that we're all being honest."

Russ leaned into Jeffrey, and Oscar didn't hide the warm little rush it gave him. They were lovely together, and Jeffrey was so good at reeling Russ in. He understood that Russ had a lot at stake. More than he and Jeffrey did, really. He had a life and a family, Jeffrey had friends and a good job. But Russ's life was riskier. More solitary. Less stable.

Hell, Russ could lose his job when the house sold, and then what? Their lover needed some stability and some reassurance right now, Oscar could understand that.

Jeffrey dragged the pad and a pen over, scribbling madly. "Okay, got it."

"You're a lefty. How have I not noticed that?"

Jeffrey laughed. "I'm good with both hands, lover."

Oscar felt himself blush, but he tried to stay focused. "Okay, I have a question."

Jeffrey eyed him. "Fire away."

"How do we make sure that this—the three of us—stays the priority? That we keep this the focus? I mean, it's good to have individual relationships, I know. But to me, it's important to remember how we are together. This is about all of together, really. Isn't it?"

"Yeah." Russ nodded.

Jeffrey did too. "It is. I hear you."

Everyone looked thoughtful, and the room fell quiet as they considered the question, which made him even more glad he'd asked it.

"Saturdays?" Russ suggested finally.

"Yeah. We could make Saturday night a regular thing."

"That would work most of the time. If I have a conflict with the girls, we could make it Friday instead? I'd let you know as soon as I know." The girls had to stay a priority. That wasn't negotiable, but he thought the guys got that.

"Sure. Yeah. One of those two nights, every weekend."

"I'm writing it down." Jeffrey started scribbling again. "So, we're, uh... we're exclusive, the three of us. Right?"

"Yes," he and Russ answered at once and so emphatically it made them all laugh. Jeffrey kept scribbling.

"What else?"

"Aren't we at the kiss and make-up part, yet?" He pulled his phone out of his pocket and put on a playlist, set it down on the table, then got up and headed for Russ and pulled him right out of his chair. "Maybe that's enough for tonight."

"You think it's that easy? Just write a few things down and it's all better?" The words were terse, but Russ was grinning at him.

"Nope. I was thinking I'd dance you around and seduce my forgiveness out of you."

"Mmm. I like the sound of that." Russ stepped close, and Oscar pulled his lover in, sliding an arm around his back and swaying to the music.

Oscar loved how Russ fell right in step, following like he'd been born to it. He and Russ moved smoothly around the living room to one full song and then another came on. He could dance and admire that smile all night, but he lost track of the steps when Russ kissed him. "Mmm."

"Damn. Look at the two of you. Can I play?" Jeffrey came over, rocking slightly with the music right alongside them.

"Of course, we both owe Russ a little love, don't we?"

"I believe you're correct, Oz." Jeffrey moved in behind Russ, and Russ moaned softly. Oscar winked at Jeffrey, and Jeffrey leaned right over Russ's shoulder and kissed him, slowly, deeply.

"Oh God, you guys." Russ swayed between them, bumping and rubbing in all the right ways.

Oscar slipped his lips away from Jeffrey and kissed Russ again, one hand in Jeffrey's hair as Jeffrey went after Russ's neck with hungry teeth. He tried to keep dancing, but there wasn't much hope for it, given Jeffrey's fingers were flattening out, warm and wide across his abs, and Russ wasn't giving up their kiss.

They moved slowly toward the stairs and made their way up—hand in hand in hand. For all that he loved his intense adventures with Jeffrey and his more romantic lovemaking with Russ, this felt so right. Like coming home. Like being whole.

They undressed each other slowly, exposing skin, touching and kissing, dropping compliments and quiet words. He loved the way they moved together, caring the most by not caring at all whose lips or neck or shoulder they were kissing, just wanting, loving, treating one another alike, worshipping skin and muscle, whomever it belonged to.

Their loving attentions turned hotter when Jeffrey slid to his knees and took Russ's cock into his mouth. Oscar gasped almost as loudly as Russ did.

"Fuck, Jeff!"

"Oh, he's good at that, Russ. Isn't he?"

"Yeah. Fuck... yeah."

He grinned and let Russ lean on him, spreading his legs wider for balance. He ran his fingers over Russ's chest and swirled his fingers over stiffening nipples, making Russ shiver for him. His own cock grew full and heavy, and he rocked it against Russ's ass, humming deep in his chest at the sweet friction. Fuck, it felt so good.

Russ was quickly getting lost in it. "Oh... oh God."

"Mmm. So beautiful, Russ. You're no one's second choice, believe that. You're our first. Our lover."

"Oscar!" Russ turned his head, and Oscar kissed him, feeling Russ's hips start to grind back and rock forward, seeking more sensation.

Oscar reached around and put a hand on Jeffrey's head, slowing him, stopping him, giving his aggressive lover a hot look. "Bed?"

Jeffrey grinned back, nodding, and got to his feet.

"Oh! Oh no, don't stop. Jeff? Oz...?" Russ was suddenly disoriented, lovely and confused, hands reaching and lips begging for attention.

Oscar reassured Russ with soft words and deep kisses, pulling him to the bed, where Oscar stretched out on his back. Jeffrey surprised Oscar, hot confident fingers taking hold of his erection and rolling on a rubber.

"Jesus! Your hands."

"They like you too." Jeffrey stroked him a couple of times, making him moan, Russ looking on the way a starved man eyed a thick steak. Russ moved to straddle him, Jeffrey tossed a bottle of lube on the bed, and Oscar only had a second to wonder what was happening before Russ was taking him inside. Oscar offered them a needy groan and pushed, slowly and steadily, into Russ's tight heat. He wasn't nearly as high as Russ yet, but it felt like fucking heaven anyway.

His eyes locked with Russ's as the man started to move. "Better?" he teased.

Russ nodded, making a sound that was part moan and part sigh, like it was everything his lover wanted. He reached for Russ's cock, but his hand was batted away before he could get a grip.

Jeffrey had stretched out beside them, hips near Oscar's shoulder, his mouth covering Russ's erection, making Russ crazy.

"Oh my fucking God!"

Oscar grinned and rolled his upper body toward Jeffrey to kiss and lick and suck Jeff's prick. And if Russ's whimper was any indication, he in turn relished Jeff's appreciative groan.

This was incredible. To be this lost in so much sensation, lost in his lovers. To be rooted in the moment by choice, by desire, and by an undeniable need. He spent so much of his time on the needs of his family, he longed for this. He wanted it like he'd wanted nothing else in forever, and he gave himself permission to enjoy every touch, every second of all of it.

The room was mostly dark except for the moonlight coming in the two small windows, and it filled with their sounds, which grew so constant after a while that he could hardly be sure which were his own.

"Fuck. Jeff, Oscar, I'm... fuck!" Russ's hips stuttered, and Oscar let Jeffrey's cock slip from his lips, so he could see the lovely grimace on Russ's face.

Jeffrey followed Oscar's lead, taking Russ's dark, straining prick in hand, and knelt to watch.

Oscar rolled his hips hard, giving Russ more, forcing himself deep over and over until Russ's constant moaning turned to a shout and ended in a long, breathless sob.

Jeffrey knelt up and kissed Russ, and Oscar just lay back and admired the view. Russ's cock was still leaking, abs working as Russ caught his breath, and Jeffrey gentled their lover down, drawing him back to reality, sweet as could be.

"Fucking beautiful, Russ."

Jeffrey agreed quickly, "Right?"

Russ stroked fingers over Jeffrey's face, then walked his hands up over Oscar's torso, letting Oscar's cock slip free, making him groan.

"Oh fuck."

Russ's kiss was deep and hard. Jeffrey made the condom disappear, then licked right up his length and bathed the head of his erection. He had to break the kiss to rake in a breath. "Jeffrey!"

Jeffrey just laughed low in his register, the sound dark. "Don't get too excited, Oz. I'm about to fuck you so hard you're going to forget your own name."

He gasped and his cock turned to concrete, the sudden ache in his balls traveling right up his spine.

Russ pulled up, eyes wide. "Oh my God."

Jeffrey muscled Russ out of the way. "Roll over. Now."

"Jeffrey, I—"

Jeffrey reached out and twisted one of his nipples, and Oscar whimpered and flipped right over onto his stomach, not even sure what was happening.

"Fuck. Jeff...." Russ sounded as stunned as he was.

"Something to jack off to on your own time, Russ." Two fingers shoved into Oscar, the lube as cold as it was slippery, and he gasped and grunted.

He was well aware of Russ's presence, and he wasn't sure how he felt about Russ watching this. His cheeks grew hot as he blushed hard. This was somewhere between embarrassing and hot. Or so embarrassing it was hot. Or something. God, where was his brain?

All he could focus on was want. He just wanted Jeffrey. He wanted everything.

Jeffrey's fingers stretched and slicked him, swirling with purpose, and moments later he was groaning with the slow burn of Jeffrey's cock diving in deep. Jeffrey pulled back on his hips, and Oscar struggled to get his knees under him as they pressed together tight, skin to skin, Jeffrey seated balls-deep inside him. "Fuck. Oh fuck." He couldn't get his voice above a whisper. He could barely get a breath.

"I hear you, Oz." Jeffrey started thrusting slowly, easing back, then driving in deep again, making him grunt. He felt Russ's fingers thread through his hair, and he tried to catch his lover's eyes, but every time he lifted his head, Jeffrey would nail him again and he'd lose it.

"So hot, Oscar." That was Russ's voice.

"He's beautiful, isn't he?"

He tried to reply, but whatever he'd planned to say was replaced by a long groan. He never thought of himself as beautiful. But then he'd never thought of himself in a triad or wanted so desperately to be fucked before either. Everything about him felt new these days. Alive.

Russ crawled down the bed to Jeffrey, and Oscar could hear them over his shoulder, kissing and whispering. Someone took hold of his cock—he assumed Russ but he couldn't be sure—and it set him off. He whimpered and begged, and Jeffrey sawed into him, trying to cut him right in two.

Every thrust sent his prick through a tight fist, and Russ would stroke a thumb across the head of his erection or tunnel through his slit. He knew what he had to look like, ass in the air, face in the mattress, fists digging into the sheets for leverage as he let himself be used, but he didn't care. He trusted them. And he wanted this so fucking bad.

"Jeff! Gonna... oh God." He felt like he was going to explode.

"That's it, baby. So perfect." Jeffrey was gulping in air behind him, and Oscar knew his lover was close too. Russ was peppering his back and shoulders with kisses and the grip on his cock never let up.

Fuck, he loved and dreaded this moment—wanting

release so badly, needing it so hard, his balls so ready to give it all up—a moment there was no possible way to hold on to. Even as part of him was thinking *No, no, not yet*, the better, and louder, part of him was screaming *Oh, fuck yes*.

And that was it. He shot hard, in shuddering waves, panting with the intensity.

"Yeah." Russ stroked him right through his climax, sending new shivers of pleasure through him.

"Fuck!" Jeffrey grunted and slammed into him a handful of times, then bent over his back and hugged strong arms around his chest. Buried to the balls, his lover came hard, grunting and panting in his ear, cock jerking and pulsing deep inside him.

"So hot." Russ's whisper barely registered, but it was enough. Enough to begin to pull him back from the hormone haze in which he was drowning. He arched under Jeffrey and as his lover left him he was able to stretch out and take Jeffrey's full weight, deliciously warm as the man still held on tight.

"Fuck, Oscar."

Russ stretched out alongside them, pillowing his head on one of Oscar's arms and moving in close. They didn't share many words after that, just touches and kisses. Eventually Jeffrey slid to his other side and the room went quiet and still as they all drifted into dreams.

CHAPTER TWENTY-ONE

Jeffrey sat at his desk, staring at his keyboard and frowning. In all his time in real estate, he'd never had so much trouble selling anything. Stable Hill was a lovely farm, in decent shape and sat on a nice-size property. Old, sure. Dated, definitely. But it wasn't in bad shape. It just wasn't a McMansion.

To be fair, he had an interested buyer. But it wasn't one Oscar was going to like. He had that developer, FHI, the same one that had been knocking at his door since Steph dropped their email on his desk. They hadn't given up; they had both money and patience. And it seemed like they were confident about how this was going to play out.

But he'd made Oscar a promise—no developers. Oscar wanted to sell to a horse family or at least a farmer. He could probably get Oscar to settle for a vanity farmer who just wanted pretty fences and property if he had to, but that kind of buyer was rare, and they always wanted the big house. "Charming" and "vintage" weren't words those people cared much for.

So that left him with... what? Nothing. Still. After more than a month.

Despite several attempts on his part, he and Oscar never finished their conversation about the house. Oscar just didn't want to hear it. But it was going to stay a sticking point, and... well, Oscar was going to ask questions soon, and he didn't have answers his lover was going to like.

The phone rang, and he picked it up absently. "Stokes."

"Mr. Stokes, it's Mr. Fraden from FHI on the line. He says he's been expecting a call from you?"

"Shit. Yes." Speak of the devil. He'd said he'd talk to Oscar and call back, but since he never did talk to Oscar.... "Put him through, thanks."

The line clicked, and he swallowed and then answered, "Jeffrey Stokes. Can I help you?"

"Yes, hello, Mr. Stokes. This is Andy Fraden of First Home Incorporated."

"Hello, Mr. Fraden. Yes, I remember." Jesus, how could he forget?

"Mr. Stokes, we are still looking to schedule a tour of your Lancaster County property. Stable Hill Farm it's called? We'd like to bring our surveyors out and make a proper offer, but we've been waiting for your call."

"Yes, I apologize about that. My client has been difficult to reach." *And somewhat impossible to get through to.*

"Well, while you're waiting, is there any harm in our just taking a look?"

"Oh. Well...."

"That way when he calls, you'll have a firm offer for him from us to put on the table, hmm? It would benefit us both, I think."

The guy did have a point. And if not for the fact that he and Oscar were lovers, he'd have made this very arrangement ages ago. "Yes. You're right, it would. How's Thursday?"

By the time they hung up the phone, they'd arranged an early-morning meeting on Thursday up at Stable Hill. He was going to have to tell Oscar. And Russ. And neither of them was going to be happy about it.

He was going to have to come up with something big to get past this one. Maybe... hm. Maybe he'd let Oscar fuck him.

Ha. Who was he kidding? He'd bring them flowers.

THERE WAS something about Wednesdays. Oscar never figured out what it was exactly in all his years of parenting, but Wednesdays were his toughest day at work, and the house was always an emotional disaster. If someone was going to have a bad day, bring home a bad grade, or end up in the ER, it was always on a damn Wednesday.

So Oscar arrived home from work ready for anything, but was really hoping for the all-clear as he hadn't gotten any irritated texts or panicked phone calls before he left work.

He should have known better.

"What the hell is going on here?" he asked, sensing the tension as soon as he walked in the door, barely ducking a flying stuffed animal. If he'd known he was going to need a suit of armor, he might have stopped for a bottle of whiskey on the way home.

"Riley stole my lip gloss!"

"I did not! This one is mine!"

"Zoe—" He barely got his daughter's name out of his mouth.

"She's a liar! I bought that with Grandma Rose last weekend!"

"Riley!"

"No, this is the one that Sherri gave me at her birthday party!"

"Girls!" he shouted, and that stopped them both, leaving them wide-eyed. "That's *enough*." He held out his hand for the lip gloss, which Riley placed on his palm without argument. "Where's your grandmother?"

"She's upstairs with Sophie."

"Sophie was crying."

Oh boy. "I don't want to hear another peep out of you two. You hear me? Enough arguing. Find something else to do. We'll get dinner started in a bit."

He put the lip gloss in his pocket, and the girls slunk off to the living room.

Oscar hung up his coat and took a deep breath.

Okay, then.

Now. What was going on with Soph? He dumped his coat on a chair and headed upstairs to find out. He rounded the banister and was surprised at how quiet it was. It looked like Emily wasn't home yet. Her door was wide-open, and he didn't recall seeing Brian's car in the driveway. He knocked lightly on Sophie's door and stuck his head in, and Rose looked up at him from where she sat on Sophie's bed, his daughter asleep in her arms.

She gave him a nod and carefully extracted herself, setting Sophie in the pillows and covering her with an afghan, then shut the door as she left the room. "I'm glad you're home."

"I handled the twins. They were—"

"I know, but what could I do?"

He nodded. "Yeah. I know. Is she okay? What's going on? Did something happen at school?"

"I think so. She wouldn't tell me. She's so... quiet right now. This whole school year. I'm worried about her, Oscar."

He nodded and hugged Rose. Of the four girls, Sophie had always been the quietest, usually the easiest, and yet the hardest to get a handle on. She was shy, certainly introverted, but so kind and thoughtful. It had been a tough year for her, and he really didn't know why. He assumed tenth grade just sucked. High school had sucked for him in general; he remembered those years being awful.

"Well, let's let her rest. Maybe if she doesn't wake up feeling better, she can skip school tomorrow."

"I'd be happy to have her home with me."

"Yeah. Thank you, Rose."

"Anything for our girls, Oscar. You know that. Anything at all."

"Oh." His phone vibrated in his back pocket, and he pulled it out. "Sorry, Rose. I need to grab this."

"I'll start dinner, sweetheart. Before the twins eat each other." She went downstairs, and he headed into his bedroom.

"Hey, you." It was Jeffrey, a welcome surprise.

"Hello, Oz."

"God, what a day. It's nice to hear from you. What's up?"

"Well, I wanted to talk with you about the farm, but that's just business. Are you okay? Bad day?"

He sat down on the end of his bed, smiling at Jeffrey's concern. "Yeah. Yeah, I'm okay. I got home to a chaotic house is all, and something is up with Sophie."

"Is she hurt?"

"Well, not physically as far Rose could tell, but she cried herself to sleep. Something must have happened at school, but Rose said Sophie wouldn't talk about it. She just cried and wore herself out."

"Poor kid. She's a quiet one too."

"She is. I'm a little concerned, you know?"

"Sure. Of course. I mean, it could be anything or nothing at that age, right."

"Fifteen is a nightmare. Did you like tenth grade?" He chuckled softly. "I just hope it's drama and not real. And I won't know now until she wakes up, maybe not even then."

"I'm sorry. That's frustrating, I guess. I can't pretend to

know what parenting is like, but I've been around Sophie enough to know she's not a big talker."

"Yeah." He sighed. "I'll know more soon. I'm just anxious. This is the hard part of parenting. Watching your kids go through stuff, knowing when to let them deal and when to step in."

"Hey, hang in there. She's home and she's safe, right?"

"Yeah. Yes. You're right. That's the important part."

There was a quiet moment, and then he pulled himself together. "So you wanted to talk about the farm?"

"I... uh. Hey. It's not urgent. We can chat about it another time."

"Are you sure?"

"Yeah, I'm sure. It's nothing you need to worry about yet. We'll talk soon. Catch up on Saturday?"

"I'm looking forward to it. Can we plan a night next week?"

"I would love that, but... text?"

"Yes. Right. I will." *Right. Make plans in the group text.* "I didn't mean—"

"I know. I forgot with Russ the other day. We'll get used to it. Let's just do it right."

"Absolutely. I'll text."

"Let us know about Sophie too?"

"Oh. Yes, sure. I'll let you know when I know something more. Thanks, Jeffrey. I really.... It means a lot that you care."

"I care about you. Of course I care about your family too."

He nodded, still smiling. "I'm really glad you called."

"Me too. You get some rest and give Soph a hug for me."

"Will do. Thanks."

"Night, Oz... I... good night."

"Yeah. Night." *Me too.*

They'd get there. They just needed a little more time.

· · ·

Russ called Miles at 2:00 a.m. for help.

His first worry had been fire because he'd been through that before, and he'd flown out of bed as soon as he'd heard all the noise, running outside shirtless and in his pajama pants like an idiot to find half the barn in an uproar. At least he'd grabbed a jacket and stomped into his boots on the way out the door.

Thankfully it wasn't anything as urgent as a fire, and there was no sign of anyone having broken in, so Russ had to assume it was a raccoon or a fox or something causing trouble. That was better, though critters came with their own issues, and they still had a dozen-plus horses to check on and soothe.

Between the two of them, they'd managed to calm everyone down, but they hadn't found their visitor. No one seemed to have any bites or scratches either.

"Thanks for coming out, Miles. Sorry to wake you, but I wasn't sure what I was dealing with."

"No problem. It's my job, man. Any idea how the critter got in?" Miles asked, pouring himself a coffee.

"I don't know. How do they ever? For all I know, he might have already been in when I locked up for the night."

"And we don't know if he ran out yet, huh?"

"Nope." *Dammit.*

"Well, why don't you go put some jeans on, and I'll have a—"

A godawful screeching sound came down the aisle, and he looked up, knowing exactly who it was. "Shit. Angel." He took off at a run, Miles right on his heels. The pair of them arrived just in time to duck a raccoon launching itself over the stall door.

"Hey!" Miles shouted and took off after the animal to chase it out of the barn.

"I need to know if it's sick!"

"On it!"

Angel was frantic. She kicked at the wall of her stall and tossed her head. Her eyes were wide, nostrils flared, ears back. She rushed her stall door, her head thrusting out into the aisle and her chest up against the wood. He tried not to panic, but she was giving every indication that she'd been bitten. He'd never seen her so flipped out, and he needed to help her get under control before she hurt herself. He grabbed a rope lead and stood a few paces from her stall door, talking to her, trying to see if she could calm down on her own before he had to intervene.

"Hey, Angel. Easy, lady." He spoke in a calm voice and drew his words out, noting the little bit of South Carolina that came out when he did that. He didn't sound much like his people anymore except when he was talking to horses or angry.

Angel wasn't having it. She tossed her head and huffed at him, striking at her stall door with a pissed-off hoof.

"Okay, beautiful." He took a step closer, a little to one side, watching her, keeping his tone calm and even and his movements slow and fluid. He didn't want to spook her. "That's a girl. Good girl."

He wasn't afraid of her. He'd calmed more crazy horses and taken more hard hits than he knew how to count. Everyone in the barn had been vaccinated, but he was still a little anxious for her, worried she'd hurt herself, worried for what the next few hours might bring. He did his best to set all of that aside and took a deep breath. In one smooth, quick motion, he reached up, tossed the lead over her neck, crossed it under her jaw, looped it up over her nose and finally crossed it under her chin in a makeshift halter. He gripped the ends of the rope together as she started to tug against the rope in protest, but he hauled on it, holding her head down until she finally figured out he wasn't letting go.

"There you go. That's it. I got you, girl."

"Little fucker took off for the rafters." Miles's words were soft so he didn't upset Angel, but they held a whole lot of pissed off anyway.

"Damn." Angel tried to tug her nose up, but he held her down. "That's a girl. Just let it go, lady. I got you. Shhhh...."

"He didn't head for the door. He scrambled his punk ass up to the loft."

"Well, Jesus fuck." He sighed. This was going to be a pain in the ass and a long night. "Call Hank. Tell him what's going on and ask him to come out ASAP. Ask him if he has a couple of traps. I got this."

"If he doesn't, my brother might. I'll handle it."

"Thanks, man."

Miles pulled out his cell and walked away from them. Angel's eyes were starting to look more normal, and she'd stopped fighting him, but he knew he had some time before he could let her go. She could spook at anything right now.

"Oh, Angel. I hope that asshole didn't bite you." He went up on his toes and eyeballed what he could of her, and everything looked fine. She wasn't acting so much like she was hurt right now either. Maybe she'd just been thoroughly pissed off at that raccoon.

An hour or so later, Hank arrived with two traps that Miles went and set up in the loft, and Russ had managed to get Angel out of her stall and into a fresh one.

"I gave her a booster," Hank told him, closing the stall door. "You'll just need to keep an eye on her. When you catch that raccoon, we'll see what the tests say. I don't see a bite, but you can't be too careful."

Oh, thank God. "I didn't see one either, but I'm really glad you got a second look to confirm it. It's hard to believe the way she just lost it. I'd never seen her like that."

"Well, she had that tangle with a raccoon before."

He looked at Hank. "No kidding? When the Griggstons owned her?" Jonas bought Angel off Carl Griggston. Hank knew all the horse people in the area.

"Yep. She was curious, the raccoon wasn't having it, and she ended up with a nasty scratch on her nose. That's where that crooked scar came from."

He'd noticed the scar of course, but he hadn't given it much thought. "Huh. That explained why she went bananas in the stall. She was pissed."

"She was probably trying to kill the damn thing."

He chuckled. "Yep, maybe."

"All right, Russ. You keep an eye out for that raccoon and call me when you catch it."

"I will. Thanks, Hank. I really appreciate you coming out at this unholy hour."

Hank laughed. "You're welcome, Russ. Seems like emergencies only ever happen in the middle of the night. You take care."

He watched Hank drive off, and then headed back into the barn. His work was nowhere near done. He needed to clean Angel's stall in case that raccoon was sick. He needed to see about Miles and those traps. He needed some clothes and some coffee.

"He's up there for sure." Miles came dragging up behind him and collapsed in one of the folding chairs.

He reached over and turned on the little heater. "You saw him?"

"Yep. Got as close as I dared with one of the traps and the other is near the ladder."

He sighed. "I need to clean Angel's stall and—"

"I'm gonna put on some coffee, man. You go put on some real clothes."

He grinned at Miles and nodded. "You want me to bring you some eggs?"

"Sounds great. I'll get started on that stall. We can't leave this crew alone until we know that raccoon's caught anyway."

"Jeans and breakfast. I'll be back in a flash."

The sun was coming up as he crossed the yard to the house. He ducked inside and took a super-fast shower to get warm, then pulled on clothes and made egg sandwiches for him and Miles.

So what if sometimes crazy shit got him up in the middle of the night? This was still a damn good life. He had good help, great lovers, everything was solid. For now. Losing the damn farm....

Shit, he needed to stop thinking about Stable Hill as his place. He'd spent the last two years settling in, the old farm sinking into his bones, but it just wasn't meant to be. There was a good possibility the new owners would let him go, bring their own barn manager, and then he'd be jobless and home-less again. He had Jeff and Oscar, but what did he have to offer them without being the one keeping Stable Hill running? He couldn't be sure he could get another job around here.

Jesus, that was enough. He was tired was all, he wasn't really this anxious about everything. He'd be fine. He always had been, even when he had nobody. He stomped into his boots, pulled on his coat, scooped up breakfast, and headed back out to the barn.

CHAPTER TWENTY-TWO

ANGEL WAS happy once they got her back in her own stall. She seemed tired, otherwise fine, but Russ stayed close all day anyway. He'd been keeping an eye out for the raccoon, but no one had seen it yet. Miles kept checking the traps in the loft —Russ was pretty confident they'd have the little fucker come nightfall.

He hadn't been expecting Jeffrey to show up with that potential buyer. Maybe they thought he wasn't really required to know? It was Oscar's place; he and Jeffrey could make whatever arrangements they needed to, he supposed.

They never even went in the house, but it still would have been polite to let him know they were coming.

His phone chirped at him, and he pulled it out of his pocket and looked at it. Speaking of Oscar....

Hey, Russ. Bringing Sophie over.

Uh? Russ stared at his phone. *Ok...?*

God, he was tired. Today wasn't a great day for Oscar to decide to bring the girl by, but Russ had suggested it, so what was he going to say? Again, Oscar's property. He was just going to have to find some patience.

Sophie didn't go to school, huh? Jeff texted back. This three-way thing rocked—nobody missed anything. *Did she tell you what was going on?*

No. Russ—she had a bad day yesterday and won't tell me what happened. Jeffrey happened to call about the property in the middle of it, that's why he knows. So, I've tried to tempt her out of her room today—going to the barn was the only thing she would agree to. Sorry about the notice.

Oh, poor thing. Well, he got it. The barn was the only place he felt safe as a kid too. He thought about Jeff, and all the time his lover had already spent with Oscar's girls. This was his shot, right?

All good. I hope I can help.

Me too. CU soon.

He snorted. That was spoken—or texted—like a man who had teenagers.

Hope all goes well, I'll check in with you guys later.

He put his phone away. Oscar wanted him to entertain a teenager who didn't feel like talking. Well? Shit, he'd had a bad day too. And so had Angel. Maybe that would mean something to Sophie.

"Caught the little asshole!"

"No way. For real?"

"He's in one of the traps up here!" Miles shouted. "Bringing him down!"

He waited at the ladder to help. "Don't bring him over that way. Maybe take the trap around and out the far door? I don't want Angel to see him."

"I hear that. It's no wonder he came flying out of her stall, you know. She probably wanted to crush him. This son of a bitch is lucky to be alive."

"Hopefully he's healthy so he can stay that way. Hank told me she had a history. I had no idea." He pulled out his phone and texted Hank.

"I'll stick him out back."

He nodded. "Thanks." Great. His day just got better. Now all he needed was a good report from the vet. The rigmarole if the thing was sick was more than he really wanted to deal with—cleaning all the stalls, replacing feed, another round of vaccinations—all of it was time consuming and expensive, and it could be a long while before they could be sure everyone was healthy too.

Okay, so what to do with Sophie? He thought about a pony ride, about lunging her out in the ring, about teaching her something about confirmation or care. In the end he decided to keep it simple. He had work to do. She could help him with it—or not—as she pleased. Something about not trying too hard felt better to him.

When they showed up, he was finishing raking out stalls with Davy.

"Are we interrupting?"

"Nothing but a good day's work," he said, coming out of the final stall, rake in hand. "Hey, Oscar."

Sophie was in jeans and rubber boots and had an earbud in one ear with a cord that led to what was likely an iPod squirreled away in her coat somewhere. Oscar was looking great in jeans and a field coat and work boots. Oh man, he wanted a kiss.

Now wasn't the time, though.

"You remember Sophie, don't you?"

"I do. Been a while, though. It's nice to see you again, Sophie."

She nodded at him, gave him a little hint of a smile.

"I've got some errands I need to run. We thought maybe she could hang out with you for a little while, Russ. Is that cool? We figured she could have a look around."

"Oh. Yeah, sure." Oscar was leaving her? "That's fine. I've got work to do, though. You up for helping me out?"

Sophie looked a little surprised. "Oh."

"Great. Thanks, Russ. I'll be back in a couple of hours." Oscar shook his hand with a soft smile, holding on just a second longer than he really needed to. "I appreciate it."

"Sure, Oscar." He made sure to smile back, though the fact that Oscar still hadn't told his girls wasn't sitting well with him.

Now was not the time for that either.

He and Sophie both watched Oscar head out, and then he just walked away from her, leaving her standing there. "Davy, you ready?" He scooped the last of the straw up into the spreader.

"Yeah." Davy started up the spreader, gave him a wave, and headed out of the barn.

"All right, Sophie. Come on." He headed down the aisle to the first stall on the end. It was clean and had a neatly bundled bale of straw sitting in the middle of the floor. He pulled out his wire cutters and snipped the wires holding it together, handed it to her, and then got to work, spreading the straw around the stall. Sophie watched, her expression hard to read. "That's it. You think you can handle that?"

"Me?"

"Well, yeah. Miles is out dealing with a raccoon, so I'm short a set of hands. You came by at just the right time." He handed her the rake and took the wire. "Pile the wires out here. Make sure you pull both wires out of each stall so the horses don't hurt themselves on it."

"Uh. Okay."

"I'll make my way down and clip them all for you." He did just that, leaving her standing there again. It didn't take long to cut all the wires, and then he came back around, intending to start filling water buckets that Davy had scrubbed out earlier, but Sophie started talking.

"You do this every day?"

"Yes, ma'am."

"It's a lot of work." Sophie kept moving while she was talking, spreading the straw around.

"Yeah, well. We ask a lot of them letting us ride them, working them, breeding them. It's our job to make sure they stay healthy and content. It's funny how fragile they can be for something so big and powerful. They need a lot of care."

"You enjoy that part?"

"Taking care of them?"

"Yeah." She scooted around him and into the next stall, and he followed her.

"I do. I mean, do I love mucking stalls? No. But I do love the horses."

"They're pretty cool, huh?"

He nodded. "Yep. Hey, I'm going to get them fed. When you're done, you want to help me water?"

"Sure, okay."

"Great. Thank you." He left her to her work and her thinking and got back to his. An hour later, stalls were done, everyone was fed and had fresh water, and he and Sophie were having some coffee and cocoa.

"So... where are the horses?"

"They're in turnout up in the big pasture."

"How long are they out?"

"Depends on the weather mostly, sometimes how much daylight. A cold winter day, it might be just the afternoon. A really hot summer day, they'll stay in out of the sun and go out at night instead. And sometimes on a nice spring or fall day, we might let them stay out all night if we can."

"Wow."

"They need to be out, you know? They're like kids. Like your little sisters. They need exercise and fresh air. If you keep them cooped up, they get bored and then they can get destructive or form bad habits. They need to be outside where they belong."

Sophie nodded, listening. "So how come that one is inside?"

"Angel?" Russ sipped his coffee and answered slowly. "Well, she had bad night."

"Horses have bad nights?"

"Sure. They have good days and bad days just like we do. They have different personalities like all animals do. A raccoon got into her stall last night, and she is afraid of them, so she flipped out. She was kicking and rushing the stall door."

"Whoa. Is she okay?"

"Yeah, we think she is. But she needed some calm, so I kept her inside today. She'll get out with everyone else tomorrow."

Sophie put her mug down and wandered down the aisle toward Angel. He started to follow but changed his mind, kicked back in his chair and sipped his coffee. He kept an eye on her, but there wasn't much trouble she could get into with Angel in her stall. He could see Sophie talking to the mare, stroking her nose, and finally Angel stretched her neck out long, and Sophie scritched along Angel's neck to her shoulders and up behind her ears.

Angel started nipping at Sophie's jacket, poking her nose at Sophie's pockets.

"She doesn't have what you're looking for, sweetheart," he said, walking up behind them.

Sophie was grinning and lightly pushing at Angel's nose. "What does she want?"

"Peppermints."

"Really?"

"Yep." He took a few out of his pocket and slipped them

into Sophie's hand. "Give her one at a time, hold your hand out flat."

Sophie took the wrapper off one and laid it flat on her palm.

"Good. Hold it out."

Gingerly, Sophie held it out toward Angel. Russ grinned as the horse daintily reached out with her upper lip and slurped the candy off Sophie's hand.

"Oh!" Sophie laughed. "Can I give her another?"

"You want to spoil her, huh? Sure." Hell, he spoiled Angel on the daily.

Sophie had a lovely smile and looked genuinely happy. There was something about her he really liked, and it seemed like Angel was taking a shine to Sophie too. Just when he was wondering what could possibly have the girl so down, she spoke up on her own.

"I know how she feels, kind of. I'm sort of stuck inside today too. I didn't go to school."

"No?"

"Stuff happened yesterday." She shrugged. "I just need to think about what I'm going to do about it."

"Can I help?"

She looked at him. "I... I don't know?"

"Well, I guess the worst that happens is I can't, right? Fire away if you want to."

"I came out to a girl I like."

Oh, come on. Really? He'd known the girl a couple of hours and... this? "Oh, wow," he said carefully.

Holy shit. Does Oscar know?

He needed something to do with his hands, so he got out Angel's grooming kit. "I was about to groom her. Want to help?"

"Oh. Uh. Yeah, okay. Sure." She looked about as thrown as he felt. He was trying so hard not to show it.

"So how did she take it?" He led Angel out of her stall and hooked her up on crossties, then showed Sophie how to hold the rubber curry comb and handed it to her. "Like this, small circles. Start up here... and work your way back. Got it? Don't be afraid to use a little pressure. Be careful to stay off her legs."

"She... I don't know. She got kind of mad. She said I was crazy." Angel leaned into the curry comb, loving the attention.

"Love is crazy." Boy, did he know that or what?

"I didn't say I loved her!" Sophie blushed and switched to the other side of the horse, where he couldn't see her.

He rolled his eyes and winced. "Sorry. Sorry."

"I said I liked her. That's all."

"Okay." *Think. Say something, idiot. Ask a question. A good one.* "So... why was she mad?"

"Because she's straight."

Oh. Fuck. "She doesn't like that you're gay, huh?" Coming out was hard. He'd gotten used to the reactions, but it never seemed to get easier.

"No. That's not why. It's that she only wants to be friends."

Oh. "So she doesn't care if you're gay?"

"Why would she care that I'm gay?"

He blinked and walked around Angel to look at Sophie. "Why would she care?"

"Yeah. Nobody cares about that stuff anymore. I mean, not my friends. Old people maybe, but not us."

Old people, maybe. It was like an episode of the *Twilight Zone*. Kids around here actually were growing up letting people be people. Whoa.

"Also, I didn't say I was gay, Russ. You just assumed that."

He blinked. "So liking girls doesn't make you gay."

"Nope. But you'd probably have to be queer to get it."

Was this conversation happening? He was so confused. "I'm gay. Did I say I was straight?"

It was Sophie's turn to blink at him. Then she grinned. "Wait. You?"

"Yeah. I wasn't trying to insult you."

"Well, we both assumed, I guess."

He felt better. "So you're... what, then? Bisexual?"

"Pansexual."

"Oh! I know what that is! That's when you like everybody, right?"

"Yep." She smiled at him. "Maybe you're not that old."

He hoped not. He switched out her curry comb for a body brush. "Long strokes, with the grain. And you can go right down her legs too."

Sophie went to town, brushing and stroking and grooming like she was born with a brush in her hand.

"You ever seen our little herd make the run back to the barn before?"

"No."

"All right. You're in for some fun, then. Let's get Angel back in her stall." He showed her how to walk a horse into a stall, then shut the door and pulled out his phone. "Just texting your dad so he'll know where you are if he shows up."

If you're looking for us, we're taking a trip up to the big paddock to send the horses home.

I'm actually in the house having a cup of coffee. How is it going?

Oh, for crying out loud. That shouldn't have surprised him one bit. *Very well.*

Sophie had trusted him, and he didn't know how confidential she'd meant it to be. He had no intention of outing her.

"Okay, ready?"

On the way out, he gave Miles the heads-up to have the barn ready. They took the walk up to the paddock, not talking much, mostly because Sophie was looking around, taking in the place. He understood why Oscar needed to sell the farm, but it would have been so good for her to grow up here, with all of this. Hopefully Oscar would see for himself now how much she loved it and at least get her some lessons.

He showed Sophie where to stand so she'd be out of the way and then leaned on the paddock gate and whistled. The horses had been meandering over anyway once they saw him and Sophie coming up the way, so it didn't take long before they were close enough to run. He swung the gate open, and they took off at a trot for the barn. When the last one was through, he closed the gate again.

"Wow."

"Right? Isn't that a beautiful thing to see?"

"They just know where they're going?"

"They know it's suppertime. They're no dummies." He grinned at her. "Still. It's fun." They waited for the dust to settle a bit and then headed back to the barn. "Your dad is at the house."

"Oh, okay."

He glanced at her. "He's a good guy, your dad."

"My stepdad, but yeah. He's great."

"Sorry. I meant that, I just... he thinks of himself as your dad. I'm sure it's hard for all of you."

"It's... bad sometimes. Okay other times. I love Oz."

He smiled, deciding that was a good place to leave it, and didn't say anything more about that.

"Do you do lessons here?"

How was he supposed to answer that one? He'd teach her, but... selling the farm. "Well, until the farm sells, I'd be happy to teach you a few things." He would too. Be happy, that is. She was a nice girl, and they shared this horse thing.

"I'll talk to Oz."

"Sounds like a plan."

He walked her through the barn so she could see everyone all tucked into their stalls and eating, and then they made their way up to the house.

"Y'all wanna stay for supper?"

"Thanks, Russ. But I need to—"

"Please?" Sophie chimed in.

Oscar looked at her, then at him with a raised eyebrow, a subtle smile tugging at his lips. "I... uh. Well? Let me call Grandma Rose."

Oscar made the call, and then suddenly Russ was hosting them for supper. This was great. He was wrung-out and exhausted, but this was great anyway.

This was—well, this would be, hopefully, one day—his family.

He'd resisted the idea for a while until he realized that he'd already thought of Oscar as family long before their first kiss. And Jeff would fit right in here, right now.

Speaking of.... "Let Jeff know you're staying?"

"Uh. Yeah."

"It's okay with me if you want him to—"

"Russ...."

Oh, shit. Sophie. She seemed into her phone, though, so maybe she hadn't been listening.

Damn.

When was Oscar going to tell the family? It had been nearly a week. He knew Sophie was on his lover's mind at the moment, but he'd been helpful with that, hadn't he? Shouldn't he be allowed to have that status?

Maybe he was just being a brat again. He sighed.

"Have you talked to Jeff yet about the people that saw the property today? They seemed pretty interested. Though I think maybe more in the land than the barn."

"Wait. People came by today?"

"Yeah, a big group. They had surveyors and suits and cameras and all kinds of shi—tuff."

"I haven't talked to him, no." A cloud fell over Oscar's face, and he started texting furiously.

Shit. Well, Russ decided he'd better stay out of whatever that was and start supper. A little shrimp and grits would go down well with everyone, right? His phone started blowing up, but he ignored it, letting his men work it out.

"Sophie? Would you mind setting the table?" He could keep her busy for a few minutes, surely. "The silverware is in the drawer there."

"I know, Russ." She rolled her eyes at him as she pushed off the counter.

"Right. Of course you do. Sorry." The girls hadn't spent a lot of time here the last handful of years, but Sophie was older. Of course she remembered.

Sophie stuffed her phone into her back pocket and pulled out silverware.

"There's still a million different placemats in the side-board. Pick whatever ones you like."

"There were always a gazillion. Grandpa said Grandma collected them."

Placemats, little silver spoons, things with her initials on them—Jonas had pointed them all out to him. It was a shame none of the girls had known Oscar's mother. The way Jonas talked about her, he would have liked to have known her himself.

Oscar finally tossed his phone on the counter with a sigh, face stormy.

"Everything okay?"

"Fine. What's for dinner?" He watched as Oscar fixed his posture and schooled his expression.

"Shrimp and grits. Are you sure?"

"Just Realtor stuff. Hmm?"

"Oh. Right." He got the hint and shook his head.

"You want me to put out anything else?" Sophie asked, leaning in the kitchen doorway.

"No, I think that's it, Sophie. Thanks."

"Thanks for helping, sweetheart. You hungry?"

"Yeah. Super hungry. I didn't eat today."

He pointed. "There's some apples in a bowl over there and some granola bars in the breadbox."

"Oh. Thanks, Russ."

Oscar looked between them. "So what did you guys get up to today?"

"Well, I'd had a long night because a raccoon got in the barn—"

"I spread straw, I helped with food and water, and I got to groom Angel. She's so sweet."

"Sounds like fun. And then you got to watch everybody run in for dinner? Grandpa and Lionel taught them to do that, you know. And every time we got a new horse, all the older ones would teach the new one where to go. Grandpa did that for years and years."

"Yeah. It was cool." Sophie was munching on a granola bar.

"You seem like you're feeling better."

Sophie shrugged. "I want to take riding lessons. Russ said he would teach me as long we still owned the farm."

"Oh." Oscar looked at him. "Well... you don't mind?"

"I don't," he said, sure of himself. "Miss Sophie and I had a nice afternoon, didn't we?"

Sophie nodded. "It was fun. I like the horses. Can I ride, Oz? Please?"

"Sure. Of course. I just have to figure out transportation and all. It's a bit of a drive."

"Thank you!" Sophie hugged her arms around Oscar so tight it made his lover's eyes pop.

"Thank you." Oscar mouthed at him over the girl's head.

He smiled and shrugged and went back to making supper, feeling pretty good about the whole thing. He could do this kid gig maybe. They weren't all that different from horses.

Oscar took Sophie into the living room to sit down, so he let them talk while he cooked. She had a lot on her mind, and her father was the one she should be talking to. Though she'd trusted him, and that made him feel all warm inside.

Supper went over really well. Turned out Sophie loved shrimp. Go him. He'd added a little spicy sausage, garlic, and cheddar cheese to the grits, and Oscar just ate it up. He was so proud of himself, he forgot he was supposed to be tired.

"Thank you for dinner, Russ. Last-minute and everything. It was so good."

"It was my pleasure, I mean it."

Sophie looked at him like she was going to say something but didn't. At least not at first. She gave him a smile and a nod. "I had a good time. Thank you for... thanks." She shrugged, and he winked at her.

"You're welcome. Thanks for the help. And the talk."

"Oz says we'll look at the calendar and figure when is a good time to ride."

"Probably a weekend morning." Oscar put his arm around her, just as proud and protective as anything. It was sweet. Such a good dad.

"That works. I'm always here."

"All right, then. I better get this girl home and in bed so she can go to school tomorrow."

Russ gave Sophie a light hug. "Good for you."

She nodded at him. "It's all good."

He leaned in for a real hug from Oscar, but his lover slipped it into a bro-hug instead. "Night, man."

It felt like a stabbing knife to his heart. "Good night." He headed for the front door and opened it. "I'll see you soon,

Sophie." She headed out to the truck, and he stopped Oscar in the doorway to look at him. "Really?"

"I'm sorry. I haven't.... I'm going to. Soon."

"Great. Call me when you do."

"Russ—"

"I'm out, Oscar. I'm not hiding anymore. I'm not interested in pretending. Either you—"

Either you love me or you don't.

"I'm not going back in the closet. Any closet."

"I'll call you, Russ. Soon. And I'll see you Saturday."

He just shrugged. They would see each other on Saturday, wouldn't they? That kind of took what little power he still had to negotiate away from him. Dammit. "Good night, Oscar."

"Good night."

He closed the front door and doubled over, bracing his hand on his knees and breathing through the ache in his chest. Fuck, that hurt—one distant hug threatened to ruin this whole day.

He took a deep breath and straightened up, then headed for the kitchen to do the dishes. He was tired, that was all. Exhausted. He was making something out of nothing. Or maybe nothing out of something... did it matter? He needed to clean up, shower, maybe have a shot of something, and then get his ass in bed.

Tomorrow was another day. Horses waited. Stalls waited. His life, whatever defined him now, waited. He'd think about that tomorrow.

CHAPTER TWENTY-THREE

OSCAR WAS tempted to call Jeffrey when he got home, but by the time he got Sophie tucked in and told Rose about their day, it was late and he was tired. He was angry too, and he wasn't sure what he was going to do about it. He'd expressly said no commercial buyers. No developers. He wanted a real farmer who would use the property as it was intended. He wasn't sure what Jeffrey was up to. Would Jeffrey have shown the property to commercial buyers without permission if he were a regular client? Someone Jeffrey wasn't sleeping with?

He hated that they'd argued over text, though, and he didn't like leaving things the way they had. That was his fault. He should have just waited until he got home or until this morning.

Not that he felt all that much better this morning—he hadn't gotten very restful sleep.

But all the girls got off to school on time, including Sophie, who was being so brave. They'd discussed her identity and her sexuality a couple of months ago. It had gone much better than his still-unfinished safe-sex talk with Emily had, but he honestly hadn't expected Sophie to act on anything for a while. Apparently he'd been naïve. The fact that she already "liked" a girl, whether she really understood what that meant or not, was lightyears ahead of what he was prepared for.

Your girls... our girls are growing up too fast, Emmett.

Fast was pretty much the theme of his life right now. Everything was changing, and some of it was so beyond his control it was unnerving.

Some of it, though, he absolutely needed to have control over. He'd taken a sick day and was driving toward Jeffrey's office, hoping his Realtor was in. He'd like to see his lover too, frankly, but they had business first. He'd texted to let Jeffrey know he was coming before he left, but he didn't wait for a reply, and many years of young children in his minivan had broken him of the habit of checking his phone while driving.

He pulled into the parking lot, still not sure what he was going to say. He didn't want to fight, but he needed to be clear. He thought he had been clear. He took a deep breath, went inside, and stopped at the reception desk.

"Good morning. I'm here to see Mr. Stokes."

"Jeff is waiting for you." The girl behind the desk smiled at him. "Last office on the left."

"Thank you." He made his way back, passing one office after another until he got to the end of the hall. Jeffrey appeared in the doorway.

"Mr. Kennedy. Come on in. Thanks for coming by," Jeffrey said with a totally impersonal tone, waiting until he was inside to close the door.

"Mr. Kennedy, huh?"

"Well, as far as they know you're a client."

"I am a client."

Jeffrey sighed. "Okay, Oz. I hear you. I know you're upset. But—"

"Did I not make myself clear, Jeffrey?"

"You did, but—"

"There's no 'but,' Jeffrey. I'm not interested in a commercial buyer. Period. But I know you know that or you would have told me who you were bringing out there yesterday."

"Oscar. Would you listen to me a minute?"

He eyed Jeffrey for a second, then leaned back in his chair. "Fine."

"Thank you. First of all, I was going to tell you the other night when I called, but then you told me that Sophie was upset and you sounded like what you really needed was for me to listen, not add to your stress. So I'm sorry. I made a judgment call, and I admit it may have been a bad one."

Oh.

Well, damn. Jeffrey had been looking out for him. He sighed. "Maybe, but... thanks."

Jeffrey laughed softly. "Wow, was it that painful?"

He grinned and shook his head. "Shut up."

"Okay. This is the hard part, but I'm hoping you hear me out." Jeffrey gestured for him to take a seat on a wide leather couch, and Jeffrey sat with him. It felt like bad news was coming.

"It's my job to help you consider your options and make a good business decision. The sale of a house can be very emotional, but the bottom line is basically a dollar figure."

"I don't need a real estate lecture, Jeffrey."

"All due respect, Oz? You do."

He sat up, offended. "There's more to this than the bottom line."

"Is there?" Jeffrey looked at him. "Why? Because you grew up in that house? Because it was your father's? You're selling it, Oscar. You can't afford to be sentimental."

"What? I thought we agreed on this. It's farmland. I want it to stay that way. The number of operational farms like

Stable Hill is dwindling every year, Jeffrey. It's important to preserve the farms we have."

"Then keep it."

He shook his head. "I can't afford to keep it." Why the hell would he be selling it if he could?

"Okay." Jeffrey stood up and paced the length of his office. "Here's what I can tell you. I'm waiting on the offer from the developers just so you can compare and so that I know you understand what you're turning down. You've had six or seven families looking for farms come through and no offers. They want more house. The property might sell but only well below asking price if you don't renovate the house."

"I don't have the cash to renovate the house, and even if I did, there's nothing wrong with it. It's a farmhouse. Maybe it needs a little spit shine. I'm still planning to paint it inside and out. That I can do. I can do a little landscaping maybe."

"It needs more than that, Oscar."

"Bullshit."

"Look, are you going to listen to me or not? I'm trying to do my job, here."

"Are you?" He stood as well. "Or are you just trying to make a buck, Jeffrey?"

"What?"

"How is it in my best interest to go completely stone-cold business on this sale if I don't want to? If I actually do care about who buys? You take a percentage, right? So you stand to make more money if I sell it high?"

"Well, of course, but—"

"So it's in your best interest, more than mine."

"Oscar, that's unfair. I have colleagues who are laughing at me because they know the money is in the developer, but I've been stubbornly looking for farmers anyway. Every Realtor who sees the place tells me the same thing. The house is losing us the sale."

"There's a buyer out there. There's someone who will love that house."

"Yeah. You."

He snorted. "Look. Do you need me to hire someone else? Take this off your plate?"

"I don't know. Are you going to continue to accuse me of trying to line my own pockets?"

He shook his head. "No. I'm sorry. It's my parents' house, you know? My childhood is in that house, and it was a good one. This is really difficult for me. It's the right thing to do, but it's difficult. I...." *God, I don't mean to be an asshole. Why am I such an asshole?* "I'm so tired of losing, Jeffrey. Losing people, losing the farm. So tired."

"Oh, Oz. Baby, I understand." Jeffrey moved closer to him, slid a hand along his jaw. He leaned into the touch. He needed it so much. "You're letting go of the past to make a better future for your girls. And a better future for yourself. For us."

"Us?" He stared into Jeffrey's eyes. They were warm, emotional.

Jeffrey nodded. "I adore your family, Oz. Spending time with them. Rose is so sweet and acts like a mom to me and those girls. I just love them all. Especially the twins. I want to be a part of that."

"Jeffrey—"

"Are you hearing me, Oscar? I love you."

He nodded. He ached so hard, he thought he might tear right in half, but he heard. And he was more sure every minute that he felt the same way. "I hear you. I do. I love you too."

Jeffrey kissed him hard. He couldn't breathe, didn't need to. He needed this more.

"*We* love you, Russ and I, both. We want... you. Them. All of it."

"Jeffrey." He took another kiss, not caring if his lover saw the tears on his face. They were real. He felt more real right now than he had in years.

"We'll take care of you. You belong to us now. Go see Russ and tell him we talked. Tell him how you feel. He needs it, Oscar. We all do."

"Okay. I will. You're okay if I—"

"More than okay," Jeffrey interrupted, smiling.

He kissed Jeffrey again. "We'll see you tomorrow?"

"Saturdays are sacred. I'll be there."

He made his way toward the office door. "I didn't want to argue. I'm sorry. I just needed to know what was going on, and... please, I don't want any more developers coming through."

"You won't see another one. These guys are going to make a bid to win it."

"You'll turn them down."

"Oscar."

"Jeffrey, turn them down. I love you. I'll see you tomorrow."

CHAPTER TWENTY-FOUR

Two DAYS back-to-back, Oscar drove through the Stable Hill gate and up the driveway. Saturday would make three in a row. Russ could get used to having his men around on the regular, even if it did mean he didn't get all of his work done. That pile of tack that needed cleaning was laughing at him from the tack room, but Miles didn't complain. The man would just nod and rally whoever was needed to get shit done. Miles had told him a hundred times that a farm manager didn't need to be mucking stalls and cleaning tack. But the farm wasn't bringing in as much money from hay sales like it used to, and he really felt like idle hands was a luxury they couldn't afford.

While it would be nice to see Oscar, Russ was a little worried. It was Friday afternoon, and his lover really ought to be at work, but instead Oscar was coming from Jeffrey's office. He had a bad feeling that meant they'd finally sold Stable Hill and Oscar was headed his way to break it to him personally.

Russ watched the minivan pull up the drive and park. God, that thing was ugly. The man who stepped out looked good, though, in jeans and a button-down, leather jacket squaring up his lover's shoulders real nice. Oscar gave him a wave and a smile through one of the front porch windows and then came on in.

"Hi." He hopped up off the couch and went to Oscar, sighing as Oscar pulled him in and kissed him, and oh, oh God—it wasn't an apology or a consolation. It was deep and slow, intense, needful. A groan rumbled low in Oscar's chest, and he answered with a moan.

"Hello," Oscar said finally, eyes on his, a hint of a smile in them, and more than a hint of heat.

He smiled back. "What's going on? Did you sell the farm?"

Oscar gave him a curious look. "No. No we haven't yet. Is that why you thought I was coming?"

"From Jeffrey's office? On a—"

"On a Friday afternoon. God. I'm sorry, Russ. Did we worry you?"

"Some." Oscar hadn't let him go. They were still in the foyer, talking inches away from each other.

"I came to.... Jeffrey and I talked, and it was a good conversation, and he told me that the two of you... that I should tell you that he told me—"

"I love you." He blurted, knowing where Oscar was going and understanding that his lover was anxious. It was okay. Like Jeffrey had said, Oscar was complicated. They had to open their arms wide enough for all of Oscar's baggage, and the man would bring it right in.

Oscar sighed and grinned at him. "I was supposed to say that first."

"It's not a race, mister. You don't lose just because you came in second." He wanted to hear it, though, so bad his heart was pounding.

Oscar laughed and kissed him again, another deep one,

and he could feel the words coming, building a path from Oscar's soul to his. "I love you, Russ. I'm yours."

"Yes." His. Finally. "I'm yours, Oscar. Have been for so long."

Oscar nodded. "Take me upstairs and let me show you."

Fuck, those words were good too. So good.

He took Oscar's hand and led him upstairs, Oscar following him, simple as could be, past what had been Oscar's mother's room and the little room that had been Oscar's once before it was his, to the big room at the end of the hall that he'd come to feel with everything in him was theirs.

His and Oscar's and Jeff's.

Oscar crowded him through the door and kissed him again, warm hands roaming over his belly. He reached down to tug his T-shirt off, and Oscar helped, lifting it up and over his head. "Mmm. One of my favorite views."

He smiled, accepting the compliment, letting it build him up. "Just a hard day's work."

"It's hot, Russ." Oscar's hands were roaming over his skin, leaving goose bumps behind as they slid over his chest, his arms, down his back.

He reached forward and pushed Oscar's coat off, then started in on the buttons of Oscar's shirt—one, another, two more. Oscar bent and took one of his nipples between careful teeth, and the pinch and burn made him moan. Then Oscar was suddenly on his knees, pulling at his belt, lowering his fly.

"Oscar." Oscar tugged his jeans down, baring his ass and making his cock smack against Oscar's cheek. He looked down, letting that sight sink in. "Fuck."

Oscar didn't reply, just raised those blue eyes to Russ's and let Russ push his cock past those lips, the head rubbing against Oscar's soft palate. "Oh God. God." He made a needy sound, one that betrayed just how much he wanted, everything he needed.

Oscar's hands traveled up his abs, over his hips and around to his ass, rubbing and massaging the muscles they found along the way. He watched his prick disappear into Oscar's mouth again and again, his balls aching and his breath shallow. Oscar devoured him hungrily, sucking and licking, teasing his hot spots with a clever tongue. "Fuck. Oscar.... Oscar!"

His lover groaned for him and gave his ass a final squeeze before standing slowly. "You taste good."

"You feel so good." He pushed into Oscar's arms and lifted his face for a kiss, wanting more. Oscar backed him up until his knees hit the bed and they finished undressing each other between kisses and smiles, laughter and moans, fingers tangling when they'd meet and hands touching everything as Oscar's blue jeans hit the floor.

He still hadn't quite caught his breath when he crawled up on the bed, then slid backward. Or maybe he had and it started all over again. Oscar was on him in a flat second, shouldering him onto his back.

Oscar looked into his eyes. "I love you."

He nodded, watching the softness he loved in Oscar's gaze turn heated. "I know."

"You will."

Oh fuck. He liked the sound of that.

Oscar began gently tasting along the line of his jaw and down the tendons in his neck. His lover's teeth found the curve where neck met shoulder, sending a shiver through him and making him groan. Each of his nipples were sweetly tortured in turn until he couldn't be still anymore. Oscar knew how that drove him mad and didn't let up until he arched and rolled under his lover, squirming and sliding his heels in the sheets.

And all the while Oscar stroked him slowly and kept him needing enough to cloud his thinking.

"Beautiful, babe. You look beautiful like this."

"Want... I love...." Sweet Jesus, he'd lost words.

Oscar laughed softly, darkly, and tapped on his thighs, his legs falling open, wide and willing. "That's it, love. So eager. You want?"

"Yes. God, yes." *Everything. All of it. Anything.*

He felt Oscar's fingers press against him, the slick cool on his skin and wondered when the man had.... "Yes. Yes, please!" Fuck it all, he didn't care. He wanted.

Oscar gave him a finger and then gently added a second, and Russ bucked against them, taking them deep.

"Look at you, Russ. All out of patience, baby? So hot."

"Yeah." He rolled, riding Oscar's fingers as his lover worked and stretched him. He didn't need much, he was so ready. So goddamn ready for it. "Come on, Oz. Fuck me."

"Jesus, Russ."

That growl in Oscar's chest that he loved so much wasn't lost on him. Oscar liked that. "Fuck me, baby. Need you." He arched, giving Oscar something to look at, and this time the growl was louder, Oscar's eyes narrowing as that thick cock pushed inside.

"Russ. Fuck, so good."

"More, Oscar."

Russ knew his words would set his lover into a roar. Oscar surged into him at first, deep and strong, thrusts hard and heavy, making them both groan and pant. But after that first burst of pure need, Oscar pulled back, lengthening the strokes and slowing the pace.

Gathering that control that made him lose his mind.

It seemed like Oscar could hang on to those reins, hold back his own need, no matter how burning. Or at least the man managed it a lot better than he could. He loved handing it over to both of his men. His eyes locked with Oscar's and they both smiled, his lover nodding to him.

Yeah. Hell, yeah.

"Tomorrow," he said, voice rough. "You and me and Jeff, yeah?" God, he wanted that. The three of them together, in love.

"Yeah. Gonna do this first, though." Oscar laid into him a couple of times, backing up those words, and then slowed again, grinning down at him.

"So good."

The slow and steady build made him dizzy and he hung for what seemed like forever on the edge of begging. He knew Oscar loved it, loved watching him. Got off on it. On him. It was everything Russ wanted.

"Is it time, baby?"

He loved the way Oscar asked him that, as if his lover didn't know damn well he was ready to scream. "Hard."

Oscar swallowed, and those bright blue eyes pinned him from under silver bangs. "Yeah?"

"Really fucking hard. Please."

"Jesus Christ." Oscar's hips stuttered, such a rare and perfect slip. He was proud of himself for the two seconds before everything got wild.

Oscar took him at his word, bending him farther and pummeling him over and over, sharing pants and grunts and heated, dirty talk as the room faded, thought faded, until all that was left was rough and animal.

So perfect.

"R-Russ. Fuck." Oscar's hips trembled and jerked, nailing him in just the right spot.

"Yes! Fuck! Yes!" That was it. He felt like he was suddenly thirsty and the universe sent him a waterfall. He was about to beg for something he already had. Fireworks went off behind his eyelids and the room got so fucking hot, he couldn't breathe.

Oscar grunted and pinned him down, hips pressing deep

and both hands on his shoulders. He forced his eyes open, wanting to see, to watch that beautiful agony on his lover's face.

They lay there breathing, smiling, taking in each other's eyes and trading kisses until all he wanted was to fall asleep in Oscar's arms.

"I love you," he said softly, drawing a line across Oscar's cheek with one finger.

Oscar caught his hand and kissed it. "I love you."

"Stay?"

"I will. I'll want to call and check in, but Rose doesn't expect me home until Sunday."

"Really? I get you all day tomorrow?"

"You get me all night too."

Oscar's words set his skin on fire. "Oh."

Soft laughter puffed across his cheek. "Let an old man nap first, love."

CHAPTER TWENTY-FIVE

JEFFREY PACED the entire length of the waiting room, one end to the other and back again, every so often poking his head around the corner and looking down the hall to see if Oscar and Russ might be getting off the elevator.

Rose sat in the only chair that had a view of the hall. Brian's parents sat stiffly against a different wall, poor Brian sitting motionless between them, looking pale and a little green, the expression on his face still as stone. He'd puked twice since Jeffrey arrived.

This wasn't just terrifying; it was also so fucking uncomfortable.

After trying Oscar's cell phone a couple of times, Rose finally thought to try Jeffrey's. She said Oscar had told her they were staying the night together. It was a little awkward when he wasn't able to put Oscar on the phone, and he had to tell her his lover was actually spending the night at the farm with Russ.

He could have stretched the truth and just said Oscar was at the farm, but he knew Rose. Then it would have been concern over why Oscar had lied, and had they had a fight—God only knew what a mother could cook up in her mind. Regardless, it wasn't his responsibility that Oscar hadn't told the family about their relationship yet.

Russ was going to have a fucking cow.

All of that was unimportant at the moment, though, because Oscar's daughter—

"He's here, finally." Oh, Rose sounded so stressed. Damn.

"Rose? Jeffrey? Where is she? Is she...? Can I see her?"

He hugged Oscar and then Russ. "The doctors are with her right now."

"What have they told you?" Russ asked him.

"Rose." Oscar went to her as she approached them and pulled her into his arms. "I'm so sorry. I should have been home."

"Hush, sweetheart. It wouldn't have changed a thing. Don't you worry about me."

"Who... who is with the girls?"

"Mary Ellen from church is at the house with them. Her husband, William, drove me over."

Oscar nodded. "You'll remind me to thank them."

"Let Jeffrey fill you in, sweetheart."

"Yes. Please."

"Let me give you the no bullshit good news first, Oscar. She's in surgery, and they're optimistic it will go well. They asked you about the surgery, right?"

Oscar nodded, eyes riveted on him.

"She's a strong girl, Oz." He waited for Oscar to nod to make sure he was being heard. Russ stepped up behind Oscar and put an arm around their lover's back.

"Give me the rest, Jeffrey."

He sighed. "She took a bad blow to the side of the head. She was unconscious when they found her, then conscious for a bit but disoriented and confused."

"How... how confused?"

Rose interrupted, to Jeffrey's great relief, laying a hand on Oscar's arm. "She couldn't answer questions, sweetheart. They're not sure why."

"She didn't remember...?"

"That's one possibility, yes. Or it could have been physical. It could have been a disconnect somewhere. They don't know yet."

"I need to sit down." Oscar pushed past him and reached for a chair, Russ holding him up slightly. They had just about gotten Oscar seated when—

"You." Oscar flew out of his chair again, heading for Brian.

"Whoa. Hey!" Brian's father stood up abruptly.

Jeffrey and Russ fell on Oscar, each grabbing an arm and dragging him back. "Whoa!"

"The accident wasn't his fault."

"Hey! Hey, hold up. Oscar, it wasn't Brian's fault. Look at me." Jeffrey made Oscar meet his eyes, if just to get them off Brian. "It's the truth, Oz. Calm down." He slowly loosened his grip as Oscar started to breathe, started to relax.

Brian's mother stood as well and put her arm through her husband's, but Brian stayed seated, still looking so miserable.

"Breathe, baby. It's okay." Russ could be such a balm for Oscar's temper.

Jeffrey slowly let Oscar go. "Brian did everything right."

Oscar took a couple of deep breaths, just nodding until those shoulders finally sagged. "Okay. I'm sorry. I'm sorry, Brian. I'm.... We're all upset, I know. I'm sorry."

Brian's father stepped closer. "I'm Ron. This is my wife, Helen. We're all here pulling for Emily, Mr. Kennedy."

"Oscar." Oscar stuck out a hand to shake. "I know. I'm—I apologize. What happened?"

"The guy didn't stop. He ran a red light. I swear my light

was green, Mr. Kennedy. I wasn't speeding or anything, I promise. I wouldn't.... I love Emily. I always take care of her. He came out of nowhere." Poor Brian sounded heartbroken.

Brian's mother hurried back and sat down beside her son, and Oscar took two huge steps forward to kneel at Brian's feet.

"He was drunk," Ron added with a sigh.

"I understand. It wasn't your fault, Brian, and I don't blame you. Okay? I'm sorry I snapped at you. I... I'm just so scared for her. I know you are too."

Brian burst into tears, and Oscar wrapped those solid arms around the kid. Russ rested a hand on his shoulder. Rose went and sat with Helen, taking Helen's hands between hers. The waiting room was quiet and still except for Brian's hiccupping sobs and Oscar's soothing words.

"Tell me this is going to be okay," Russ whispered to Jeffrey.

"It will be okay." Jeffrey needed to say it so he could believe it himself.

Oscar was just finally stepping away from Brian when a doctor in scrubs came out. "Which one of you is Emily's father?"

"I am." Oscar hurried over, and Rose joined him. "Oscar Kennedy."

Jeffrey held his breath.

"She's out of surgery. She did beautifully. We didn't run up against anything that overly concerns me. It's still a head injury. It's too early to make promises, and she will need a little time, but I'm quite optimistic."

Oscar nodded and covered his face with both hands.

"Thank you, doctor," Rose said for him. "Oscar just arrived. He's a bit overwhelmed."

"I completely understand." The doctor looked at Rose

this time. "We won't allow her to wake up until tomorrow at the earliest, and when she does, she could be disoriented in any of a handful of ways. We can talk more about that tomorrow. Would you like to see her?"

"Yes." Oscar was quick enough with that reply.

"Follow me, Mr. Kennedy."

"One second, please." Oscar moved back over to Brian. "The doc said she's out of surgery and she did great."

Ron sighed, relieved. "That's good news."

"It is. They're going to let me see her. Are you okay?"

Brian shrugged silently.

"We have to think positively, kiddo." Oscar gave Brian's shoulder a squeeze, then looked back at Jeffrey.

"I'll come back and get you guys in a bit, okay? Unless... I mean, you heard, right? She's not going to wake up until at least tomorrow. You could go home and get some rest."

"Like hell." Russ's words sounded rough, but the affectionate smile that went with it wasn't at all.

"We'll be here, Oscar. Go see Emily."

Oscar nodded and put his arm around Rose's shoulders as they followed the doctor.

Ron looked at Jeffrey. "I think we're going to take Brian home."

"Of course. We'll keep you up-to-date."

"Can I see her tomorrow?" Brian was still so pale, and his eyes had dark circles under them, but the kid looked like he was breathing now at least.

"I don't know what they'll allow, but I will let your folks know as soon as we get word."

"Thanks."

"Are you...? Which of you is Oscar's boyfriend? It's you, Jeffrey, right?" Helen asked slowly.

Jeffrey smiled. "I am. And so is Russ."

"So... oh!" Helen gave him a smile. "Well, Oscar has lots of support, then."

"He does."

Ron started moving. "We're pulling for Emily. She's a sweet girl. We like her very much. Good night."

"Night." Russ tugged on the brim of his baseball hat.

Jeffrey looked around the waiting room. "Guess it's just us, now."

Russ led him over to a couch in one corner of the room, and they sat—Jeffrey with his arm around Russ, who rested a tired head on his shoulder. "Oscar was a wreck on the way over. He was saying all kinds of crazy things—how he shouldn't have stayed with me, that getting involved with us was a bad idea, he needs to focus on his family. He kept saying how much he appreciated the ride, like I was someone he shouldn't be asking for a favor."

Jeffrey took a deep breath and sighed. "You know he didn't mean any of that, babe. That was guilt and worry and fear talking. It's like promising God you'll be a better person when something bad happens if he'll only make it all right. It's something you say to make yourself feel better."

"I hope so." Russ sighed. "I really hope you're right."

"Me too."

Russ was asleep in seconds, and Jeffrey was envious.

Russ woke up alone on the couch in the waiting room. He blinked, still bleary-eyed and disoriented from a nap he hadn't meant to take. He knew he should make himself wake up and find his men, he wanted to see Emily and be there for Oscar, but his eyes felt thick, his back was stiff, and he just wasn't ready to move quickly.

He sat up and ran his fingers through his hair, yawned and

stretched, and scratched the back of his neck. God, he needed some coffee in the worst way.

"Good morning."

Jesus.

Not alone after all.

Startled, he blinked again and looked over in the direction the voice had come from. "Uh. Hey." He nodded to Rose. They'd only been introduced in passing the very few times Rose had made it out to the farm, but he knew who she was. Truthfully, that burned him more than it probably should right now. This wasn't about him.

"Hay is for horses." Rose looked at him expectantly.

What? Was he really being schooled by a little old lady at 4:00 a.m.? "Yes. Sorry, ma'am, I forgot my manners." *I did just wake up and all.* "Hello, Miss Rose. I'm Russ White." He watched her, hoping that was better. He thought his mother would have been happy with that. How formal did she want him to be?

Rose smiled, looking pleased. "I remember. It's nice to see you again, Russell."

Russell. Only his mother called him Russell. "I'm awfully worried for Emily. I'll be keeping her in my prayers."

"Thank you, Russell. I appreciate that. Send one or two up for that dear boy too, if you can spare them."

What was his name? Brian? He was pretty sure it was Brian. Poor kid. "Yes, ma'am. Will do. How are you hangin' in? Would you like a ride home? I have my truck."

"Aren't you darling. No, thank you. Oscar said he needed some things from home. I'm going to wait for him."

He nodded. "Do you know where I can find a cup of coffee?"

"I don't. But I think Jeffrey does. Oscar just took him to see Emily. Did you want to join them?"

"Oh. I... uh." *Yes and no.* He wasn't sure how Oscar would

feel about it, and he didn't want to make things more compli-cated right now. They had things to talk about, words that needed to be said, but it could wait until they were all rested and things were less scary with Emily.

"Russell?"

Oh God. She used his full name again. Did that mean he was in trouble? "Yes, ma'am?"

"Can I ask you a very frank question?"

"Oh. Well... I...." She raised an eyebrow at him, and he knew there was no refusing her. "Yes, ma'am."

"Thank you, Russell." Rose smiled at him and leaned closer. "Are you... you're Oscar's lover, then?"

Oh God. Oh God. Please come back, Oscar, and save me. "I—"

"His *other* lover, I mean."

Oh, no, no. Oh, this wasn't how this was supposed to go, was it? Oh, help. "Yes, ma'am. Oscar told you?" He knew damn well Oscar hadn't, but what was he supposed to say? This was the strangest conversation he'd ever had.

"No," Rose replied carefully. "No, he did not, I'm afraid. But it seems he should have, since he was with you last evening."

Russ's cheeks lit on fire. "It's... we're...."

Jesus Christ.

"It's quite all right, Russell dear. I don't expect you to explain. I think I should probably ask Oscar to do that."

"Yes, ma'am." *Thank you, God.* He was on the stuttering end of embarrassed as fuck now.

There was a long silence. He was trying to figure out how to politely excuse himself and go find coffee or go after Jeffrey and Oscar, anything to get him off this couch, when Rose cleared her throat and looked at him again. "Why don't you come to dinner? Normally I'd suggest Sunday, but this weekend is... no. No, so next Sunday, then? Once we have

Emily home and things have settled a bit. Yes. You'll come then, won't you?"

Oh. Should he say yes? Was he supposed to? Would Oscar want him to? "I... thank you, ma'am, but—"

"But nothing. I'm cooking and you're invited."

"Yes, ma'am. I'll be there." *Okay, got it. You don't say no to Miss Rose.*

CHAPTER TWENTY-SIX

INSTEAD OF spending that Saturday together at the farm, Jeffrey and Russ spent the day at the hospital with him, taking turns getting naps and food and helping him deal with the doctors. In the days that followed, one of them was with him nearly all the time. Oscar couldn't bring himself to tell them to go home, not seriously anyway, although he would have preferred to be alone. It was hard to think with them sitting so close, bringing him coffee and water, reminding him to get out of Emily's room and walk.

While Emily lay in her hospital bed, letters from colleges were coming in. Acceptances across the board. Rose had brought a few to the hospital, but he felt that Emily's state of mind was still too fragile and her short-term memory still a bit off, so he hadn't shown them to her yet.

Otherwise, though, she was doing well. After nearly a week, she was able to sit up for some of the day, they were allowing her to move around her room with assistance, and she'd finally gotten the long-awaited shower she'd been begging for. She'd be going home soon. Sometime in the next couple of days, the doctor said, perhaps even tomorrow.

But he needed to think. He needed to reconsider what he was doing, how he was spending his time, whether this relationship was fair to his girls. The answers weren't that clear. He needed to focus now on Emily and what was best for his family. For the time being at least, it would be quiet once he got her home, and then he could figure himself out.

"Knock, knock."

Oscar blinked and looked up, mustering a smile. "Hey, Rose."

"Hello, dear. Oh, Oscar. You look so tired." Rose came in and sat with him, taking his hand in hers.

"She's doing better today. She was awake a little while ago, and we were talking and watching TV."

"How are you, sweetheart?"

"I'm fine. She just gets tired so quickly. They think we'll be able to bring her home in a day or two. I guess I need to talk to the school. She won't be able to go back for at least another week, maybe two. And work. I need to talk to work."

"Oscar."

Work had been good about everything, and he had lots of time saved up that he could use, but it was still stressful. "Thank goodness for you, Rose. I don't know how I would do this without you."

Rose sighed. "Oscar. How are you?"

"I'm okay. I just need to get all these ducks in a row, you know? There's a lot to think about." They'd done the nurse-maid thing before, he and Rose, with Emmett. The last six months or so when they knew the trial drugs weren't helping and Emmett had refused further treatment, they took shifts so Oscar could keep working. Someone needed to. Rose would look after Emmett during the day while the kids were at school, then get the girls settled with after-school chores and homework. Then he'd come home and take over with Emmett and the girls while Rose made dinner. They'd get

everyone in bed, Rose would retire, and he'd do the dishes....
God, if he thought about it, he could remember everything.
But if it hadn't been for Rose—

"Oscar? Oscar, you need to sleep. Take a shower. Eat something."

He nodded. "I will." He could use getting his arms around his girls for more than five minutes, actually. Maybe hear about their days.

"Why don't you go now? I can stay for...." Rose looked at her watch. "Oh. The twins will be home from school in a bit, and I should be there. I have a little time, though."

"That's all right. Jeffrey and Russ are going to come sit with Emily for a few hours tonight so I can get home for dinner and see Soph and the twins."

"Oh, that will be nice. They miss you."

"I miss them too."

"I invited your Russell to dinner next Sunday, after things have settled down."

Oscar glanced at her. "Did you?" Oh, boy. She wanted to have this conversation now?

"He's a nice young man."

"He's not that young."

Rose looked at him over the rim of her glasses. "Oscar."

"He's twenty-eight. He's a grown man."

"Let's see, he was... barely ten when Emily was born."

"Stop that."

Rose chuckled, pulling some needlework from her bag. He thought it was crochet, but he could never keep all that stuff with yarn straight.

"Sophie speaks very highly of him, you know, and she is looking forward to riding with him. She told me all about how he'd put her to work in the barn and about the sick horse."

He looked at his mother-in-law. "They made a connection at the barn after... that horrible day at school."

"They did, and he made quite an impression on her."

"He's remarkable."

"Very sweet. And so very in love with you."

Okay, so this was less of a conversation and more of a reckoning. "You are far too perceptive for your own good, woman."

Rose appeared to ignore that comment, fingers and eyes busy with her yarn. "You'll forgive me if I don't quite understand how this works."

"Oh, yes. You're forgiven." He grinned.

"Don't be funny, son."

"Sorry." He wasn't, really. He loved calling her out when she was being coy. It made her so mad, it just made him laugh.

"You have a lot of family already. But two lovers?"

"Oh, Rose. Did you say 'lover'? Emmett would be so proud of you."

She dropped her hands into her lap. "Are you going to explain it to me, Oscar, or not?"

He blinked at her and smiled, and she smiled back, and then they were both laughing. Rose shook her head at herself like she didn't have words.

"I will. But it won't be easy because I'm not sure I understand it myself. The easiest bit is that I love them both, one as much as the other. I feel as if either one of them alone would be wonderful, but not... enough. And they look at me differently. I think it's the same for them."

Rose's fingers were busy-busy, and she didn't say anything for a long time.

In fact it wasn't Rose who answered him at all. "So, wait. You have two boyfriends now, at the same time?"

Oscar turned his head abruptly, and Rose looked up from her crochet, as shocked as he was.

"What? Are you okay, Oz? What's wrong?" Emily reached up and felt her face with her fingers. "Do I have a huge zit or something?"

Oscar snorted. "No, honey. You surprised me. I didn't know you were awake."

"Well, I'm glad I am or else I wouldn't know you were finally dating."

Oscar had no idea what to do next. "Finally?"

"I was worried about you. What have you been waiting for? It's not like Dad is coming back."

Oscar looked at Rose and then down at his hands. Out of the mouths of babes. Not that Emily was a baby anymore, far from it. "I have you girls to think about, to look after. It didn't seem right, and I didn't want to upset you."

"Sophie and I were hoping you were dating Jeffrey."

"He is, darling," Rose chimed in.

"Oh, yay!"

"Hoping?"

"You know how weird it was that I was dating and you weren't? Weird. Who's the other one?"

He felt like this snowball had started rolling downhill and it just kept getting bigger and bigger until his legs weren't long enough to keep up. "Russ. He's the—"

"Oh, the horse guy? At Grandpa's farm? I remember him, kind of, but Sophie told me all about him. She said he was cute."

You actually met him. Yesterday. The short-term memory thing was kind of scary, but the doctors promised him it was normal.

"He's adorable." Rose leaned forward like she was conspiring with Emily. "And young."

"Rose!" Oscar sighed.

"What? Oz! How young?"

He rolled his eyes. "Russ is twenty-eight."

"Oh. That's not young, Gram. God. That's almost *thirty*."

Oscar looked at Rose and winked, and they shared another laugh.

"I like the sound of that laughing." They all looked up at Brian, who was leaning in the doorway, smiling at Emily.

"Brian!"

Oscar was on his feet. "Shh. Emily, you need to stay calm."

"Hey, Em."

"Brian, she really needs to—"

Brian leaned over the opposite arm of Emily's hospital bed and kissed her. Right in front of Oscar, on the lips, like he wasn't standing there. It was a nice kiss, but....

"Oscar, you should go get some coffee."

"No, I really—"

"And I'd like some tea." Rose stood up. "Come on."

Brian and Emily were talking softly and smiling at each other. It was sweet, but he couldn't leave them alone, could he? "Emily, make sure you—"

"Come along, Oscar."

"But—"

"She's not listening to you anyway."

He looked back over his shoulder as he left the room. Rose was right. Emily wasn't paying attention to anyone but Brian. Right now, Brian was her whole world.

CHAPTER TWENTY-SEVEN

SUNDAY NIGHT supper had been a big deal in Momma's house growing up. Russ was pretty pleased to have been invited to Oscar's, and nervous too. Yeah, he and Sophie had an understanding, and he and Miss Rose did too. He wasn't really nervous so much about meeting the older girl, Emily, and the little twins for the first time either. It was more the whole thing, the whole picture—his lovers, the kids, his... well, basically his mother-in-law, he guessed, all at one table like a real family. A nice big family.

Yeah. Excited and nervous. But it was good. It was all good. It was about time he was invited, time he felt included. He knew Oscar hadn't meant to exclude him exactly, he understood that the relationship the three of them had was hard to explain, but it was the three of them, after all. He tried not to be upset that Emily's accident had forced the issue instead of Oscar just speaking up for him. Doing the right thing wasn't always easy.

He'd showered, shaved, brushed his teeth, found clean jeans, a button-down, and his better pair of boots. He didn't have dressy ones, but these were in good shape and clean, so they'd do. Then he grabbed his keys and got in his truck.

It wasn't a bad drive; long, but easy on a Sunday, and he cruised into Oscar's neighborhood right on time. Wow. This was regular suburbia over here. The houses were big, with shiny SUVs in everyone's driveways, and sidewalks and green lawns. Some of the houses had three-car garages. Some had swimming pools. He drove past one neatly lined-up mailbox after another until he got to Oscar's house, number 141, gray with black shutters, lovely if slightly more modest than some of the others. Well looked after. It was a nice house.

This was why Oscar wanted to sell the farm, huh? To keep this house with neighbors and neat little mail boxes.

He saw Jeff's Mercedes parked in the driveway, so he pulled in and parked behind it, figuring that was a fairly safe bet. Sophie met him at the door with a big smile, and he found he was glad to see her. The logistics had been complicated, and sometimes he had to drive Soph home or pick her up, but they'd found a way for her to spend more time with the horses, riding and talking. She was a shy kid but a smart one, way smarter than he was. Smart like her dad.

"Hey, Soph."

"Hey, Russ. Look. Before there are a lot of people around, I want you to see something." She handed him a sketchbook before he'd been through the door one second. The book was open to a picture she had drawn of a horse... not any horse; that was definitely Angel. "Wow, that's Angel, for sure. Look at that. You didn't tell me you were an artist."

"I'm not. I just draw. But I knew you'd recognize her."

"Of course I recognize her. She's my girl." For a little while longer anyway. Damn. He was going to miss that mare.

"Sophie's a little young for you, Russell."

Sophie looked horrified. "Grandma!"

He looked over at Miss Rose and gave her a smile. "Yes,

ma'am. Sophie was showing me her drawing." He leaned down so Rose could kiss his cheek.

"Hello, dear. I'm so glad you came."

"Thank you for inviting me."

"Well, for some reason Oscar kept... forgetting."

"He's an old man. It happens."

"Hey, now." Oscar stepped up behind Rose and rested his hands on her shoulders.

"Come along, Sophie. I need you in the kitchen." Oh, Rose was good.

"Gotta make dinner." Sophie smiled at him and then followed her grandmother off.

Oscar gave him a warm smile. "I'm not that old."

"Compared to me, you're an old-timer."

"Yeah? I keep up with you all right."

Jeff wandered over, hands in his pockets. "Some men age like a fine wine."

"Okay, guys. Thank you. You're both here at my invitation, remember."

"Wrong! Miss Rose invited me." He looked over Oscar's shoulder. "Can I kiss you hello, or is that weird?"

Oscar laughed. "These girls already had two dads, remember? And I'm finding that three seems to be less of a stretch than you might think."

Russ leaned up and kissed Oscar first, then Jeffrey, and came away smiling. He felt just fine.

"Come on in and meet the rest of the crew." Oscar led him into the little living room. "Hey, Zoe? Riley?"

Two identical heads popped up from working on a puzzle on the floor. "Is that him?"

"That's your other boyfriend?"

"Girls, this is Russ. Russ, this is Zoe, and that is Riley."

"Lord, I am never going to get that right, am I?" Although....

"No one ever does." Both girls shrugged.

"Well, hold up. Give me a second." He looked at them both carefully, nodding sagely. "Zoe, your right eye is a little flatter and wider than Riley's. And Riley's got a kink here in her lip and a tiny little scar on her jaw. How'd you get that, honey?"

"I fell down the outside stairs last winter. It was icy."

Zoe stared at him. "You're like a wizard or something."

"No, I had to learn to tell horses apart real quick. I've had practice."

"Set the table, girls!" Rose's voice came in from the kitchen.

"Come help us, Russ?"

"Please?"

"Zoe...." Oscar tried to save him, but he didn't really want saving. This was the good stuff. The stuff he'd been missing out on. He smiled, letting Oscar know it was all right.

"Well, I can't say no to two such beautiful little ladies, can I?"

Riley took his hand and hauled him away, leaving Oscar and Jeff laughing behind him.

"Sucker!" Jeff called after him.

They had no idea. Five minutes as a captive to Riley and Zoe and he'd never had so much fun setting a table.

"Grandma Rose." Riley's eyes were humongous. "Don't ever let Russ set the table by himself."

Rose played along. "No?"

"He doesn't know his right from his left! And he's old!"

"So old," Oscar joined in, laughing softly.

He hung his head. "It's all true, and I kept forgetting which one was the fork and which was the spoon, didn't I, Zoe?"

"I showed him twice. I think he failed school," Zoe said seriously.

Sophie jumped right in with "Good thing you're good with horses," and he smiled.

"Right? They don't use forks."

Honestly, he loved every second of this. Every damn second.

Brian showed up right before supper was ready, and he helped Emily down the stairs. He was right there, making sure she didn't trip, ready to help her if she needed it. That girl was a trouper. It was really good to meet her when she was actually aware of what was going on. She'd been sort of out of it for their brief meeting in the hospital. She was a beautiful girl, and Brian was totally taken with her. Anyone could see it.

"Oh, lasagna!" One of his favorites, and he hadn't had it in ages and ages.

Oscar laughed, but it was Jeffrey who chimed in, "Rose makes it for everyone Oscar is trying to win over."

"Such a snitch, Jeffrey. And here I thought you would keep my secrets."

He smiled at Rose. "It's amazing, Miss Rose, but totally not necessary. I'm already won."

Jeffrey nodded. "I was too, Russ. Oscar just didn't know it yet."

"Aw." Russ caught Oscar blushing but didn't tease him. "That's sweet."

Dinner went by quickly with lots of conversation and laughter. It was everything he'd missed about family and he counted himself lucky to have even a taste of it back.

When they were done, he got up to help clear, and so did Brian and Jeffrey, and pretty soon the three of them were shuttling dishes and drying while Oscar washed. The kitchen was sparkling in no time.

"Oscar, sweetheart, I'm going to take Zoe and Riley off to bed. Brian already took Emily upstairs. Sophie is reading."

"Thank you, Rose."

Russ jogged over to her and offered a hug, which she accepted. "Thank you so much for dinner. It was delicious."

"You're very welcome, dear. Come back again soon, please. Now that I know about you."

Oscar winked at Russ. "You didn't know I was in the dog house, did you?"

"Oh bah. I only wish you'd told me earlier."

Jeffrey smiled at Rose. "He was worried you wouldn't approve."

Rose snorted. "I understand that, I guess, but I know how hard it is to fall in love again after you lose your spouse, as I have yet to do it myself. My Emmett felt lucky to find Oscar, and Oscar is lucky to have found not one, but two kind, handsome men who love him. Emmett would tell you both you're very fortunate to have found Oscar too."

"We are," Russ agreed quickly.

Jeffrey leaned over and kissed Rose on the cheek. "Thank you, Rose."

"There's no need for the dog house." Russ stepped in this time. "Oscar was worried about the girls too. You know?"

"Oh, Oscar." Rose took Oscar's hand and held it. "Just be happy, sweetheart. That's what matters, isn't it? That's the best example you can set for a child."

Oscar kissed her hand and kept it together, somehow. Russ was pretty impressed.

"Good night, everyone." Rose smiled at each of them. "Sleep well."

They all watched in wonder as Rose left the room.

CHAPTER TWENTY-EIGHT

ONCE ROSE understood the nature of Oscar's relationship with his lovers, a grand conspiracy formed. She'd already had Jeffrey's cell number and now she had Russ's too. Oscar didn't stand a chance. The three of them plotted to get him out of the house and out to the farm the following Saturday, despite his protests that he should be home with Emily.

Rose insisted he go. She was downright immovable about it. Jeffrey and Russ had been texting him all morning, making sure he was coming. Jeffrey even asked if he wanted a ride.

Finally, he'd left the house out of sheer annoyance. But the closer he got to Stable Hill, the more he wanted to see his men, not in a hospital, but somewhere they could be themselves. No one, not even Rose, was telling him it was wrong to want this. To need these men. Maybe they were right. Maybe he needed this night.

He pulled up next to Russ's truck and hopped out, making sure this time to take his phone inside with him. "Oh, it smells so good in here."

"Jeffrey is cooking." Russ came right to him and felt like home in his arms.

"You feel good."

Russ hummed against his chest. "I'm so glad you're here."

"I am too. I was wrong. This is exactly what I need."

Russ kissed him, soothing him, shifting his focus even further away from the stress of the week.

"Hello? The kitchen wench would like a kiss too."

Oscar laughed against Russ's lips.

"He's so impatient." Russ grinned back.

"Coming, wench."

"Not yet you're not." Jeffrey curled a hand into his shirt and pulled him in as soon as he got close. Oscar heard himself groan like it was coming from someone else. It was low and heated and entirely Jeffrey's doing. "Oh, that was very nice, Oz. Keep that thought for after dinner."

Jeffrey was so good at that. So strong.

"What are you making?"

"Chicken Parm. Pasta. Humongous salad."

"My request." Russ grinned. "Beer?"

"Sure. Thank you. It sounds great, Jeffrey."

"How's Emily?" Russ handed him an open beer and leaned on the counter, watching him.

"She's okay. No school again this coming week, but after that, she should be okay to go back as long as she takes it easy. She has some recovery to do, you know? I'm just grateful it wasn't worse."

Jeffrey nodded. "She was lucky. So was Brian."

"Oh, that poor kid. He feels terrible, and I can't seem to convince him I don't blame him. He apologizes to me every time he sees me."

"It probably scared him half to death." Russ took his hand.

"Yeah, it did. We talked a little about it. He's dealing with some difficult things. The guilt especially. You know, he told me that he let her down."

"Because he was supposed to be taking care of her?" Jeffrey was stirring something on the stove.

"That's what he said. I just told him she loved him."

"You're a good father, Oscar."

He shrugged. "I'm winging it, but I do okay."

"It's too bad Sophie won't be riding tomorrow." Russ squeezed his fingers.

"She's super excited, though. I'll bring her out again soon."

"You don't mind the driving?"

"No, actually. Time alone in the car with Sophie is great. She actually talks." Some of Oscar's best moments with his girls happened in the car.

Russ smiled and nodded knowingly. "No wonder we get each other."

Oscar appreciated the relationship Sophie was forming with Russ. They connected over horses, but Russ seemed to have a way about him that she responded to. It was good for her, and good for Oscar too, because she was such a mystery.

"Okay, Russ. I need you. Oz, you set the table, please?"

"Set the table. So domestic." It felt for a minute like they all lived here. He got placemats and silverware and very happily helped get the food on the table too.

"This smells so good." Russ danced out to the table with a plate and sat down. "Hurry up, boys, or I'm starting without you."

He laughed. "It does smell good."

"No starting yet, Russell Morton White, or I'll take you over my knee."

Oscar blinked. "What? Morton?"

Russ rolled his eyes. "I am so sorry I said anything."

"Russ told me one sweaty night after... you know." Jeffrey's eyebrows waggled. "Pillow talk."

"God." Russ sounded horrified.

He squinted at Russ. "Morton? Like the salt?"

"It was my grandfather's name. Can we eat, please?"

Jeffrey laughed. "Maybe we should call him Morty."

"Morty!"

"I swear to God, y'all, I'll go sleep in the barn."

Jeffrey laughed. "Damn. That's a good threat."

"No kidding, right?"

Russ looked smug and grinned at them. "You'd miss me."

"We would." He shook his head. It was hard to believe he was even having this conversation.

"Can I eat now?"

"Hey." Jeffrey raised his glass of wine. "To us."

Russ raised his beer. "To Saturday nights."

"To family." He touched his wineglass to Jeffrey's and then to Russ's beer.

"You can eat now."

"Finally!" Russ dug right in. "Oh my God, so good."

Oscar and Jeffrey laughed.

DINNER CONVERSATION was light and lively, and Oscar couldn't recall ever having this much fun washing dishes.

"So I'm walking by the barn, and I'm just about to call it a day, and I hear this howling. And the first thing I think is it's another goddamn raccoon, right? So I go looking, follow the sound, you know?"

"Okay...." Jeffrey had been wiping down the table in the dining room but reappeared in time for the punch line.

Russ dropped a dishtowel down on the counter for emphasis. "It was coming from behind the new siding. The contractors walled up one of the fucking barn cats."

"What?" He stared at Russ. "You're kidding."

"Nope. And I couldn't tell which one either. Turned out to be Tilly. I had to rip the siding off to let her out."

His homeowner's brain kicked in for a minute. "They came to fix it for free I hope."

Russ rolled his eyes.

"Right, I just…. Sorry." He shrugged and chuckled.

Jeffrey put his arms around Russ. "Are we done here? Because I have plans for family game night."

He laughed. "Twister?"

Jeffrey rolled his eyes. "Got it in one, Oz."

"Be nice, or I'll go sleep in the barn with Russ."

"Ooh, there's an idea." Russ slipped away from Jeffrey and into his arms instead. "What do you think, baby?"

"Hey!" Jeffrey protested.

Oscar raised an eyebrow. "You're thinking we should give him something to think about?"

"Yeah. To watch."

Jesus, that idea was… it made him blush and it turned him on at the same time. He rested a couple of fingers behind Russ's ear and pulled Russ in for a kiss.

Jeffrey watched them, moving slowly closer. "Pretty, but what is this? Mutiny?"

"I believe it's a called a conspiracy. Whoa. Or maybe it's an assault." He laughed, pretending to try to fend off Russ's hungry kisses when he really wanted every single one.

"Come on, Oscar." Russ took him by the hand and led him to the stairs. He looked over his shoulder at Jeffrey and shrugged, grinning. Who was he to deny Russ anything?

"Traitors." But Jeffrey followed them, riding their wave of testosterone up the stairs to the big bedroom.

"You've got it all wrong, Jeffrey."

"Yeah? So let me in there."

"No." Both he and Russ replied at once and then turned to stare at each other.

Russ gave him a grin. "Just caught on?"

He had. Jeffrey was so strong, the man was an irresistible

force sometimes, and he was looking forward to having a little of that control back. Making Jeffrey watch, hands off, would be fun.

Russ tugged at his shirt as they made their way down the hall toward the bedroom. He followed, fascinated by this flirty side and how much Russ also seemed to get off on the idea of keeping Jeffrey at bay.

He glanced over his shoulder at Jeffrey again, laughing softly until Russ cupped a hand over his crotch through his jeans, making his head snap back around and his whole existence suddenly narrow in.

"Russ."

"That's it, Oscar. Eyes on me." Russ pushed at his shirt, and he reached back and tugged it off over his head. "That's better." Russ did the same, baring smooth skin and tight abs.

Sure. Eyes on Russ. He could handle that. This was what Russ wanted, after all. To show off a little, make sure Jeffrey understood what they had together, to make sure Jeffrey knew they wanted him to be a part of it.

He reached for Russ and smoothed a hand over those tanned abs, keeping focus. When he and Russ started this, he wasn't sure he'd be able do it, but now it had become this insane turn-on, the idea that they were being watched. God, the notion made him a little nervous. Excited. Hard. He was well aware of the eyes on him, Russ in front of him and Jeffrey, hovering off to one side, close but not interfering.

He pulled Russ in, kissing and touching warm skin. Russ sighed and arched his neck, and Oscar went after it, lips traveling along Russ's jaw. Jeffrey made an approving sound from just out of arm's reach, and he grinned and nipped at Russ's chin.

Russ hooked fingers into his waistband, arching and offering up skin everywhere his lips traveled, over Russ's throat, across prominent collar bones, over one shoulder. He hooked his hands behind Russ's back for support and bent to one nipple, sucking it into his mouth.

"Ah. Oscar." Russ's breathless words were followed by a groan from Jeffrey, but he wasn't the least bit inclined to look over. Russ was in his arms and everything right now. He pinched Russ's stiff nipple between careful teeth, and Russ went up on tiptoe with a whimper. "God."

"Gorgeous. Damn, Oscar," Jeffrey whispered.

He hummed. "Mm. I think Jeffrey likes it."

"Yeah, me too. God. And he's going to love this." Russ put hands on his chest and levered him away, looked down between them, and both hands started in on his jeans. They loosened his belt and his fly, pushed the waistband over his hips until the jeans fell to the floor. He kicked his shoes off, stepped out of them, and his briefs followed.

Jeffrey hummed and stepped closer. "Oh, that's a lovely view."

"Look, don't touch, mister," Russ admonished, and Jeffrey stepped back again.

"So not fair."

"Uh-huh." Under no such orders, Russ grabbed his bare ass with both hands, his lover's jeans rubbed against sensitive bits, the rough denim making him groan. He dropped his hands to Russ's waist and carefully popped the top button, but Russ stepped back suddenly and grinned at him, shucking the jeans quickly.

He held his hands up in the air, grinning. "I can't touch either?"

Russ laughed, his thick, hard cock bobbing. "Just making it easier, baby. Come on."

He followed Russ to bed and climbed up next to Russ's tan body, where they could stroke each other as they kissed.

He heard Jeffrey sigh somewhere out of his line of vision,

and the sound of a zipper and Jeffrey's soft moan were unmistakable.

"Got him," Russ whispered.

He chuckled at the glee Russ was taking in this game, but it didn't last long. Russ started making a trip down the length of his torso with a hot tongue, and he rolled onto his back to give the man more room. "Yeah." God, he loved Russ's mouth. He placed a hand on Russ's head and gently steered that tongue lower, over his flank and into his curls.

Russ moaned for him and tasted the base of his cock, and he moaned back, arching as his cock swelled and stretched away from his body.

"Look at that," Jeffrey whispered.

"Russ, please."

Russ didn't make him wait. That tongue drew up his shaft and circled the head. His mouth dropped open and he rolled his head back as Russ took him in, starting with just the tip, and then taking him deeper, little by little until the head of his prick was rubbing against the roof of Russ's mouth over and over, making him groan.

"Fuck. You two...."

He'd forgotten for a second that Jeffrey was there, but at this point it was hard to focus on anything. Russ had him panting, had him wanting, and he rolled his hips, pushing his cock deeper into that wet heat. Russ made a soft sound and pulled off him, grabbing a rubber and lube from the nightstand.

"Yeah. Yes. Russ." Words. God.

Russ rolled the rubber on, grinning down at him, and they all moaned as Russ lowered himself down onto his cock, getting ready to ride him. His hands flew to Russ's hips. "Fuck. Oh, fuck."

"Take him, Russ." That was Jeffrey's voice, and Oscar expected Russ to counter, but instead Russ whimpered like

Jeff had actually touched him, then grabbed his own prick, stroking as he moved. "That's it. Deeper."

Christ, Jeffrey's voice was dark and smooth, and it just poured over both of them in thick waves, adding to the experience, making them both hotter. Russ grunted and his eyes crossed as their bodies met ass to flank, his cock buried so deep he could barely breathe.

"Fuck, Oscar." Russ's voice was rough, shaky, but he started to move, and Oscar watched, fascinated by the furrowed brow and the way Russ was biting his lip.

"So good, baby."

"Ride, Russ." Jeffrey's words were drawn out and low and lit something in him, something bright and hot.

"Fuck yeah. Ride me, baby." He arched up under his lover, and Russ cried out. It wasn't long before Russ was working and he was bucking underneath, both of them breathing hard and focused on each other. It was so good until suddenly he wanted... more. He needed to really move.

"Down." He ordered, and Russ moved, rolling smoothly to his back and reaching for Oscar again.

Russ looked up at him, heat and need in those eyes. "Come on, baby."

"Russ." He dove back into Russ with a groan, and slipped right into a strong rhythm, watching his lover move and arch under him. "Beautiful."

Then things got confusing for a minute as he felt hands on his back, and he turned his head to find.... *Oh. Jeffrey.*

Cool slick fingers slipped over his hole and one pressed inside, and his rhythm faltered, hips stuttering. He took a deep breath, his head dropping to Russ's chest, and he went with it, all the sensation, sinking deep into Russ and then pressing back to ride Jeffrey's fingers. "Jeffrey."

"Jeffrey." Russ's voice was husky. "Do it. Please. I want to feel it."

"What?" He lifted his head, catching Russ's eyes, but his question was much too late. He groaned heavily as Jeffrey slowly pushed inside him, breaking his rhythm altogether, making him stop and breathe. Russ moaned and arched under him. "Russ. Jeffrey. Oh. Oh God."

So full. So full and so deep. So much, his head was going to explode. He heard Russ's and Jeffrey's sounds, moans and grunts, and he reached back, steadying and slowing Jeffrey's hips. "Wait."

He shifted his knees and folded Russ's higher, and then he took control for a bit, rocking back and taking Jeffrey deep, then rolling forward, sinking into Russ. The room was full of breathy pleasure, some of them urgent and shuddering, some long and deep, all full of desire and emotion.

"Oscar! Jeff... Jeffrey. I need...."

Jeffrey grunted in answer and surged into him, forcing him that much deeper into Russ. His own cry nearly drowned out Russ's shout and Jeffrey's satisfied grunt, and he surrendered, letting Jeffrey take control, overwhelmed by their sounds and the press of their bodies, giving in to the need.

He hung over Russ as Jeffrey picked up the pace, looking deep into Russ's eyes and reading such love there. "Russ." His lover's name was all he could manage, but it must have been enough. Russ nodded to him, smiling.

Jeffrey shifted behind him, hit everything just right, and Oscar's eyes flew open wide. "Yes! Oh fuck."

"More!" Russ shouted, arching and bucking, and Jeffrey practically pinned them together, fucking him hard and right. "Gonna... oh!"

He wrapped a hand around Russ's cock and stroked his lover through a wild orgasm, Russ's ass gripping him, muscles working to push him over too. He was just one... second... behind.

"Fuck!"

His shout and Jeffrey's were right on top of one another and as he came, hard enough his vision narrowed, he found himself helpless to do anything but moan through it and take everything Jeffrey could give him.

By the time things calmed a bit and the freight train in his ears had subsided, poor Russ was so gone, his lover was almost sobbing. He patted Jeffrey's hip, and Jeffrey nodded, slipping free and stepping back so he could do the same for Russ.

"Oh...," Russ whimpered, and trembling hands reached for him.

"Just a.... Hang on, baby." He quickly disposed of his rubber and climbed back into bed, pulling Russ close. Jeffrey was only a moment longer, and the three of them cuddled close, tangling arms and legs, Russ cradled between him and Jeffrey. The three of them shared kisses and a chorus of "I love you" until they'd caught their breath and none of them could keep their eyes open another second.

CHAPTER TWENTY-NINE

OSCAR WOKE up with his arm around someone and his ass pressed up against someone else, so sore and so content he didn't even want to consider moving. God, what a night. He'd wanted so much and needed more and gotten it all, from all sides, all at once. It had shorted him out, scrambled something inside him, and reset his compass completely. There was no doubt in his mind this was exactly where he belonged.

These men loved him. These men were the perfect mix of personalities, of strength and honesty, of trust and desire. He couldn't imagine one without the other, or even either of them being without him. Their balance was everything he needed.

He knew it was the same for Jeffrey and Russ. He was more convinced than ever that they felt it the way he did, that this was real, this was solid, this was their own very special kind of love.

Russ stirred next to him and sighed, and Oscar kissed his temple. That earned him a smile, and Russ rolled onto his back, green eyes looking up into his.

"Good morning," he whispered, in case Jeffrey wasn't awake yet.

Russ gave him a sleepy, happy smile. "Good morning."

"Morning." Jeffrey's voice floated over his shoulder, the word muffled and mumbled. He and Russ laughed softly.

"Maybe he worked too hard?"

Oscar snorted. "I'll remind you that I am the senior of the three of us. If I can handle it, he can."

"Gentlemen." Jeffrey sat up on one elbow, looking over his back. "You're forgetting that the two of you tried to kill me last night."

"Oh, that's right." Russ laughed. "I thought you'd be able to handle it."

Jeffrey snorted. "Hell, no!"

"I think, actually, that the two of *you* nearly killed *me*." Oscar could still feel himself buried deep inside Russ's tight heat and ached from the perfect burn as Jeffrey took him at the same time.

Oscar arched back, asking Jeffrey for a kiss, and he got one. Then he leaned forward and passed it on to Russ. "Coffee?"

Russ nodded. "Shower."

"Clean sheets."

He grinned. "Meet downstairs for brunch?"

"You're on."

They had their marching orders, but they didn't rush. They got up and moved slowly, jostling and kissing, fingers sliding over each other's skin, touching one another. Russ headed for the shower and Jeffrey started stripping the bed. Oscar pulled on sweats; he was on a mission.

Coffee.

He trotted barefoot down the stairs, every creak and groan of the old staircase familiar from his childhood. He knew just where to step so the third one from the top didn't pop when he took his weight off it, and so the last one didn't creak and shift and wake up his parents. Once upon a time he'd been the master of sneaking out of the house.

He almost always got caught coming home, but hey, sometimes it was better—and more fun—to beg forgiveness than to ask permission.

He crossed the living room to the kitchen, wishing he'd thought to pull on his socks because the floors were chilly. He should have remembered that too, all the mornings he'd hopped around from foot to foot, making his oatmeal, and Mom sending him upstairs for his slippers and his bathrobe.

Young man, go put some clothes on.

He started a pot of coffee and grabbed a banana from the bunch on the counter, then ate it thoughtfully, letting himself visit his memories while the house was quiet. Homework at the dining room table, reading his comic books in the little nook by the fireplace with an afghan over his knees. They'd always had dogs; it was weird that there wasn't a dog stretched out on the entryway rug and another by the woodstove. Mom always had flowers on the sideboard, and Dad's pipe and tobacco used to sit in a little dish on the telephone table by the back door.

The coffee mugs were the same, though. The dishes, silverware, almost everything functional about the kitchen. Even Mom's dishtowels and the weird little sunflower cookie jar that still smelled like cookies even though there hadn't been any in it since Dad got sick.

He poured himself a cup, then went out to the living room to drink it, and sat on the couch. He and Russ had gotten rid of Dad's big chair. Neither one of them could stand to look at it, let alone sit in it, and it wasn't fit for guests, anyway, as beat up as it had been. He remembered the day they'd done it, how relieved they both had been to discover the other couldn't deal with it sitting there empty either.

Maybe he should have known then that there was something between him and Russ, way back then, after Dad's funeral. Maybe Russ did. He wondered if they had gotten together back then, whether they'd have welcomed Jeffrey in the same way.

Things happen for a reason.

That was Dad talking. Dad never explained the reasons, he'd just always said there was one. For everything, including losing Mom—even losing Emmett—and maybe there was. Oscar couldn't say for sure it wasn't true, but it made him crazy no one ever told him what the reasons were.

There was a ruckus of feet and voices in the stairwell, and then his lovers appeared, both freshly showered, dressed, and smiling.

"Hey, did I miss an invitation?"

"I didn't invite anyone. Ooh. I smell the coffee." Russ laughed and went straight for it.

Jeffrey came to him first, and he stood up for a kiss. "I barged in on him. Sorry."

"Don't be. It's my turn, though. Have some coffee. Think about breakfast. I'll be quick."

"Sounds good."

He finished his coffee and hopped in the shower, humming as he scrubbed and shaved. He pulled a clean T-shirt and undies from his bag, then found yesterday's jeans and pulled them on. He looked at the giant, neatly made bed with the clean, new sheets Jeffrey put on it and smiled again. The first time he'd seen it was so strange, this huge bed in his parents' room, but now it was their room and their bed, and he was happy with that. It was going to be a shame to lose the house. He had no idea where that bed might end up.

It sounded like the guys downstairs were having a good time. Their voices were starting to carry. That didn't seem fair, he'd already missed the shower, so he pulled on his sneakers, grabbed his empty coffee mug, and made his way back down for breakfast.

"I need more coffee. Did you guys decide what we're eating?"

The room went silent as he appeared at the bottom of the stairwell. Russ looked at Jeffrey, then at him, then ducked his head and went into the kitchen.

What the hell?

"Everything okay?" Had they been arguing?

"Yeah, fine. I think Russ was going to make omelets. Why don't you go get more coffee."

"Okay...." Something was up. He gave Jeffrey's arm a squeeze as he walked by, making his way into the kitchen. Russ was scrambling eggs in a bowl, and the counter was covered in veggies. He ran a hand over Russ's shoulders and then poured himself a cup of coffee. "Can I help?"

"Sure. There's spinach and mushrooms and scallions, and I wanted to dice up some of that sausage."

"Great." He took a sip of his coffee, noting that Jeffrey hadn't joined them. He started cleaning the mushrooms. "Were you two arguing?"

Russ didn't answer. He set the bowl of eggs by the stove, got out an omelet pan, and then joined him at the counter to chop sausage.

They'd had such a perfect night together. What in the world could they possibly have been arguing about? "I'm starving. This is looking good."

"I know you like a big breakfast. This is easy anyway."

They worked in silence for a while until everything was chopped, but Russ never seemed to relax, and Jeffrey hadn't reappeared at all, not even for more coffee. That was just wrong. Jeffrey could drink the entire pot by himself.

Once Russ was cooking, he made his way back into the living room to check on Jeffrey, who was looking out a window at the morning sunshine. "Don't you want some more coffee?"

Jeffrey looked into his cup. "Yeah, I guess I do."

Oscar sighed and took the mug from him. "What's going on?"

"He didn't tell you?"

"Russ isn't talking at all. He's making some killer omelets, though."

"Who knew the king of peanut butter and jelly and canned soup could make an omelet?"

"I know. It's funny, right?" There were a few things Russ did well with. If it involved scrambling eggs, Russ could pretty much pull it off.

"I'll get you more coffee."

"Thank you, love."

As worried as he was, he let himself smile at that and headed back to the kitchen to fill up Jeffrey's mug. He didn't know what the protocol was here. Should he make them talk? Should he stay out of it? Were they not talking because the argument was about him, or was that just being paranoid? Should he leave and let them finish hashing it out?

"I don't know what I'm supposed to do here, Russ. You're not talking; he isn't talking.... I don't want to make anything worse, I'm not saying it's even my business, but this is awkward for me, and I don't know how I should be handling this."

"He has something to tell you."

"What?" That didn't sound good. "He does?"

"Go on, ask him to tell you what he told me." Russ was plating omelets and handed one to him, then picked up the other two.

"This looks fantastic."

Russ met his eyes, gave him a strange, sad grin. "Thanks. I think you'll like it."

"I know I will." He followed Russ out into the dining room. "Come eat, Jeffrey. I got you more coffee." Ask now? Ask after breakfast? Dammit. Having two lovers was complicated, and they hadn't discussed any rules for this. He decided to wait and let everyone get some food in them before bringing it up.

"Thanks, love."

They all sat down and he dug in, trying to ignore the tension and enjoy what really was a fantastic omelet. "This is great, Russ. Thank you."

Russ nodded. "My hungry man."

He'd gotten about halfway through his breakfast when he noticed Jeffrey was barely eating. He sighed. "Okay, what, Jeffrey? Tell me what you told Russ."

Jeffrey looked up sharply, eyes on Russ before moving to him. "All right. Are you serious about selling the farm?"

What? "Of course. It's not what I want to do, but I can't afford to keep it."

Jeffrey looked at Russ again, then back at him. "I have a buyer."

"Oh?" Oscar turned his head slightly, eyes narrowing. "That's a good thing, isn't it?"

"First Home Incorporated. They want to take the buildings down and turn the land into an adult housing community."

"A commercial buyer."

"Yes."

God fucking dammit. "We discussed this."

Jeffrey nodded. "We did."

"Then you already know my answer."

"Oscar. I think you need to seriously consider the offer."

He glared at Jeffrey. "No."

"See?" Russ interrupted.

Jeffrey pushed back from the table. "Russ—"

"All he's thinking about is the bottom line, the dollar figures. He's not thinking about what you want, Oscar."

Jeffrey put a hand up. "Hold on."

"You know what he wants! Why are you insisting on bringing people here that you know Oscar won't accept? And while we're at it, don't you ever use me like that again. Oscar didn't know they were coming, and you brought them anyway. I let them in, let them see the place, thinking you'd already cleared it with him."

"Wait. Russ, that's not—"

"Hey!" Oscar stood up, getting their attention. "I'm sitting right here, guys."

They both glanced at him and then away again. Russ poked at his breakfast, and Jeffrey picked up his coffee.

He sat back down, looking from one to the other. Selling this farm was stressful on all of them, if for different reasons. The fact that it was coming to this only made him more convinced he needed to sell it soon. He needed it out of their hair so they could move on with their lives.

"Tell me, Jeffrey. Explain it to me."

Jeffrey sighed and nodded. "I know what you want, Oscar, and I understand why. In a perfect world, I would find a buyer for this place who would love it for their own family like you do. But that's just not the reality of the market we're in right now, babe."

Russ snorted and took a bite of his omelet, and Jeffrey took another sip of his coffee.

"The one barn is fantastic, the horse barn. But the other is only half-built, the little cottage over here needs a new roof, and I'm sorry, Oscar, but this house in its current state isn't appealing to buyers."

Fuck. Okay, he tried to listen, tried to hear what his lover was telling him. "What are my options?"

"Your...? Oscar."

He held a hand out to hush Russ. "Just give me the options, Jeffrey."

Jeffrey stared at him, glanced at Russ, then sighed. "None of them make financial sense."

"Money." Russ snorted into his coffee mug. Neither he nor Jeffrey responded.

"Jeffrey, I don't care. I need to know what they are. I want to make a good decision. The right decision."

"Okay." Jeffrey nodded. "All right. So the first thing you could do is put an addition on the house that includes another bathroom, paint the exterior, finish the basement, and upgrade the kitchen. That's one option. Another is that I could lower the price of the property significantly, and I might find a buyer who could then afford to tear the house down after they buy and put up something else. Any way you slice this, it's not going to turn out the way you want it to, and you're going to lose money. The buyer who's interested—"

"The developer," Russ added.

"Yes, Russ. It is a commercial buyer, but their offer is above asking, and they'll forgo building inspections because they're going to remove them anyway. That's going to save you some costs too, Oscar. And you can sell everything salvageable yourself too. The horses, the equipment, they don't want any of it. If you're looking to use the proceeds to put the girls through college, this is the way to go."

"And, of course it makes you some money too."

"Russ." He put a hand on Russ's. He would never make an issue of Jeffrey's right to a commission.

Jeffrey just shook his head. "Of course I'm going to make some money, but I've already lowered my usual commission. I need to take something. I've spent a lot of time on this sale, and I do have to pay my rent."

"Russ, let's be fair. This piece is a business arrangement,

and we have to keep these things separate to some degree."
He watched Jeffrey, doing his best to reserve judgment and let
the man speak.

"Oscar, if you were nobody to me, if you were just another
client and I was looking to make a giant sale, I'd have
convinced my client this was the way to go a long while ago.
I'd have told them I wouldn't find a residential buyer. This
would have been over by now. But I know how important the
farm is to you, and I've tried. Longer and harder than I would
have for anyone else. I'm not suggesting this lightly."

Oscar nodded. He wasn't happy, but it couldn't be easy for
Jeffrey to tell him things the man knew he didn't want to hear
either.

"There is one other option that might make more sense.
You could sell the house in Ardmore instead."

"What?" *Emmett's house?*

"I could sell that in a heartbeat. Great neighborhood,
good schools. I could get you a good price." Jeffrey raised an
eyebrow.

He shook his head. No, that was Emmett's house. The
girls were raised there and would have to be uprooted, the
farm needed work and upkeep. He had no idea how the
schools were. While he loved the farm, that made no sense.

"I can't afford that either."

"Well, you have your options now. I'm just asking that you
think about it seriously. This is, as you said, a business deal.
You have to let the emotional attachment go. If you're selling,
it's not going to be yours anymore, you know? They could
decide to renovate the house on their own. They could turn
around and resell it. They could do anything they wanted to."
Jeffrey looked at him seriously. "You need to think about *your
goals*, you know what I mean? Your reasons for selling. Make a
decision you can live with."

He didn't want to lose the farm for himself. He needed to

sell it for his family, and his family always came first. When he thought about it that way, that simply, it was really a no-brainer decision.

"Does it matter to anyone that I'm losing my job in this deal? I mean, this is all well and good for your family, Oscar, and for your rent, Jeff, but I'm left out in the cold here. It took me a good long while to find this job, and I don't know what my next one might be. Not to mention, I'm losing four-teen friends who are living out there in that barn. And I'm losing the only place I've called home since I left South Carolina." Russ pushed back from the table and stood up, shaking his head. "I know it's not about me, but this is." Russ gestured to the three of them. "Y'all will be perfectly fine after the sale, right? A little more cash in your pockets, a little less stress on your shoulders. But what about me? I'll be homeless and unemployed."

"You can move in with me," Jeffrey offered quickly.

"I don't want a handout, Jeff. I need a goddamn job." Russ stomped off with his plate into the kitchen.

Jeffrey stood up and followed Russ. "It's not a handout, Russ. I love you."

Oscar watched them go, not really meaning to tune out their discussion, but damn, he had a lot to think about.

Think about your goals.

That was the best advice right there, wasn't it? There was a reason he'd put the farm on the market, a good reason and long before there was anything between any of them. He had a family to support, and as much as he loved both of these men, he had a responsibility to those girls. To Emmett's girls. The only right decision was the one that benefited them the most.

He loved Russ, and he certainly understood what losing a home felt like. Losing the farm was sad. It was closing a beloved chapter of his life. But those girls had entire lives of their own ahead of them. He and Jeffrey would never just abandon Russ—Russ wouldn't be homeless, wouldn't want for anything, and would have time to find another job. They'd figure something out.

He was going to sell the farm.

He got up and made his way into the now-silent kitchen. Jeffrey had his arms around Russ, who was leaning into Jeffrey's chest, looking as sad as on the day of Dad's funeral.

Jeffrey gave him a helpless look that sat awkwardly on Jeffrey's face and settled uncomfortably into his strong shoulders.

Oscar set his plate down and looped his arms around them both. Jeffrey raised an eyebrow at him, and he gave his lover—and his Realtor—the nod.

CHAPTER THIRTY

JEFFREY PARKED out in front of the Stable Hill farmhouse, next to Russ's truck, and grabbed his duffel bag off the front seat as he climbed out of his car. He let himself in the front door, knowing the place was never locked, and went upstairs to the bedroom, where he quickly changed out of his suit and into jeans, a T-shirt, and a pair of hiking boots. It was that or sneakers, and these at least looked like he belonged outdoors.

He ran his fingers through his hair and headed back downstairs, this time going out the back door toward the stables. It was a beautiful day, and the place was busy, though honestly, he wasn't a barn guy, and he couldn't tell what was going on. There were guys sitting at a picnic table, sorting through what looked like reins maybe. There were guys in the barn carrying rakes and hay. The stall doors were all open, and there wasn't a horse in sight.

Russ was in sight, though. His lover had on a dirty base-ball hat, a pair of sturdy jeans, and a T-shirt with a sweat stain on the front. He was standing by a small stack of hay bales.

God, Russ worked hard and looked damn good doing it.

Jeffrey took a few steps closer. "Hey, babe."

Russ looked over, dark clouds forming in his green eyes, then picked up a bale of hay, fingers tucking under the wire. "I'm working." He took the hay into a stall, cut the wire free, then brought it back out and tossed it into a pile.

"I was wondering if you had time for some lunch."

Russ picked up another bale. "Nope."

Shit. Okay. Russ was more upset with him than he'd thought. "Already had your peanut butter and jelly, huh?"

"Yep." Russ dropped that bale in the next stall over and cut the wires, adding them to his pile.

"I texted you earlier, but you didn't get back to me."

"I'm working."

"Where are the horses?"

"Turnout."

He sighed and tucked his hands into his pockets. "Seems busier than usual around here."

"Yep." Another bale, another stall.

"Is there something special going on?"

Russ glared at him. "The guys are going through the tack and the equipment to see what we can sell. I figure it won't be much use to the over fifty-five crowd."

Ouch.

"You know, I did the best I could."

"I'm not questioning that."

"This farm is costing Oscar money every day it's not sold."

"I know. I'm not questioning that either." Russ picked up another bale and carried it to another stall. This time he followed Russ in.

"Can we just talk a minute, please?"

Russ sighed and wiped his forehead on the shoulder of his T-shirt. "Well, you've got me cornered, so talk."

"You're going to be fine, you know. You can move in with

me and then find another job. Move in with me and stay, I mean. I'd like that."

"You've got it all figured out, huh?"

"It makes sense, Russ."

"It might, but you're not the one being told how this is going to work. You have a place, and a job, and selling this farm is going to make you a little money. Selling Stable Hill puts me out of work and out of a home." Russ shook his head. "What happens next isn't up to you."

"Russ, it'll be okay. You will move in with me. We'll make sure you're good."

"Did anyone ask me if I wanted to? If I wanted you to make sure I'm good?"

He blinked at Russ. "Well, don't you?"

"I don't know."

What did *I don't know* mean? "I'm not sure I understand."

Russ shrugged. "I applied for a job."

"Yeah? That's great. Where?"

"Tennessee."

Wait.

Shit, where did the air go? Jeffrey forced himself to take a breath. "Ten... nessee?" *What? No.*

Russ nodded. "Busy barn, forty horses. They breed and give lessons. Fancy operation. Pay's really good."

"Oh." *Think. Change his mind.*

"I'd been thinking about it before we all... got together. It's not a new idea. This place had started to feel pretty much like a dead end for me after Jonas died. Some of those horse farms in Tennessee and Kentucky are grand."

"I'm sure. So... that's better than moving in with me." He didn't care for the ache in his chest.

"I'm not a teenager, and I have some pride, Jeff. It's solid work and a good situation, where people aren't making decisions for me."

"Offering to help and making decisions for you are not the same thing."

Russ looked at him for a long moment. "Are you going to let me out of here? I have work to do."

He stepped aside wordlessly, letting Russ by. "Don't go to Tennessee."

"Why not? You and Oscar have this all figured out. You'll be fine."

"Really?" He stepped close to Russ, right into his space. "Is that what this is about?"

"Yes. It is. Partly. And the other part is about this farm. Why doesn't anyone understand what I am saying? Why can't one of you listen? I understand that it's not really mine, I don't have any kind of money in it, but it's my home all the same. I'm... rooted. I put down real roots here."

He didn't know what to say. Oscar was selling; the man had set his priorities and that was that. How could he not respect needing money for those girls? He reached for Russ and pulled him into a hug, not letting go when Russ made a halfhearted attempt to protest.

"And then there's Angel. Jonas left her to me when he died. I'd have to find a place to board her, pay for her boarding.... I mean, if I found the right job, I could keep her on that farm."

Angel. Did he know about Angel? That had to be the horse Sophie was talking about Sunday night.

"I'll help you with Angel too."

"Jeff—"

"I love you and I want you to stay. Oscar loves you. You brought us all together, baby. We don't work without you." That was the truth. He and Oscar were hot as fuck in bed, and they loved each other, but on their own, the two of them weren't enough. They were a triad, not a couple. Every piece mattered.

Russ gaped at him, blinking for a moment, and then finally shook it off and looked away. "I'm... I need to get back to work."

Jesus Christ.

"Promise me you'll think about this."

"I've done nothing but think about it. I'm thinking. I'm also working. You need to go."

Fuck. The lawyers were all involved now. Oscar had signed the Letter of Intent first thing Monday morning. Late this afternoon Oscar's attorney sent him a final copy of the Purchase Agreement, and it was ready to be signed. Oscar probably had it in his hands right now. They'd set a deadline of this coming Monday to get the deal done, and then it was just a matter of getting the money sent around and the real estate papers signed. The farm was already all but sold.

He understood Russ's feelings about handouts, but he hadn't intended any such thing. He wanted Russ to know how important this was to him. How important Russ was to him, their relationship was.... He wanted to live together. All of them one day, when Oscar was able, but until then, why should he and Russ live apart? Russ could move in, and he'd give Oscar a key so his lover could come when not with the girls. His apartment could scrve as their new place. It could work. He really thought it would work.

Russ had gone back to the bales of hay, picking them up and dropping them in each stall down the lane, no longer acknowledging his presence. He sighed and turned back up toward the house, feeling... sad. And a little panicked. Maybe a little heartbroken.

This is why he didn't do relationships. He hated feeling this way. Who needed this uncertainty and worry? Who needed to lose sleep over someone else? Multiplied by two?

By the time he'd gathered up his things upstairs, he wasn't sad anymore; he was frustrated. Keyed up. He needed a drink.

He got in his car and raced down the drive, so ready to tear up the town. He stopped at the end of his driveway, flipped to Grindr on his phone, and stared at it.

Yeah, right. Who was he kidding?

He sighed and deleted the app.

CHAPTER THIRTY-ONE

OSCAR LOOKED at the paperwork on his passenger seat, feeling sick to his stomach.

Just... sick.

Sorry, Dad.

He wanted to throw up. He wanted to cry.

He wanted to put his girls through college.

All right, suck it up. This was your decision.

He hated selling to commercial contractors, but he'd started to wonder if it really would feel any better if he were selling to a family? Either way he was selling his childhood home.

A friend at work told him about how she and her sisters agonized over selling their family's home. She said they all knew it was the only decision they could make, but the signing was emotional. This house was right in town too, and she had to drive by the neighborhood on her way to work every morning. He supposed this was better than that. Once he sold Stable Hill, there would be no reason to head out that way anymore.

He grabbed the envelope and got out of the car. It wasn't

going to get any easier sitting out here.

The house was quiet, Rose was at dance with the twins, and he knew Brian was sitting with Emily, keeping her company. She'd been back at school this week, and it had gone pretty well, but she was tired and really needed extra help at home. They'd talked about getting a part-time nurse, but so far Brian had very willingly—and lovingly—filled in when Oscar and Rose couldn't be home.

Things happen for a reason.

He couldn't imagine why this had to happen to Emily, or Brian, for that matter, but if ever there was a man he could pick for his eldest daughter, Brian would fit that bill.

Growing up so fast. All of them.

Sophie was in the living room, reading, exactly where he would have expected her to be. "Hey, Oz." She smiled when she saw him, but her smile faded quickly. "Are you okay?"

Did he look as sick as he felt? "I'm not feeling great."

Sophie put down her book. "You want some tea? I was thinking of making some anyway."

That made him smile a little. "Yeah, that would be nice. Thanks."

"Come on." Sophie got up and took his hand, then led him to the kitchen. "Is it your head? Your stomach?"

"It's... I don't know." *Everything.* He didn't want to say much. He wasn't going to burden her with his issues.

"What's that?"

"Oh." He looked at the purchase agreement in his hand and set it down on the counter. "It's the paperwork I have to sign on Monday to sell the farm."

Sophie left the kettle warming on the stove. "Monday?"

He nodded. "Yeah."

"You found someone who wants the horses?" Sophie asked softly.

"No, honey. Russ will have to find homes for them all."

"They can't stay on the farm? The new family doesn't want them?"

"Well, no. They can't stay because it wasn't bought by a family. It was bought by a developer."

"So... wait. The herd won't stay together? It's not going to be a farm anymore?" Sophie looked right at him, tears welling in her eyes.

"No. It's not what I wanted, but—"

"What about Russ? And Angel? Oz, she's Russ's best friend."

Oh, poor girl. He knew she loved to ride, but he hadn't realized she'd be so upset about this. Was it the farm? Was she worried about Russ?

"We love Russ, Soph. We're going to take care of him. Don't you worry. He's going to live with Jeffrey."

"And Angel?"

He wished he hadn't allowed this conversation. He'd planned to tell everyone later tonight after he'd thought about what he should say. He didn't have answers for her right now. "I'm not sure about all of that yet, Sophie, but—"

"Oz!"

Oscar sighed, trying to stay calm when part of his heart wanted to break. "Russ will find Angel a good home, sweetheart. And the rest of the horses too."

"You guys have to find a way to keep Angel at least. Please?" Sophie held his gaze, tears in her eyes.

He had no idea how he'd pull that off. "I'll do my best, okay? I wish I could promise you, but... I can promise I'll do my best."

The kettle whistled, making them both jump. Sophie turned around and poured two mugs, and he watched her, wishing yet again that Emmett were here. Or... even Russ. Russ would know what to say to her; Oscar was sure of it.

Sophie set a mug down on the counter, right on top of his

paperwork.

"Maybe you could sell this house to a family instead?"

Could he— What? Jeffrey had made the same suggestion, but..."This is our home, Sophie."

"Stable Hill could be our home."

"No, it's—no."

Sophie set her tea down hard enough it startled him. "Why not? And how come nobody has asked us about this? Me and Emily and Grandma Rose?"

"This is our home," he insisted. "Your father and I had a plan."

"You're not listening, Oz!"

He blinked at her. Sophie never raised her voice. Never. "Sophie?"

"You're not listening."

He stood up, trying and failing to hold back his own emotion. "This house is where you grew up. Your father— your father and I raised you here! Our memories are here. Our life together is here, honey."

Dammit.

He hadn't meant to shout. "Soph."

Sophie stared at him for a long moment, then reached out, dumped his tea on the paperwork, and stormed out of the kitchen.

"Sophie!" He grabbed a dishtowel, tossed it onto the spill, and took off up the stairs after her. "Sophie, hang on!"

She didn't wait. Sophie ran down the hall, easily leaving him in the dust, and slammed her bedroom door.

"Dammit, Sophie!" He huffed out a breath and shook his head as the house fell back into silence. He really didn't think things could get any worse.

"Oz?" Emily's voice drifted from her bedroom into the hall.

He sighed. Or maybe they could. "What's up?" He poked

his head into Emily's room, trying to find a smile for her.

"Damn, Mr. Kennedy. You look like crap."

He snorted, but for some reason Brian's honesty made him grin. "Thanks, Brian."

Emily swatted Brian's knee. "You okay, Oz?"

"I'm fine," he lied. "Sophie's mad at me."

"She's been kind of off this week."

"She has?" He really needed to get the farm off his plate. He was too preoccupied. "I guess I've been—I hadn't noticed."

"Is it the farm?"

He nodded. "It's okay. I've got a buyer now. All I have to do is sign the papers and it'll be done. We can all get back to normal."

"Are you sure?" Emily's voice was soft but confident. Brian stayed quiet beside her, rubbing her back.

He blinked at Emily. "What?"

Emily spoke up again, her voice stronger this time. "Well, I'll be leaving for college soon. Sophie actually loves the farm, and the twins are young still. They'd probably love it out there too."

Oscar shook his head. "I tried to explain it to Sophie. This is our home. Your father's house. All our memories together are here." He sighed. "It's our home."

"Oz." Emily patted the bed beside her, and Brian moved out of the way so Oscar could sit. "Oz, Daddy is in here." She rubbed a hand over her heart. "All the good memories are in here."

He thought about that and slowly put his hand over his own heart like Emily.

"Oz, Sophie loves those horses. And she says Russ gets her. She hasn't been this happy since Daddy died."

He looked up sharply, meeting Emily's eyes, Sophie's words echoing back to him.

You're not listening, Oz.

He wasn't listening. He hadn't ever asked the girls what they wanted. Not one time. He was so focused on keeping everything normal for them, giving them what he thought they needed, that he'd never considered what they wanted.

Emily shrugged. "I don't care so much about the horses, truthfully, but I care about Sophie. Don't sell the farm."

"I... I care about Sophie too," he said thoughtfully.

"Oh, I know! I didn't mean—"

He blinked and took Emily's hand quickly. "Oh, I know, honey. I know that."

"And you. I love you, Oz."

Don't cry. Do not cry in front of your daughter.

Yeah, too late. He was already crying in front of his daughter. He blinked the tears from his eyes. "I love you, Em. I'm sorry."

Emily reached out and hugged him hard, and he held her close—his buddy, the only one of Emmett's girls to really remember Emmett the way he did. He felt like that hug did them both some good.

"Russ wants me to keep the farm too."

"What does Jeff want?"

"Jeffrey wants—" *What does Jeffrey want?* "Jeffrey wants me to... make the right decision. To be happy."

Just be happy, sweetheart. That's the best example you can set for a child.

Rose, Sophie, Russ, even Jeffrey—they were all right.

And Emily was a thousand times smarter than he had ever been.

In trying to preserve for his family the life they'd had with Emmett, the stable life their girls had had, he'd nearly destroyed something that could make them all happy again.

Damn, getting to work from Stable Hill was going to be a killer commute.

CHAPTER THIRTY-TWO

OSCAR DIDN'T wait for Monday. There was no point to letting it sit until then. He wanted it over with so he could concentrate on patching things up with Russ and smoothing things out with Sophie. He needed to spend some time putting his unconventional, quirky, wonderfully perfect little family back together.

He grabbed his phone off his dashboard and his wallet from the glove compartment and slid out of the car, then hurried into Jeffery's office.

"Hello, Mr. Kennedy. Good to see you." The receptionist gave him a smile.

"Hi, Evie."

"Do you have an appointment? Jeff didn't mention—"

"No, no I don't. I texted Jeff to say I was on my way over, and he said he'd fit me in."

"Oh, okay. Hang on. I'll let him know—"

"Oscar?" Jeffrey called to him from down the hall. "Come on in."

"There you go." Evie smiled. Oscar gave her a wave and headed down the hall.

Jeffrey held the door and followed him in, then closed the door behind them. "What's up, Oz? Is everything okay?"

He looked at Jeffrey. There was no point in mincing words. "What if I don't sign?"

Jeffrey blinked at him. "What if... you mean on Monday? Is there something wrong with the purchase agreement? They'll be frustrated, but I can ask their attorney to put it off a couple more days."

"No. At all." Jesus Christ, his heart was pounding, but he suddenly felt like he could breathe again. "What if I don't sign it at all? Ever."

Jeffrey sighed and rubbed his forehead. "Uh. Well, the deal would fall through, obviously, and—"

"But I don't have to?"

"Well, no. The LOI has a provision stating it's non-binding. You can walk away from the deal anytime until you sign the PA."

"Perfect. Will you move in with me?"

Jeffrey didn't look any less frustrated with him. "I... uh. That house is pretty tight as it is, Oscar. I don't think Russ and I would help matters."

His lover was right about that. The twins shared a room, and Rose's room was barely bigger than a walk-in closet.

But....

"Stable Hill has five bedrooms and a guest cottage."

"Stable Hill? You want... wait." Jeffrey took him by the arm, steered him over to the couch, and sat him down. "You're asking me to move out to the farm? You mean all of us?"

"All of us. And Rose can have the cottage. We can fix it up for her. It will be worth putting some money into it if we live there."

"And sell the house in town?"

Just as Jeffrey had suggested a couple of days ago.

He hadn't been ready to listen then, but his girls were brave and smart. Emily convinced him, and when he talked with Sophie, she... well, he hadn't seen her smile like that in ages.

"Yes. If I fire you, can I rehire you to sell that house instead?" This could absolutely work. Rose was on board, the girls... now he had to talk to—

"Oscar, have you... talked to Russ?"

"No. He won't answer the phone, and he's not returning my texts. I know he's mad at me." He was about to talk to Russ. He'd needed to find out if he could get out of the sale first.

"I hadn't either, so I dropped by yesterday."

He'd thought about doing that, but he didn't think he'd be welcome. "I wish I'd known. I feel like an even bigger asshole now."

"Don't. He didn't really want to see me, and he didn't let me stay long."

Oscar shook his head. "I have to get over there, I know. We need to talk."

"I asked him again to move in with me, and he... Oscar." Jeffrey sighed, that bewildered smile fading. "Russ applied for a job in Tennessee."

"He... what?" *Tennessee?* "Like the state of Tennessee?"

Jeffrey nodded slowly. "I asked him to think about it. I told him I didn't want him to go."

"He can't go to Tennessee. I have to go see him. Wait. Did you say yes?"

"Did I say... what?"

"Will you move in with me? On the farm."

Jeffrey gave him a doubtful look. "I... I don't know, Oscar. Me, on a farm? I'm not really a farm kind of guy, you know? I could... I could think about it."

Think about what? Oscar pinned him with a knowing look. "The place needs work, but together we could fix it up."

"Yes, but—"

"You could stop paying rent." He knew Jeffrey. Appealing to the man's financial sense was always a good move. There was no mortgage on the farm anymore. Dad had paid that off years ago.

"That's true. And the farm is free and clear."

"Jeffrey." He took his lover by the shoulders. "Keeping the farm will keep Russ from going to Tennessee."

"Well, he might not go anyway. I mean, I did ask him to stay."

"Oh, for crying out loud. I'm going to talk to Russ." He kissed Jeffrey, then stood up and headed for the door.

Jeffrey got up with him. "Right, okay. Coming."

He grinned but didn't say a word. This was the answer. This had to work.

THE DRIVE out to Stable Hill was as entertaining as it was nerve-wracking.

It started out with Jeffrey following his minivan in that flashy Mercedes, but that didn't last long. Jeffrey passed him as soon as the opportunity presented itself so he had to follow instead. That was fine on the local roads, but the ten minutes they spent on the interstate was like the Flintstones trying to keep up with the Jetsons.

Jeffrey took off as soon as they hit the on-ramp. Oscar had tried to keep up, but at seventy-five miles an hour, his ancient minivan rattled and shook, and the engine protested. The thing sounded like it was being launched into outer space. So he slowed down and toddled along just at the speed limit. Jeffrey finally got the hint and pulled into the right lane to wait for him, but he swore he could see smoke coming out of the man's ears.

Eventually, they pulled into Stable Hill's long, winding driveway and parked in front of the house. His minivan, Jeffrey's Mercedes, and Russ's pickup, all lined up like they belonged there.

Which, of course, they did.

He could picture Rose's ancient but trusty Camry parked at the cottage, and the cars of various boyfriends or girl-friends or whoever was in their future, lined right up next to his. Good thing it was a big driveway.

He met Jeffrey on the porch, and they went inside together and found Russ sitting on the floor, eating lunch in front of the TV. "Hey, baby. What's on?"

"Powerpuff Girls."

He exchanged a look with Jeffrey, who shrugged at him. "Do you have a minute?"

"Okay." Russ sounded skeptical and looked at them suspi-ciously. "What is this, an intervention? Shouldn't you be at work?"

"I called out sick." Oscar sighed. Russ still sounded so hurt. It was in his voice, in the set of his shoulders. "Jeffrey and I came from his office."

"Ah." Russ took a bite of his sandwich and looked at the TV. "So that's that, then? When do I have to be out?"

"Hey." He sat down on the floor next to Russ. "Babe, I haven't signed the agreement. I have to ask you a question."

Russ turned his head slightly and looked at him. "You haven't?"

"No, and I'm not going to. I decided to take one of Jeff's other suggestions." He reached for Russ, but his lover leaned away. He didn't push, and dropped his hand back into his lap. "Russ. I want to know something."

"No. No, Oscar, don't put this on me. Do what's right for your family."

"I am. And I've already made up my mind. But I want to know... will you stay?"

There was a long pause while Russ studied his face. "I... don't know. Just because you're not selling the farm?"

"Dammit, Russ. No! Because I love you. We love you. Because I finally listened, and I heard what you and Sophie and Emily were telling me. Because you're an important piece of this family. Not because I need you at the farm. God." He stood up and paced away. He wanted to be reassuring but he didn't want to play games.

"Oscar." Jeffrey followed him.

"I got a good offer in Tennessee."

Both he and Jeffrey froze. He thought for a second his heart had stopped, it ached so hard.

"They want me to start right away. If I'm going to turn that down—"

"My offer is better," he countered, rushing back over to Russ. "Much better."

Russ stood and met him. "Tell me."

"I want to move everyone to the farm and sell the house in town instead."

Russ stared at him. "What? You're... moving here?"

"You know I can't afford to keep both places." He rested a hand on Russ's hip. "But you were right about Sophie. She's happy with the horses, and I don't want to risk that when we're just starting to find her again." He tightened his fingers and pulled Russ closer. "I love this old farm. She doesn't want me to sell it. And I can't lose you."

"Stay here and keep my job." Russ repeated it like he needed to make sure it was real.

"But better than before, because it will be your farm too. Your home."

"Home." Russ rested against him, head on his chest.

"Yes. Our home. All three of us, Rose, the girls, the horses... all of it."

Jeffrey's voice was soft as it floated over his shoulder. "Stay, Russ."

"Please." He stepped back so Russ could look into his eyes, so his lover could look deep inside him, to see that he was sincere. "Please stay."

Russ swallowed hard, hopeful eyes searching his. "I will. I'll stay."

CHAPTER THIRTY-THREE

Never, ever.

Not once. Not one single time in Russ's whole life had he celebrated Valentine's Day.

It was a ridiculous holiday, when you were supposed to buy presents and flowers for your sweetheart and act like you loved them more on that day than every other day of the year.

His truck bounced along the curvy driveway up to the house, and he just shook his head. The whole idea was stupid. There was no way he could love his men any more than he already did. He wasn't even sure he could pretend it was true.

But those girls? Those girls he loved more every single day. Every time Emily kissed his cheek, took off with Brian and left him worrying. Every time Zoe and Riley asked him to play guitar for them and they sang along. Every time Sophie hauled her ass back up on Angel after a fall? He fell a little more in love.

So this Valentine's Day? Damn right he was celebrating.

He pulled up next to Jeff's fancy car and parked so close Jeff was going to have to climb over the passenger seat in the morning to get in. Now that was love, right? He had a little chuckle, hauled the chocolate and the flowers off the seat next to him, and headed inside.

"Oh, it smells good in here, y'all!" The girls insisted on lasagna, having branded it the dish that made him and Jeff fall in love with Oscar. Didn't matter whether it was actually true or not. It made the girls smile, so he was all about it.

"You got the stuff?" Oscar popped up off the couch and hurried to help him.

"Yep. I got the pretty things and the yummy things. For the girls and for Miss Rose too."

And a new little box of rubber things for us.

There were a lot of Cupid's arrows in this relationship after all.

Oscar took the flowers to put in water, and he put the chocolate on the sideboard.

"How close are we to dinner?" Russ was hungry.

"My goodness, Russell, you are an impatient young man." Rose called from the kitchen, teasing. She liked to tease him, and he'd nod and "yes, ma'am" her because she liked that too. It made her smile.

"It takes a lot of energy to keep up—"

Oscar shot him a look.

"With the horses." He stuck his tongue out at Oscar, who gave him a thumbs-up.

"Dinner is, in fact, almost ready, Russell dear."

"I'll get the girls to come set the table." Oscar started toward the stairs.

"Let me?"

"Sure."

Russ gave Oscar a quick kiss, too quick to be enough for either of them, and headed up.

He poked his head into his old room, which Rose was using until her cottage renovations were done, sometime in the spring. The room that had been Oscar's mother's now belonged to the twins and had enough room for bunkbeds and their dressers. When Rose moved out, Emily was going to move into that little room since she'd be off to college in the fall, and the twins would each have their own room for the first time in their ten years.

Sophie was well settled into her room at the back of the house, which had a view of the stables and a couple of the turnout pastures too. He'd promised he'd build her a window seat by one of the windows so she could read and enjoy the view at the same time. She wanted to help on the farm more, but he hadn't offered an opinion on her plan to ask Oscar if she could be homeschooled. That was Oscar's bailiwick.

Emily's door was ajar, and he knocked on it softly. "Dinner, Em."

"Thanks, Russ."

"Thanks, Mr. White."

Russ cringed. *Mr. White?* He understood polite and all, but he'd told Brian at least a handful of times to call him Russ. Hadn't happened yet.

"Dinner?" The twins popped out of their room, all smiles.

"Miss Rose said to come get you."

"Yay!" The girls chased one another down the stairs.

He knocked on Sophie's door last.

"Uh-huh. I'm coming."

He waited a few seconds and knocked again.

"Uh-huh."

"This is why God made bookmarks, Sophie."

Sophie rolled her eyes at him and made a show of sticking her bookmark into her book.

"Oh, very nice."

Sophie trotted past him toward the stairs. "Don't you have better things to do than stand there?"

He grinned at her and followed. "Not really."

There was quite a ruckus downstairs between setting the table and handing out the flowers and candy. He could hardly believe how much bigger the house felt with more people in it. It didn't make sense. But he looked around, poking his nose into the living room before heading through the dining room toward the kitchen. Jonas built this house to be full, and though the old man's family may not have ever been as big as Jonas had wanted, it was full to bursting now. He hoped Jonas would be proud to have them all there.

Zoe ran over and hugged him. "Thank you. Happy Valentine's Day!"

"Happy Valentine's Day to you, squirt."

"Oz says you're the one who found the daisies?" Sophie smiled at him.

Russ let himself be proud. "I remembered you said they were your favorite."

"Thank you. I'm glad you're our new dad, Russ. One of them."

New dad. He sure hadn't seen that coming, not one bit. He'd never in a thousand Sundays have believed he'd be somebody's daddy one day. Not even a stepfather. "Me too, Soph. I mean that. Happy Valentine's Day."

"Happy Valentine's Day." Sophie hugged him and hurried over to help Riley finish setting the table.

He wandered into the kitchen, or tried to. It was busy, with Jeffrey helping Rose put food into serving dishes and Oscar and Emily shuttling food out to the table. He'd gotten so used to living alone, he hadn't even noticed he was lonely. Jeff and Oscar filled places in his soul he hadn't realized were so hollow. Standing here watching them, listening to the girls, he had everything he wanted. More than he had ever hoped for.

He was grateful, dammit, and like Jonas taught him, he was going to live up to the privilege. No, he didn't bring in a paycheck, but he knew his worth. He kept Stable Hill running. It was his farm now, and he loved every damn minute of work he put into it. He was living the dream.

Rose handed him a pair of floral oven mitts. "Russell, be a dear and take that lasagna pan out, would you? And ask those girls to have a seat."

"Yes, ma'am." He picked up the dish and carried it out to a hot plate in the center of the table. Emily was setting out garlic bread next to a big salad. There was also some sautéed shrimp and a bowl of zucchini and yellow squash. Oscar followed him with two bottles of wine, and Jeffrey set out glasses.

"Hey, y'all. Miss Rose says to have a seat, please." That was all it took. Everyone listened when Rose gave an order, even Jeffrey and Oscar, who sat too.

"Is that everything, Miss Rose?"

"Yes, dear. Sit, sit."

He would—right after she did. He held her chair for her at one end of the table.

"Thank you, dear." Rose sat, and then he squeezed in beside the twins on one of the benches.

"Roses and thorns?"

Riley laughed. "Oz! It's Valentine's Day! The only thorns are on the roses."

VALENTINE'S DAY dinner turned out to be a nice new family tradition.

The tradition was going to come with some extra hard workouts at the gym, but Jeffrey felt like it was worth it.

Now they were all stuffed to the gills, Russ and Brian cleared the table, Oz started doing dishes, and because he'd helped Rose with dinner, Jeffrey got to hand out the heart-shaped cupcakes he'd picked up on his way home to the women of the house, including Rose.

Rose was particularly grateful, but it wasn't really the cupcake she appreciated most, he knew; it was the thought. Little things weren't little to her, he'd learned, and Oz had impressed upon him and Russ that taking care of Rose, lightening her load and giving her some well-deserved time to relax, had to be a high priority.

They'd only been living at the farm for a month. At his suggestion, they were holding off on putting the new house on the market until spring. That meant they got to celebrate the winter holidays in the other house one more time. The short time they'd spent at the farm so far had been fairly intense. He'd had to drive all over creation for a living before the move, and with his flexible schedule, he wasn't finding the adjustment so terrible, but going from living alone to living in a full house, while it was great, was taking him some time to get used to. They'd had a lot of other things to work out between them with the move too, like the girls' schooling, and Oz's commute, but this was a case where extra hands, and extra minds, really did make a difference. So far they'd found solutions. Some of them were temporary fixes, but he didn't doubt they'd figure everything out with time.

The last month had been intense in other ways that went beyond logistics as well. The triad arrangement suited him, he'd known that for some time, but his last one hadn't felt like this. He was an equal voice with Russ and Oz, an equal partner and lover, and he loved them equally. The way he loved Russ didn't feel the same as the way he loved Oscar, but it was love all the same, real and deep and essential. They'd talked about it a couple of times, and they all seemed to be having the same experience. The individual relationships were strong, but the three of them together were stronger.

He knew Russ still struggled a little with the weight and

responsibility of family, but Jeffrey had taken to it like a house on fire. Rose felt like a mom to him from the first time they met. He hadn't been brown-nosing at all that evening in the kitchen, singing the U of M fight song. He'd genuinely enjoyed her company. The girls, the twins especially, had found a way right into his heart. Zoe and Riley reminded him that life was fun. That clothes could be washed, music was made for dancing, and there was no law that said you couldn't eat peanut butter from the jar with a spoon.

The girls had taught him—already, even in their short time together—not to take himself so seriously.

That didn't mean, however, that he approved of the pretzels he kept finding on the leather seats in his car.

"Pink or purple?"

"I'm sorry, Riley. What was that?"

Rose winked at him, like she'd known all along he'd gotten lost in his head.

"Uh. Purple?"

"Perfect! That one has glitter in it! Be right back!"

He looked at Rose, whose knowing grin was wider than the Grand Canyon. "What did I just agree to?"

"Sounds like you chose the sparkly purple nail polish."

Oh, hell. "Really? What are you getting?"

"A lovely marine blue that I gave Zoe for her birthday."

He narrowed his eyes at her. "Oh, you are shrewd."

"You'll learn."

"Come on, Oz! Russ! Come sit!" Zoe was wrangling his men, dragging them from their duties in the kitchen and out to the couch in the living room.

"You'd best go sit, dear. Before Zoe—"

"Jeff!" Zoe rolled her eyes at him. "You're supposed to be sitting!"

He hurried to the couch to the sound of Rose's delighted laughter.

"On it." He grinned and made a nuisance of himself, wiggling his butt right in between Russ and Oscar.

"Brat." Oscar poked him in the arm.

"Hey!"

"What's the matter, babe? Did Oscar wrinkle your shirt?"

"Shut up."

"Jeffrey! We don't tell people to shut up." Zoe gave him a stern look.

"I'm sorry." He could feel Oscar and Russ holding in their laughter on either side of him.

"I'm back!" Riley set down a handful of nail polishes on the coffee table, then picked the sparkly purple one back up to give it a shake.

"Sophie!"

"Right here, Ri." Sophie sat in front of Russ and picked up a very dark color.

"Did you pick something Angel will like?" Russ grinned at her.

"Midnight blue. It's iridescent."

"That'll do."

"Sit still, Jeffrey. Last time you were too wiggly." Riley took his hand.

"Got it."

"Yes. Don't be wiggly, Jeffrey," Oscar admonished him seriously.

"I see you're getting your signature pink?"

"What else?" Oscar smiled at him and leaned a little into his shoulder.

He could totally sell a house tomorrow wearing purple glittery nail polish. Right?

Right.

EPILOGUE

"LOOKING GOOD out here."

"Yeah? Thanks. It's been fun putting it together."

Bringing back his mother's vegetable garden had been one of the many things Oscar had been looking forward to once he'd decided to move out here. Once spring had finally sprung, he'd gotten in there with Russ and Jeffrey, and the three of them had hacked and tilled it under with manure. Yesterday he and Russ had replaced a couple of posts and put up new screening to keep the critters out, while Jeffrey was at the old house with a crew of stagers, getting it ready for sale. Today he'd built the trellis. Next weekend if it was warm enough, he'd start planting.

He looked at Jeffrey. "How did the open house go?"

"Fantastic. I'm fairly certain I'll have offers for review by the end of the week. Maybe even as soon as tomorrow."

Whoa. He stared at Jeffrey. "Are you serious?"

"It's a desirable neighborhood. The house has been well-maintained. The schools are good…. I expect you'll get over asking."

Jeffrey had gotten out of his lease pretty quickly once

they'd convinced him to move out to the farm. It hadn't taken much. Russ reminded Jeffrey that he'd been in the house wearing a suit numerous times without getting covered in horse shit, Oscar handed their lover a glass of wine, and that was pretty much all it took.

"Where's Russ?" Jeffrey squinted toward the barn like he already knew the answer.

"Out riding with Sophie."

"And the girls?"

Oscar grinned. He loved how interested Jeffrey had become in the girls. He was like a little sheep dog. "They are visiting Rose at the cottage, and Emily said something about showing Brian the tractor barn."

"Showing him the tractor barn, huh? Is that what they're calling it these days?"

"I don't know. Why don't you go see?" Oscar grinned at him.

Jeffrey laughed. "Hell, no. That's your job, Dad."

"If I don't see them in a half an hour or so, I'll storm in there." Oscar really hoped they showed their faces soon. He and Emily had finally finished their very uncomfortable and embarrassing discussion about birth control—during which he'd had to pretend to be neither uncomfortable nor embarrassed—and discussed that she should respect her body and come talk to him anytime. That was really all he wanted to know. This Dad gig was wonderful except when it came to that kind of stuff. But he figured since he'd now done it with Em, Soph would be easier, and he'd be a pro by the time Riley and Zoe stepped up to the plate.

"You have a dinner plan?"

"Grilling burgers." He looked at his watch. "I should probably fire up the grill soon, huh?"

"You want me to make the burgers?"

"Sounds great. Let me just put the tools away, and I'll be right up to the house."

Jeffrey leaned in and kissed him, and he returned it with interest. One of the best things about moving in together was the casual touches, the affection. Not everything had to be planned anymore.

Though some things still were. There were a lot of women in the house now.

"You look happy."

Oscar smiled. "I am happy." He had everyone he cared about under one roof, his financial issues were far less daunting, and he hadn't slept this well in ages.

"See you up there, babe." Jeffrey headed back to the house.

Of course there were things to work out. The girls would be going to private school next year because the public school out here was regional and humongous, and they wouldn't get a bus in any case. Also important was that the school they'd chosen would be a bit more understanding of their family situation. So there was school transportation, rules the three of them had had to discuss about parenting, tuition to pay, and other things. They'd already run into issues here and there, but they were staying patient and working it out.

If we all stay honest....

It had been his instinct from the beginning. The first time he went to Jeffrey's apartment, he made sure Russ knew he was going and understood why, and it had worked for them ever since. Stay honest, deal with things as they come up. It was an idealistic goal, maybe, but they were all trying.

He put his tools away and ran into Russ and Sophie on the way up to the house. "Oz!" Sophie came running over and hugged him. She smelled like a barn, and he loved it.

"Hey, how was the ride?"

"It was so much fun. Russ jumped the brook on Angel."

He raised an eyebrow, and Russ sighed. "Not really on purpose."

"Something spooked her."

He laughed. "It happens. Go on in and get your water, Soph."

"Thanks for the ride, Russ!" Sophie disappeared into the house.

He hadn't been back riding yet himself, but he was going to try it out again after the garden was planted and he had more weekend time.

He hooked an arm around Russ, who smelled like horses, and he was sweaty from working in the garden. Man, his family got filthy out here. It was great.

"Jeffrey is making burgers."

"You want me to start the grill?" Russ gave him a hopeful look.

"I was about to, but if you—"

"I'm on it. It's my thing."

That was true. Russ loved to grill more than anyone he'd ever met, and the man was good at it. "Thanks, babe." Oscar stole a quick kiss before he let go, and that won him a smile that made him look forward to later.

He spotted Brian and Emily making their way up from the tractor barn, hand in hand, and breathed a sigh of relief. She had her own room now... with a door on it. That was worrisome enough. But escaping to the tractor barn was a whole other level of parental concern.

He waited for them. About three months after the accident now, Emily's hair was growing in well, and she'd gotten a cute cut that was longer on the noninjured side and just long enough to cover the scar from her stitches on the other. It was cute and worked well on her.

"Hey, Oz." Emily gave him a kiss on the cheek. "Brian is hungry."

"Hang on!" Brian laughed. "Whose stomach was growling so loud, again?"

"Shut up."

"Uh-huh." They both laughed.

"Come on, we'll get *Brian* a snack before dinner." By the time they headed up the steps, Russ already had the fire started. "See? Burgers coming soon. Would you two mind making a big salad?"

Emily nodded. "Sure, Oz. No problem."

"We got this, Mr. Kennedy."

Emily was doing very well, but he watched as Brian rested a hand on her lower back and followed her up the stairs anyway. Subtle but concerned, looking out for her. She'd really found herself a good one.

"This needs a little time to burn before we can throw the food on."

"I think Jeffrey is still—"

"Oz!"

Oscar looked up at the sound of his name. *Riley?*

"Oz! We made cupcakes with Gram!"

Ah yes. And Zoe. "You did, huh? Are they dessert? Where are they?"

"Gram is bringing them. She said to run ahead and tell you."

Oscar grinned. He figured that was code for Rose needed to breathe for a minute. "Why don't you two run in and see if you can find the tablecloths for the picnic tables?"

"Okay!" The girls tripped over each other like puppies heading into the house, and he just shook his head.

"Those two."

Russ laughed, hooking an arm through his. "They're going to be a whole lotta teenager, Oscar. You better get ready."

He shook his head. "Please. Let me get Sophie squared away before we go there."

"Would one of you gentlemen help me with—"

"Coming, Miss Rose." Russ leaped down the back steps and took the tray of cupcakes from her.

"Thank you. You're such a dear."

"Someone's getting first dibs on dessert," Oscar teased, holding out a hand for Rose to steady her on the steps.

"Thank you, sweetheart. Oh, I walked past your garden. It's looking lovely. Your mother would be pleased."

That made him smile. "You think so?"

"I certainly do. I would be if it had been my garden." Rose gave him a pat on the arm.

"We're having burgers, but not to worry, Russ said, looking adorable holding that tray of cupcakes. "Oscar made sure we had a piece of chicken to put on for you, Miss Rose."

"You all are too good to me."

She deserved it. This new arrangement had been even better for her than he thought it would be. She had much more time to herself, time to relax. He often found her reading on the porch or taking a walk on the grounds to see the horses. They still needed her sometimes, but with all these adults around, she wasn't his only backup anymore, and he thought she was enjoying that. "Come on, Rose, let's get you some tea."

Russ held the door with one arm, balancing the cupcakes on the other, and Oscar led Rose into the house, stepping right into the busy kitchen. Emily and Jeffrey were laughing and chopping veggies for the salad, and Brian was making burgers. He squinted.

"What happened in here?"

Jeffrey and Emily just looked at each other and cracked up.

"All right. Okay." Brian shook his head. "They don't trust me with a knife."

"Oh dear. Maybe we don't want to know?" Russ suggested.

Rose agreed. "Bright boy."

"Iced tea. Got it." Oscar filled a glass with ice and then opened the fridge and pulled out a pitcher to fill it.

"Sophie, look!" The twins dragged Sophie into the kitchen, and suddenly they had a full house. Russ set the cupcakes down on the counter so the girls could show them off.

Rose appeared at his elbow. "These farm kitchens were made to serve a crowd, but maybe not to hold one," she said knowingly, taking her tea glass.

Oscar put the pitcher back in the fridge, grinning.

"But you just have to make room for family."

He put his arm around Rose and kissed her cheek. "Thank you for doing that."

The kitchen was full of movement and smiles, laughter and love. Russ headed toward the back door with the burgers and with Sophie on his heels. Jeffrey and the twins had dug right in and were sharing cupcakes before dinner. And Emily and Brian were—

Jesus.

"Not in the kitchen, lovebirds."

"You do it," Emily countered.

He had to grin. She had a point.

Rose took his hand. "Emmett would be as proud of this family as I am."

Rose's generosity and love always left him breathless. "You think so, huh?" He looked around at his family and smiled. "I think you're right."

Enjoyed Stable Hill? Try Wrecked!
Sometimes even a cowboy has to come home.

Interested in learning more about Jodi's books? Want free fiction, release news, anecdotes, coffee and drink recipes...? Join Jodi's newsletter!

What's Up with Jodi?
http://bit.ly/whatsupjodi

A NOTE FROM THE AUTHOR

Hey there!

I just wanted to take a minute to say thank you for taking the time to read Stable Hill. I hope you enjoyed it. I know everyone is busy and our TBR (to be read) lists are out of control, so it means a lot to me that I ended up at the top of your pile this time.

If you have a moment, please consider dropping by the retail site where you purchased Stable Hill and leaving a review. All honest reviews are much appreciated.

If you're looking for more of my work, why not join my newsletter? Just go here: http://bit.ly/whatsupjodi.

Thank you for reading!

Jodi

COMING SOON

Land of Enchantment
By Jodi Payne and BA Tortuga
Just Released!

East meets west. City meets country. Though there's no denying opposites attract, can a college kid from New Jersey and a New Mexican cowboy learn to speak the same language, let alone trust each other?

When Mason Wild heads west to escape his past, he doesn't have a plan or a penny to his name. Luckily he finds a job with a roofing company run by a rodeo cowboy who's kind, easy to work for, and even with his jaw wired shut, hotter than July in the high desert.

Bull rider Levi Yost knows what it's like to be down on his luck. He's not much older than Mason, but he's been around the block a few times, or at least around the rodeo arena. He takes a chance on the kid, giving him a job and a place to live on his ranch. The two of them discover a surprising amount of common ground, but trouble has a way of finding each of them. Mason has to learn to be fully honest with Levi, who in turn has to realize he's not just riding out for himself anymore.

———

Soft Limits: A Deviations Novel
By Jodi Payne
Coming in November!

Fans of the iconic Deviations series will fondly recall Bradford as the beloved owner and Master of the elite and exclusively male BDSM club that anchors the series, and also as the wise man who introduced Tobias and Noah.

Dominant Bradford's story is one defined by sudden opportunity, unimaginable heartbreak, and new-found purpose. His calling is to provide a safe and supportive environment for men in the lifestyle. Bringing Doms and subs together is his superpower, yet he feels fated to be alone himself.

In this prequel to the series, you'll discover how Bradford is first drawn to Nikki, a beautiful and hungry young man living on the streets, and the unexpected ways Bradford grows and changes while helping Nikki understand a world of strange, new desires.

Deviations readers already know the outcome of Bradford and Nikki's journey together. Soft Limits is a deep-dive into Bradford's story, into what makes the Dom tick, and how he ended up with ownership of the club. It also introduces Nikki, the sub that tests Bradford's patience, steals his heart, and soothes his soul.

———

First Rodeo
The Cowboy and the Dom Trilogy, Book One
By Jodi Payne and BA Tortuga
Coming in October!

When a killer strikes, Texan and former rodeo cowboy, Sam O'Reilly, loses his older brother. Unbeknownst to Sam, James was also the lover and sub of a sophisticated New York City Dom named Thomas Ward. Sam comes to the city determined to stay until he can bring the murderer to his own brand of justice, while Thomas' more ordered mind is hoping for a legal solution. Neither man expects their connection to the other, but having each lost someone irreplaceable, their hearts are crying out for comfort almost as loudly as their bodies are screaming for each other.

Some yearnings refuse to be ignored, but transcending their differences to explore the fragile connection between them will prove to be a steep a hill to climb—the first of many. As Sam and Thomas take the first tentative steps on the rocky path that might lead to a relationship, the killer steps out of the shadows...

And this time, his sights are set on Sam.

ABOUT THE AUTHOR

You're gonna love this guy...

JODI takes herself way too seriously and has been known to randomly break out in song. Her men are imperfect but genuine, stubborn but likable, often kinky, and frequently their own worst enemies. They are characters you can't help but fall in love with while they stumble along the path to their happily ever after. For those looking to get on her good side, Jodi's addictions include nonfat lattes, Malbec and tequila any way you pour it.

Website: jodipayne.net
Newsletter: What's Up with Jodi?
All Jodi's Social Links: linktr.ee/jodipayne

MORE BOOKS BY JODI

Gay Romance
Stable Hill
Creative Process
Linchpin
Whence He Came
Soft Limits: A Deviations Novel (coming November 2019)

With BA Tortuga
Land of Enchantment
Wrecked
Heart of a Redneck

The Cowboy and the Dom Trilogy
First Rodeo, Book One (coming October 2019)

The Collaborations Series
Refraction
Syncopation

With Chris Owen
The Deviations Series
Submission
Domination
Discipline
Bondage
Safe Words

Lesbian Romance

Best Lesbian Love Stories, Summer Flings
Sapphic Planet